DEE ROSE

D1742941

THE
HANGMAN
RETURNS

The Hangman Returns
All Rights Reserved.
Copyright © 2020 Dee Rose
v3.0

This is a work of fiction. The events and characters described herein are imaginary and are not
intended to refer to specific places or living persons. The opinions expressed in this manuscript are
solely the opinions of the author and do not represent the opinions or thoughts of the publisher. The
author has represented and warranted full ownership and/or legal right to publish all the materials in
this book.

This book may not be reproduced, transmitted, or stored in whole or in part by any means, including
graphic, electronic, or mechanical without the express written consent of the publisher except in the
case of brief quotations embodied in critical articles and reviews.

Outskirts Press, Inc.
http://www.outskirtspress.com

ISBN: 978-1-9772-2244-2

Cover Photo © 2020 Dee Rose. All rights reserved - used with permission.

Outskirts Press and the "OP" logo are trademarks belonging to Outskirts Press, Inc.

PRINTED IN THE UNITED STATES OF AMERICA

PART 1

"WHERE'S THE HAND?"

Jericho dived over the bar in the empty pub. His massive back bounced off the edge of the bar, but his huge arms cushioned his fall. The pub was dim, with light emanating from the front doors. It was small, with a few wooden tables and chairs scattered around. Jericho liked that. It was easy to make stakes out the broken wood. An old jukebox and dartboard made the place appear older than it really was. Three dead bodies lay on the floor. They were badly decayed with fang punctures on their necks.

The door leading to the bar resembled batwings. They were short double doors with spaces between the top and bottom and swung open in the middle. As Jericho lay prone on the floor, he heard the doors squeak open and multiple footsteps move across the hardwood floor. Jericho figured he could take on a few vampires, but he was hurt. *And dammit! I left the Sword of Caine in my room. Stupid. A slayer should never be without his most important weapon.* He was also concerned that his latest apprentice, John Shack, was missing.

Jericho sighed and ran his fingers through his blond buzz-cut. He checked the pockets of his green and black camouflaged clothes to make sure he was ready. He knew he couldn't hide forever. Besides, he knew the blood that dripped from his wound would attract the vampires. But something was different. Vampires in the United States hadn't been organized since he dispatched the Sickleby clan a few years prior. *Sure, Kofee, the new vampire boss has organized them in the last year, but they're actually hunting me, the vampire slayer. This is unheard of.*

The town, Joplin Wyoming, was the kind of town vampires held up in because it was cut off from the main cities, so it was no surprise they were there. However, their ambush was perfect and surprised even Jericho. It was obvious vampires had taken over and either fed on all the townsfolks or turned them into vampires.

After a few minutes, Jericho heard the footsteps stop in front of the bar. Jericho had recognized the voice of one of the vampires from his hotel room, a vampire known as Dante. He was a tall black, balky, and deep-voiced vampire with an afro and thick sideburns. Jericho's forehead frowned as he heard a thud hit the floor. He didn't know what it was, but he guessed and hoped he was wrong.

"Come out, Caine." Dante's thick voice rang out. "We just wanna talk."

"Yeah, we've got something you might wanna see," another said.

Jericho stood to face the creatures, four in total, and confirmed his thoughts. "I see you've found my apprentice. He's looked better." Jericho tried not to stare at the blond man lying lifeless on the floor.

"You know, I was saying the exact same thing on the way in here." Dante threw his head back and laughed. "He put up a good fight if it means anything to you, but he's dead none-the-less."

"I think that goes without saying, leech." Jericho looked around to keep the other vampires in sight. "But I have to know one thing."

"Wait a minute." Dante held up his finger. "The great and powerful Jericho Caine has a question for me? I'm honored."

"Enjoy it while it lasts, blood breath," Jericho said. "Because you'll be dust in a few minutes."

"I heard you were funny." Dante folded his arms. "But please, continue."

"Who's running your little operation?" Jericho asked. "There's no way you guys have put together the type of muscle I've been seeing lately."

"I'll answer that for you," said a voice from behind the vampires.

The vampires stepped aside from the door. The smiles on their faces let Jericho know things were about to get interesting. The clunking sound of boots and what Jericho determined were spurs got louder as the person approached. A tall, pale man, about six-foot ten inches, strolled through the door. He wore dark shades, a long black leather coat, and his long black hair reached his shoulders. Visions of BA, the Bad Angel, immediately rolled through Jericho's mind when he surveyed the man.

"Well, well, well. Jericho Caine," the man said as he stood beside Dante.

"I remember you, don't I, tall-stack?" Jericho asked. "What's your name again?"

"The name is Cometus. Over the years, I've just been known as The Comet or just plain ole Comet." Comet walked closer to Jericho. "I'll bet you're thinking right about now that you wish you had the Sword of Caine."

"The thought *did* cross my mind." Jericho took a step backward until his back was up against bottles behind the bar. "But what are you doing here? I didn't know fallen angels ran with vampires."

"In due time, Mr. Caine." Comet turned to walk away but stood with his back turned to Jericho. "But I think my fanged friends want to have a little talk with you first. You have something that I need. So, when I see you again shortly, I'll tell you what you want to know when you're in more of a talkative mood."

Jericho watched as Comet walked out the swinging doors. Jericho knew he had no time to think. He turned his attention back to Dante and the other vampires. There were two vampires to his left, one to the right. Dante stood in the middle of the bar. Jericho attacked first and launched himself at the vampires to his left. The vampires slid to the side and allowed Jericho to fall between them. When he got back to his feet, the vampires looked at each other as if they expected more. That's when they realized what happened. They looked down and saw wooden stakes sticking out of their chests. They looked at each other, then back at Dante as they burst into ashes.

Jericho then focused on Dante and the other remaining vampire. Dante was calm, but the other vampire's eyes moved from left to right, looking at the exit and Jericho. Jericho stared at Dante and raised his eyebrows a few times and smiled. He knew he had just caught the vampires off guard by dusting two so quickly. However, he couldn't understand why Dante was so calm. Then, as John's body twitched and shook, Jericho knew why. John rose to his feet. *They turned him into a bloodsucker, dammit!*

"No. No. No," John said softly. "This can't be."

John stared at the ground first. He looked down at his

hands and watched as his fingernails grew longer. He then looked up at Jericho with a confused expression on his face.

"Surprised, Caine?" Dante smiled. "You didn't really think I'd walk in here and face down the most famed vampire slayer in history without a trick up my sleeve, did you?"

"Actually, I did." Jericho continued to look at the bewildered John. "But he knew the consequences so…"

Dante's mouth and eyes opened wide as Jericho took another stake from his inner jacket pocket and threw it at John, who was still disoriented. The stake struck the new vampire in the heart. John disintegrated almost immediately. The other vampire jumped on Jericho's back. He bear-hugged and pinned Jericho's bruised arm against the slayer's body, leaving Jericho attempting to toss the vampire off his back at half strength. The vampire's fangs were close to Jericho's neck, and the slayer could feel the vampire's hot breath on his skin. Finally, Jericho slipped his good arm below the vampire's arm, reached back, and put his hand in the vampire's open mouth. He ripped out the vampire's jawbone. The vampire released his grip and fell face-first to the floor. Jericho pulled out another stake from his inner jacket pocket, plunged it down through the vampire's back and through his heart. Dust.

When Jericho looked up, it was just in time to see Dante's heels running out the door. Jericho gave a quick glance at John's ashes. *Dammit, John.* He and John were acting on a tip they'd received from a retired marine and former Dark Hunter who resided in the neighboring town of Casper. When Jericho and John arrived, Joplin was almost a ghost town. It was the second such town Jericho had witnessed in similar shape. About two hours after Jericho and John had arrived, they were attacked and separated. Jericho knew he could take care of himself. He hoped John had paid attention in training and could do the same. Jericho was wrong.

Jericho shook his head to break up his thoughts and then pursued Dante. When Jericho got outside, he immediately stopped. Waiting for him in the empty street, flanked by ten more vampires, was Comet and Dante.

"I guess it's time for that conversation now, I see." Jericho sighed. "Looks like it won't be a private one either."

"Probably not." Comet spread out his arms as he looked from side to side at the vampires that stood behind him. "I have to hand it to you, Caine; even having to kill your apprentice didn't stop you."

"He knew the risks." Jericho pulled out another stake. "Now, tell me what you want so we can finish this."

Comet took a few steps closer. "I knew you weren't just a loud-mouth when you dispatched my brother and good friend of mine. I'm sure you remember Kota—the first and only vampire angel?"

"What?" Jericho braced himself in his fighting stance. "This is your revenge, I take it? He had it coming. Just like you, if you don't tell me what you're doing wiping out these small towns and hanging out with bloodsuckers."

Jericho studied Comet's face. No emotion. Being an angel, Jericho knew Comet had to have a weapon. All angels had one. He remembered BA's battle-ax and Gabriel's and Michael's flaming swords. He also agreed with Comet; Jericho wished he'd had the Sword of Caine right then. Comet continued his slow pace toward Jericho, so Jericho went on the attack first. He ran toward Comet and Comet merely waved his hand, sending Jericho backward and crashing to the concrete.

Jericho breathed heavy while clutching his chest. "What kind of angel are you? I've only heard of a few who have that kind of power."

"I'm one of the first angels." Comet stopped and looked at the sky. "I was cast out for being on the wrong side of the Great War in Heaven. And this? Well, I can do this to any human. Without the Sword of Caine, you're no threat to me."

A spark of electricity flashed in Jericho's eyes. Comet was right. He needed his sword to take on an angel. He turned back toward the hotel and held out his hand. However, an invisible force knocked Jericho backward about five feet again. He landed on his back and spat up blood.

"Tisk. Tisk. Tisk." Comet crept up to Jericho. "I've studied you and know all your tricks now, slayer."

Jericho got to one knee. "That's painfully obvious."

"Before someone gets hurt, I'll get to why I'm here and why you're still alive to even be having this conversation." Comet reached down and picked up Jericho by the jacket collars. "You remember Kente Cromwell and Hangoctuforre, don't you?"

"Yeah. What of it?"

"Well, power doesn't just disappear because we think we've destroyed it." Comet gently placed Jericho down to where the slayer could stand. "Hangoctuforre needs the Hellfire Ring to return and launch another assault on Earth. I want that ring, Caine."

Jericho straightened his jacket. "What? And you think I have it?"

"Don't insult me, slayer," Comet said. "Where's the hand? I've just been waiting for the right time to claim it. But you and your Death Brother buddy, Padilla, have been inseparable until now. It was either this or go after the Book of the Dead."

"Ha. Ha. Ha." Jericho shook his head. "And you chose *me*? That fall from Heaven must have knocked you silly."

Jericho punched Comet in the face. Comet's sunglasses flew off and broke as they hit the ground. Jericho clutched his hand as he felt a bone in his finger pop. Comet's pale face didn't flinch but turned red. He picked up what remained of his glasses and tossed them to the side. He then backhanded Jericho and sent the slayer crashing onto the hood of an abandoned red car. Comet jumped into the air and landed with his knees on Jericho's chest. The air in Jericho's body escaped, and he lay motionless as Comet slapped him across the face two times.

"You're pressing your luck, Caine." Comet stepped back to the ground. "But I need you. I'll give you three days to hand over the ring. On the third day, wherever you are, I will return at midday. If you don't give it to me." He shook his head. "I will reap unspeakable destruction to everything and everyone you know. You have my word on that, vampire slayer."

Jericho breathed heavy and tried to sit up as he watched Comet walk back to the group of vampires. The fallen angel raised his arms. The wind picked up, and a small tornado swarmed over the brood. When the miniature tornado dissipated, they were gone. Jericho lay back on the hood of the car. *So that's what it's like to fight an angel. What do I do now?*

Jericho thought about how he'd come to possess the hand. Kente Cromwell Sr. had died, made a deal with the demon lord, Hangoctuforre, to return to Earth from Purgatory as the vengeful Hangman. He was charged with delivering the souls of his killers to the underworld.

Upon escaping the midway place, Purgatory's guardian, the Bad Angel, or BA pursued the Hangman back to Earth. They continued their immortal battle from there. However, unbeknown to the Hangman, Hangoctuforre had planned yet another assault on the Earth. The demon lord used demons and vampires to wage a war that engulfed the Hangman, BA, Jericho, and Father Tom Padilla, the demon hunter. Together, they defeated Hangoctuforre and banished him back to the underworld.

Unfortunately for the Hangman, he had to return to Purgatory. BA chopped off the Hangman's hand, which held the Hellfire Ring, one of the three rings of power. Now, the ring was once again at the center of Hangoctuforre's attempt at returning to Earth.

Springfield, Connecticut

Kente Cromwell Jr. checked the mailbox just outside the metal fence that surrounded his house. He stooped down to look inside the box. There was nothing. He turned and waved across the street at his neighbor, Diane Johnson, who was checking her mail as well. As he walked up the stairs and into the front door of his white-painted house, he dropped his backpack by the shoe rack of the entrance.

"Mom, I'm home," he said to no response. "I'll be in my room. Call me when dinner's ready."

Kente walked up the stairs. His room was the first one to the left at the top. He walked into his room and closed the door behind him. He dove into his bed face-first and decided he needed a nap. As he lay in bed, he realized that he hadn't heard anything or smelled food cooking. He got back up and headed down the stairs.

Kente made it to the living room. "Mom? You here?"

He stopped. His mother, Dorothy Cromwell, sat quietly on the couch with a blank expression on her face. She'd just turned forty-five a few days earlier. She was a black woman with a short perm and a little heavyset. She rubbed her hands across her yellow day-gown with red roses. She nodded toward the stranger sitting in the adjacent recliner chair.

"Come in, Kente," the stranger said. "Come join us for a little family get-together."

The stranger wore a red suit, red tie, red shoes, and red top hat. He had a goatee and oversized black eyes. It was obvious that he was tall from his folded legs, and his head was larger than normal. He twirled a metal staff in the form of a snake with ruby eyes.

"W-What's going on, Mom?" Kente asked. "Is everything ok?"

"Sure, it is." The stranger stood and motioned for Kente to sit. "Where are my manners? Let me introduce myself. My name is Damian. Damian Red."

"Ok." Kente moved over to his mother. "What can we help you with?"

"You have something that my boss wants." Damian crossed his legs. "If you give it over like a good little boy, maybe I'll let one of you walk out here alive today."

Kente opened his mouth wide. Damian was threatening to kill him or his mother...or both. They hadn't been in a situation for years where he had to use his ring, the Ring of Light.

The ring was given to him by the Hangman, his father. But the ring was in his pocket. He had no use to wear it, but he always kept it with him. Now, someone had put them in a predicament where he needed it and he didn't have it on. *Maybe I can slip my hand in my pocket and put it on without being noticed. But dammit. If he knows I have the ring, he'll know what I'm up to. I've got to come up with something quick. Look at Mom, she's terrified.* Kente slowly eased his hand toward his pocket.

"Easy, kid." Damian put up his hand. "We don't wanna make a mess of things in here. Now sit next to your mother before you do something you'll both regret."

Dorothy slid over a little but not too close to Damian. Kente sat next to her and clasped his hands together in his lap.

"The ring, kid." Damian put out his hand. "I'm sure you've figured out what this is about by now. And to be totally honest, I'll be taking one of you as insurance."

"You can have the ring," Kente said. "But neither one of us is going anywhere with you."

Damian's eyes glowed red. "You know your dad made the mistake of pissing us off once. Don't follow in his footsteps. It won't end well. There's worse things than death, young man."

"Ok." Kente stood and walked around the coffee table. "Take me with you, and you can have the ring. Just leave my mother alone."

Damian smiled. Kente swallowed, and his Adam's apple raised high into his throat. He believed he'd made an acceptable plea to Damian. He looked at Dorothy. She was crying and shaking her head.

"No, Kente," she pleaded. "I've lived my life. Don't sacrifice yours for mine."

"I'm sorry, Mom," Kente said. "Dad's mistakes have ruined this family once. I can't let it take you as well."

"Enough!" Damian held out his staff, and the ruby lights glowed red. "Why are you two acting as if you have a choice in the matter?"

Damian shot a red beam of light, and it struck Kente in the chest. Kente crashed into the wall behind him. Energy rushed through his body that made it hard for him to move. He managed to stick his hand in his pocket.

Dorothy stood and screamed. "No! Kente!"

"You need to worry about yourself, Mrs. Cromwell." Damian jammed the sharpened end of the staff's tail in Dorothy's side. "Tactu mortem (death touch)."

Just as the words left Damian's mouth, a green beam of light struck him in the shoulder and sent him crashing through the wall. Damian landed on the outside of the house and slammed into the neighbor's fence. Kente rushed over to his mother. She wasn't bleeding from the staff, but she fell to the couch and began to shake as a white foamy substance ran down the corner of her mouth. Kente sat next to her and held her head.

"I'm cold, son," she said. "B-but I f-feel no pain."

"No, Mom." Kente rubbed her forehead. "Don't' go. Please. Don't leave me alone."

"I'm going to j-join your father."

"Please, Mom. Don't go."

Dorothy's skin turned gray, and her body became cold. Her eyes closed even as Kente tried to open them back up. He pressed her face to his chest and wept. He rocked back and forth, holding her body until a breeze from the hole in the wall rolled across his neck. *Damian Red.* Kente gently rested his mother's body on the couch and stood. He looked out the hole. Damian was gone. The neighbors looked out their window into the Cromwell house.

Kente turned his gaze back to his mother's lifeless body. Tears streamed down his face. He was alone. First his father, and now his mother was gone—killed by someone seeking vengeance from his father. Kente looked down at the Ring of Light on his finger and balled his fist. The ring, an emerald, glowed green and lit up the house with green electricity. The light engulfed Kente.

"Ahhh!" He raised his hands in the air. "Ahhh!"

The electricity subsided, but Kente was still glowing green. *I will avenge you, mom. I will turn this world upside down until I find and kill everyone responsible.*

Part 2

ORIGINS:
ENTER SUSAN TAKI

San Diego, California

Three men in black suits circled two blindfolded women. The women were duct-taped to wooden chairs with tape around their mouths in an abandoned house. They were tied at the ankles and their wrists behind their backs. One was a twenty-year-old white woman with blonde hair and an all-pink outfit. The other was an Asian woman in her mid-twenties, wearing green Chuck Taylor tennis shoes, blue jeans, and a *Punk Rock Rules* t-shirt.

The men hissed as they pulled out their identical knives. They pulled the blindfolds off the women's faces. The women, wide-eyed, looked at each other and then back to their captures.

"You two should feel lucky," the younger man said. "You are a tribute to the King of the Underworld."

"Yes," another began. "We will gain favor by continuing to deliver souls to him even as others have forgotten them."

"Now, don't fight it." The younger man forced the blonde woman to stand. "You're going to die. The manner in which you die is up to you. It can be brutally or from just submitting."

The Asian woman tried to talk even though her voice sounded like mumbles through her duct tape. The younger man cocked his head to the side and then pulled the tape from her mouth.

"Are you trying to speak, little lady?" he asked

She sighed. "It's funny that you mention brutality or submission. That's what my life is all about."

The three men looked at each other with confused expressions on their faces and then back to the Asian women. She smiled. They then all burst into laughter.

"I'm kinda confused." The young man tapped his knife on his leg. "If I'm not mistaken, we have the upper hand here."

"Then I have you right where I want you," she said.

She shot up to her feet and snapped the tape constraining her legs. The top of her head cracked the younger man in the chin. He fell to the floor. The other men hissed louder. Their eyes turned black, and they grunted.

"Who are you?" one of the demon-possessed men asked.

"The name's Susan Taki, sucka." She broke loose from the rope that bound her hands. "And you clowns have fallen into my trap."

One of the demon-possessed men launched at her. She stepped to the side, grabbed him by the back of his jacket, and used his momentum to toss him across the room. The other man, a shorter, portly man, grabbed the blonde woman and led her up the nearby stairs. Susan prepared to follow when a hand grabbed her by the back of her shoulder and spun her around.

He wiped the blood from his mouth. "You've just made the biggest mistake of your life, bitch."

"Oh yeah?" she asked. "We'll just see about that."

Susan lifted her large t-shirt and exposed her skin-tight,

one-piece bodysuit. She pulled nunchucks from the small of her back and whipped them around until she was in her fight stance. *Good thing these suckas thought we were just some helpless victims and didn't search us.* The nunchucks were all black with a red ling in the middle of each.

The demon launched at her with his knife. She swung the nunchucks and popped him in the forehead, which caused a blue electric spark upon contact. He dropped to one knee. Susan spun around and roundhouse kicked him in the face. He crashed to his side on the floor. Before he could recover, she jumped down and sat on his chest.

She then placed her hand over his forehead and closed her eyes. "Extraho (extract)."

Susan opened her eyes. An electric current flowed from her eyes and down through her hand. The demon began to shake. His demon essence, a yellow smoke, tried to leave out of his ears, but the electricity wouldn't let it. He stopped hemorrhaging, and Susan released his head. Her eyes turned black but then back to normal.

The man on the floor grabbed his head and shook it. His blue eyes had returned as he breathed heavy. He frowned as he focused on Susan, who was still sitting on his chest.

"My God. Get off me!" the man yelled. "What's going on?"

"You were possessed by a demon, jackass." She stood and held out her hand. "A thank you would be nice."

"A demon?" he asked. "How? When?"

She pulled the man to his feet. "What's your name?"

"Charlie."

She wanted to smile as she was overjoyed that Charlie was alive, but held it in. She didn't know if any of the men that were possessed were still alive. Usually, humans didn't survive being possessed for long periods of time.

He pointed behind Susan. "Look out!"

Susan spun quickly and backhanded the demon she'd tossed across the room. He smashed into the wall again. He got to his feet and inched toward Susan.

"So, you're her," he said. "The girl that steals demon's essence."

Susan whipped around her nunchucks again. "And you're the demon that's about to join the list in my hurt locker, sucka."

The demon raised his hands, and a gust of wind broke the windows in the dining room. The glass levitated off the ground and hovered in front of the demon. He thrust his arms forward.

"Hit the deck, Charlie!" Susan said as she held her hands up and created an invisible field in front of herself. "I can't block them all."

When Susan turned around, her mouth hung open as Charlie lay on the floor bleeding, with several pieces of glass protruding from his body. One large piece of glass was lodged in his forehead. His eyes were open with a shocked expression on his face.

Susan lowered her head and shook it. She then turned her attention back to the demon. The demon powers she'd absorbed from earlier had worn off. The force field disappeared. She had to rely on her Kung Fu skills the rest of the way. She bounced around and rubbed her thumb across the nose like her idol, Bruce Lee.

She raised her hand and beckoned the demon to attack. "Bring it on, sucka. You're going to pay for that."

The demon raised his arms again. The windows in the kitchen began to shake. Susan jumped and spun in the air. She whipped around the nunchucks and smacked the demon in the face. He fell to one knee and wiped the side of his face. She ran and grabbed him in a headlock with one arm and placed her hand on his forehead with the other.

He struggled to get free. "Nooo!"

"Extrho," she said.

Susan's eyes lit up again, and energy flowed from her hands to the demon's head. The lights flickered for a few seconds as Susan's eyes turned black. When the energy stopped coursing through her body, she dropped the demon corpse on the floor. However, unlike with Charlie, the human host had long since died. Susan laid him down gently and shook her head. She sighed as she peered down at the body. Two of the demon-possessed men had died.

She turned to the steps. She'd forgotten about her assistant Kay. The young woman had been Susan for three months, and Susan promised Kay nothing bad would happen. Susan ran up the stairs. The first door on the right was locked. Susan kicked it in. She spotted Kay lying unconscious on the floor in the center of the room. Susan rushed over and knelt beside Kay and tapped her on the face. Kay's eyes flickered as she awakened.

"Where is he?" Susan asked. "I'm going to make him suffer for this."

"I-I don't know." Kay put her hand over her forehead. "He tossed me to the floor and headed for the window. At least that's what I remember before I passed out."

"Well, let's get you up and out of here."

"Ok, Susie." Kay sat up against the wall. "Just let me rest for a second."

Susan sat against the wall as well. She moved Kay's hair to the side where a knot had started to grow.

"Are you sure you're alright?" Susan asked. "Demons are filthy creatures."

"I'm fine, I think." Kay leaned forward and rested her hands on her knees. "But tell me something, Susie. I've always wondered. How did you get involved with this stuff in the first place?"

Susan leaned back against the wall. "Woo. That's a long story—one I haven't had to tell in a while. But I'll give it a shot."

Susan's Story

The year was 1976. My father, David Allen, was a cook and Petty Office First Class in the US Navy. He was stationed in Japan for eight years where he met my mother, Oshi Taki. She was a seamstress in a dry cleaner's just outside of the Okinawa Naval Base. He was being promoted to Chief Petty Officer and needed his new uniform pressed. He was tall, white, well built. He had a brunette buzz cut and goatee. She was short with long, flowing black hair and a small mole on her right cheek. They hit it off almost instantly. I was born four years later—a half white, half Japanese girl.

My father transferred back to the United States when I was three. My mother didn't want to move, but she didn't want to break up the family, so she agreed to move as well. Her family was upset about the move, especially her sister, my aunt, Ahmya Taki. She hated my father for moving us away from Japan and vowed to bring us back one day.

As I got older, we heard less and less from our family in Japan. I'd become a black belt in Kung Fu. I was good. I'd won several tournaments on the national stage and became proficient at using almost all martial arts weapons. I became especially skilled in using nun-chucks.

One day my mother decided to give me a present for my eighteenth birthday—a trip back to Japan. I was excited. I hadn't been back since I was three, and I was curious to see what I'd missed out on. Aunt Ahmya met us at the airport. My dad had been retired for ten years and worked at a naval shipyard in San Diego. We got off the plane; Ahmya hugged my mother and me. She frowned at my father and turned her back on him.

"Wow!" Ahmya said as she looked at me from head to toe. "You've grown exactly as I pictured you."

"Thanks, Aunt Ahmya." I hugged her again. "I've been looking forward to this trip for months."

Ahmya put her arm around my shoulder and walked with me. "When we get some time, I want to talk with you and show you the real reason you've come back to us."

My eyes tightened. I didn't know what she meant. I just wanted to meet my mother's family because my father was an only child, and I'd visited his mother and father several times in the States. I ignored what Aunt Ahmya had said for now. It didn't seem that important as we walked to the parking lot to get in the car.

The drive back into town was uncomfortable. My mother sat in the passenger side seat and my father and I sat in the back seat. I continuously looked in the rearview mirror and watched as Ahmya continued to glare at my father. I looked at him. He knew my mother's family was still angry with him.

We went to my mother's childhood home. They still lived a few miles away from the base and still operated the dry-cleaning shop. My grandmother showed me to my room and introduced me to relatives that I didn't know. My grandfather sat in his favorite chair. I was told he almost never moved from it.

"When you've settled in." Ahmya walked up to my room door. "Come find me, and let's catch up."

I nodded. "Ok. I'll do just that, Aunt Ahmya. I may need to take a nap first. I'm exhausted."

"Take your time, my dear," she said. "I've waited this long. I can wait a little while longer."

Ahmya walked away. A strange tingle rushed through my body. Part of me wanted to hurry and find out what she meant. The other part of me felt an eerie presence when she spoke. I decided to take the nap instead. It was a long flight, and I was tired. She was right. It could wait till later.

New Hampshire

It was around midnight, and two men sat on crates in an alley, rummaging through a purse they'd just snatched from a woman at the bus station. They made grunting noises but didn't' speak. One of the men was older and wore an old dirty brown raincoat with missing buttons. He was a white man with long and stringy gray hair. Gray stubble and smeared dirt covered his face. He wore gloves with the fingers cut off and combat boots. The other man wore jeans and a blue t-shirt. He was younger with frizzy brunette hair and a full beard.

Once they finished going through the bag, they tossed it aside and counted the money they'd fished out of it. The younger man put the money in his pocket and patted the older guy on the back.

"Was that worth it?" a voice from behind the men said. "A few bucks and that's it?"

The men stood and turned toward a shadowy figure. He

wore a black hoodie sweater, black pants, and boots. His face was covered by the hood.

"Do you have a problem with two entrepreneurs, my friend?" the younger man said. "Because if you do, we can do to you what we just did to that purse."

The stranger pointed. "I don't have a problem with him. But I do have a problem with you…demon."

The older man's head whipped around to the younger man as he staggered to the side. "What's he talking about, Jim?"

The stranger smiled. "Oh, you didn't know that you were unwittingly palling around with a demon? I still don't know why yet, but I'm sure with a little persuasion, I'll find out."

Jim's eyes turned black, and he raised his hand toward the stranger. The stranger whipped out his hand and shot a green beam of light from his ring. The beam knocked Jim against the building. The constant beam of green light consumed Jim's body and pressed him against the building. The stranger approached with caution as the older man backed away.

"Who are you, demon?" the stranger asked. "And what are you doing here slumming with the homeless?"

"I'm not telling you jack, Junior." The demon smiled as he looked down at Kente. "Oh, you didn't think I knew who you were once you flashed that ring. Think again. Everybody's looking for you."

Kente squeezed his fist tighter, and the beam of light grew brighter. Jim screamed out in pain until his body went limp. Kente released the beam, and Jim's body fell to the ground. He slouched over and looked to the sky. His demon essence began to pour from his ears.

"Oh, no." Kente pointed his ring at the demon. "It's not

going to be that easy." Kente shot another beam of light at the smoke-like essence and evaporated it.

"Ha. Ha. Ha." Kente nodded. "Thought you were going somewhere. None of you will survive."

An empty milk carton smacked Kente in the face. He looked up and saw the older man who threw it, standing a few feet away.

"What did you do to Jim, you bastard?" he asked. "He wasn't a demon. He was a good boy."

"He was a demon, you idiot."

"He was my friend, and you're going to pay."

The older man charged Kente. Kente threw a right punch and struck the man in the jaw, causing him to fall onto empty boxes. He tried to get up, and a green beam of light struck him in the chest. He reached down and rubbed the spot where the beam hit him. His eyes opened widely as he looked up at Kente. His body began to turn to liquid and then ashes.

Kente put his hands on his hips. "Serves him right for be-friending a demon. So, the underworld is looking for me and the ring. Planting demons in the unlikeliest places. Well, let's see if they can take it from me. I'll kill anyone who is bold enough to take me on. I will find and destroy Damian Red. No matter what it takes."

Susan's Story

Later that night, I sought out Aunt Ahmya. I found her sitting on the back porch overlooking the ocean. She sat in one of two red cloth chairs. She was wrapped in the blanket with a bright-colored flower design. I stood at the back screen door and watched the back of her head. I didn't know if she was awake.

"*Ah, Susan.*" *She motioned her hand for me to come over.* "*Come sit next to me.*"

I walked out and sat in the empty chair. "*Nice night.*"

"*Yes, it is,*" *she said.* "*I love peaceful nights like this. It's perfect for what I need to show you.*"

"*And what's that, Auntie?*"

Ahmya pointed to a wooden crate that sat in the middle of the backyard. "*There. Your destiny lies in that box.*"

I stood, looked at the crate and then back to Ahmya. "*What is it?*

"*Go have a look.*"

I walked down the few steps of the porch and cautiously made my way over to the box. I bent down and leaned my head closer to the crate to listen for any noises emanating from it. I heard nothing. I reached down and ran my fingers around the edges of the top. I pulled off the top. A man with a steel collar around his neck popped out. I jumped backward. The collar was chained to the ground, so the man's movement was restricted. I stared at him for a while. He was a skinny and tall Japanese man with short black hair, and his face appeared disfigured. He hissed and stretched out his hands, still attempting to reach me. When he opened his mouth, that's when I saw the fangs.

I looked back at Ahmya. "*What's going on?*"

She stood and walked out to the yard. "*There's no need to be scared, Susan. It is he who should be afraid of you.*"

"*Are you crazy?*" *I asked.*

Ahmya reached out and flexed her hands toward me. Her eyes turned black. An invisible force surged through my body. A dark tent fell over my eyes as well, even though I could still see the surrounding area. I turned to the vampire. He backed away and stepped back into the wooden box. His eyes were wide, and his mouth hung open. I turned back to my aunt. She had one hand out towards me and one hand up to the sky.

Electricity lit up in Ahmya's eyes. "I am a follower of Natasha of Normandy, the leader of the Fallen Sorcerers. You have the gift, my dear, and it's time for you to embrace it. You just need a little help."

Electricity flowed from Ahmya's hand and across the backyard into my body. I shook uncontrollably and fell to the ground. The electricity continued to flow through my body as Ahmya walked toward me. She lowered her hands, the electricity stopped, and she stood over my body.

"Arise, my dear." Ahmya gestured for me to stand. "Become who you were born to be."

I stood, and my eyes returned to their natural brown color.

I took a deep breath and exhaled white smoke. "Wow! What now?"

"Now do what you were born to do." She pointed at the vampire. "There's usually a simpler way to destroy vampires, either a stake to the heart or decapitation. You merely have to touch his forehead and drain his essence."

"Drain his essence?"

She nodded. "Yes. And once you do that, you will gain more power and can use it to your advantage."

I turned my attention back to the vampire. He had balled up in the fetal position inside the box. I walked over and looked down at him. I wasn't afraid of him anymore. He jumped up and launched at me. I spun around and backhanded him out of reflex. He fell back to the ground and held his jaw. I jumped down and sat on his chest. I looked back at Ahmya.

"Go ahead, my dear," she said. "Do it."

I was hesitant as my hand shook while I place it on his head. He squirmed around. I was surprised that his vampire strength wasn't strong enough to push me off, but then again, he was in a weakened state. I finally cuffed my hand around the vampire's forehead. He tried to shake his head to remove my hand, but I pressed down even harder. After a few seconds, nothing happened.

I looked up at my aunt again. "Aunt Ahmya? Why isn't anything happening?"

Ahmya smiled. "I had to make sure you were ready. Now close your eyes and imagine your body is a glass that you are filling with water. Let the power flow from your hand to your inner self. Say the word, extraho. It is the Latin word for extract."

"Why Latin?" I asked.

"It is the language for all great magic," she replied.

The vampire tried to bring his legs up and push me off him. I shot my elbow back and blocked them. I then chopped him in the throat and then punched him in the face. His body went limp as he finally submitted. He lay helplessly on the ground. I placed my hand back to his forehead and imagined I was a glass, just as Ahmya had said. I closed my eyes and tilted my head back. I could feel my eyes turn black again. A white light originated from my hand and engulfed my entire body. I felt energy flowing from the vampire and into me. It was intoxicating. Once the energy stopped, and I removed my hand, the vampire had turned to brown ashes. I jumped to my feet. I'd never seen anything like that.

My aunt and I walked back to the porch and sat in the twin chairs. She had a smile on her face. I knew I'd made her proud.

"Now what, Aunt Ahmya?" I asked. "That was incredible."

She reached over and grabbed my hand. "Relax and let the energy pulse through your body. Since you now know what you can do, it's time to tell you who we are and your next assignment."

"Assignment?"

"Yes," she said. "It won't be easy either, but I'm sure with your skills and new abilities, you'll make me proud. I am a witch."

My eyes and mouth popped open. "No way."

"Yes, my dear," she continued. "I am Ahmya of the West. My name also means, Black Rain."

"Does this mean that I'm a witch as well?" I asked.

"You have the gift," Ahmya said. "Your grandmother Oshi was also a witch. We learned years ago that the gift skipped your mother and fell to you. We belong to a powerful coven that was started by Natasha of Normandy, leader of the Fallen Sorcerers. She was the oldest witch in existence before she met her demise a year ago."

Ahmya turned in her chair to face me, took my hands and squeezed tight. I stared into her eyes and saw visions of what I assumed were witches that belonged to our coven. I could feel a weird sensation running from her hands through my body.

"Now, you must prove that you belong with us." Ahmya released my hands, crossed her legs, and leaned back in her chair. "You must kill the wretched creature that destroyed our beloved mother, Natasha."

"Who or what is the thing that killed her?" I cocked my head to the side. "Must have been something very powerful."

"He's a filthy man who masquerades as a priest." She stared into my eyes. "He goes by the name of Father Tom Padilla. But trust me, he is no priest. And he is also very, very tough."

"I've never heard of him," I said. "And I read about the supernatural world as a hobby."

"You don't need to know him." She stood and beckoned for me to stand as well. "Just kill him."

"But a priest?" I stood and put my hands on my hips. "Even if he's pretending to be a priest, must be a good person if he's pulling it off."

"He fashions himself as an exorcist. He is using that title to murder innocent people, Susie. He must be stopped."

I shrugged my shoulders. "But why us?"

"It is our sacred duty, my dear." She put her hands on my shoulders. "We lost Natasha trying to stop him. It is your turn now.

"I will investigate this."

"No!" Ahmya snapped. "Just do it. Avenge our mother and bring him to justice. Also, he has a large leather book in his possession. It's imperative that we get it. But killing him is our main focus."

"Ok. Ok. Where can I find him?" I asked.

"His main dwelling is in New York." She put her hand on my shoulder. "He operates out of church there. Don't forget. He has all of them fooled. But don't be fooled, my dear. He's an evil killer."

"Well, I guess it's time to pay that sucka a visit." I bowed my head to my aunt. "Will you be coming with me?"

"I wish could," she said. "But I must stay here and tend to other business for our cause."

"Ok. Aunt, Ahmya." I hugged her. "I won't let you down."

We stayed a week in Japan. Ahmya had given me a lot of information on Father Tom Padilla. I knew where to find him, and I studied most of his cases. On the surface, he seemed like a good exorcist and an ok guy. But he'd killed the head of our order, and I was tasked with hunting him down and making him pay.

After a couple of days of hanging around San Diego, just to keep up appearances, I got on a plane with one small bag and headed to New York. I wondered what I would do or say when I came face to face with Tom Padilla. I understood he was a great exorcist, but I was no demon. When I landed, I hailed a taxi and headed to the church I was told he frequented. It was in the late afternoon, and the streets were busy. I walked up to the double wooden doors of the church and used the metal ring out front to knock. The parking lot was in the back, so I didn't check to see if *the church was occupied. I just knew the doors were locked, and I had business to take care of. One of the doors opened, and the squeaky hinges forced my eyes to squint.*

"May I help you, young lady?" *A young priest stuck his head out.* "My name is Father Jeramiah. Unless it's pressing, I'm sorry, but we're closed today for renovations."

"I'm here to see Father Tom Padilla," *I said.* "I have urgent business with him that can't wait."

He stepped out further and looked around. "Father Padilla is expecting another guest and insists that he can't be disturbed."

"But I can't stress enough how urgent this is." *I leaned to the side to look inside the church.* "Surely, he can make time for me."

"Can I help you?" *a deep voice from behind me asked.* "If it's as important as you say, maybe I can give you a hand."

I turned quickly and saw a huge muscular man standing behind me. He was about six feet, five inches tall, with a blonde buzz cut and wearing black and gray army fatigues. He wore black combat boots and had a black duffle bag strapped over his shoulder.

"I'm sorry." *He extended his hand.* "My name is Jericho—"

"Caine," *I cut him off.* "You're Jericho Caine, the vampire slayer."

He looked in both directions and put his finger over his lips. "Shhh. You are really loud for such a small person."

"Oh my God." *I shook his hand.* "The one true slayer. I've followed the rumors of your exploits for the last couple of years. You are my hero, sir."

"Ok." *He gestured with his hand for the Father Jeramiah to leave.* "You know me, but who are you?"

I tried to calm my nerves. "My name is Susan Taki. But you can call me Susie. If I may ask, what are you doing here, Mr. Caine?"

"Please," *he waved his hand,* "call me Jericho. And I'm here to see my friend, the guy you're looking for, Father Tom Padilla."

"Your friend?" My eyes tightened. "But that can't be."

"Why not?"

"He's evil and using this church as a front."

Jericho threw his head back and laughed. "Tom Padilla? Evil?" He laughed again. "If Tom is evil, then there are no good people on this earth."

"Um. I don't know what to say," I said. "Are you sure?"

"Lady, I don't know who's giving you your information." Jericho walked past me and pushed open the door. "Come on. Follow me and see for yourself. And whatever you have in that bag, I'd suggest you keep it in there until you get to know him."

I was busted. He was the vampire slayer and I wasn't fooling him. He and Tom Padilla were friends. Aunt Ahmya didn't even mention the slayer to me. Either she didn't know, forgot to mention him, or Tom Padilla was fooling even Jericho Caine.

As I followed Jericho through the church, I wondered if I should pull out my nun-chucks or wait until I saw Padilla. The church was quiet and dim. The only light shined through the pane glass windows from above. The front pews in front of the pulpit were being refurbished. We walked down the center aisle to the back offices of the church. We stopped at a room with a closed door. Jericho kicked the door hard and laughed.

"I like messing with the priest," he said. "He hates when I do that."

Tom flung open the door. "Jericho! How many times have I told you not to do that?"

Tom wasn't what I imagined. He was a younger man, about six feet tall and a medium build. He had black hair that reached down to his shoulders. It was slicked back as if he'd used too much hair gel. He had lighter skin, but I could see that he was Latino. He wore an all-black suit with black shoes. An oversized gold crucifix hung around his *neck from a black beaded rope. He didn't wear a priest's collar, and I wondered why he was called a priest.*

"Are you gonna just stand there belly-aching, Tom?" Jericho smiled. "Or are you gonna let us in?"

"I think I want to stand here and belly-ache some more," Tom said. "Now, who is this, another assistant?"

"Oh." Jericho gestured to me. "This is Mrs. Susan Taki. Apparently, she's come here to kill you because someone told her that you were evil."

Jericho burst into laughter again. Tom looked at me and then at Jericho. He burst into laughter as well. I could feel my face turning red, as if I was being left out of an inside joke. I entered the room and sat in a chair in the far corner and stared at Tom from head to toe. I didn't see anything special or threatening about him. Natasha was the queen of our order; how could this ordinary-looking man defeat her. There had to be more to him.

I allowed myself to slump into the chair as my guard came down. The one thing the priest had going in his favor that day was the slayer. I admired the slayer and actually felt a slight crush growing as well. Jericho was cute…in a rough kind of way. So, I decided to wait, or at least until I got the priest alone.

"But enough about me." Susie punched Kay in the gut. "Let's talk about you…demon."

"B-But, how did you know?"

Susan pulled out her nun-chucks and pressed them against the demon's throat. "About halfway into the story when your breathing turned into grunting, and your skin began to turn pale. Now, is Kay still alive?"

The demon's voice became deeper and menacing. "She's dead, bitch. I broke her freaking neck before I took her body. Now, let me go."

The demon pushed Susie's nun-chucks away, grabbed Susie's arm, and tossed her across the empty room. The demon, down on all four arms and legs, rushed over to Susie, but Susie kicked the demon in the face. The demon rolled over on the floor, clutching it's jaw. Susie ran over and whipped around her nunchucks, popping the demon in the head and face. Sparks lit up the darkened room with each blow.

The demon's voice transformed back to Kay's voice. "No, Susie. Please don't."

"You bastard." Susie repeatedly punched the demon in the face. "How dare you?"

The demon slumped over on the floor. Susie bent down to one knee and put her hand on the demon's head.

"Extraho (extract)."

The demon's essence flowed into Susie's body, and the blue electricity lit up the room. A tear ran down Susie's face. She'd broken her promise to Kay. Even worse, she'd inflicted bodily harm on Kay's body to destroy the demon that had possessed her.

Part 3

THE HELLFIRE RING

Baltimore, Maryland

Two days had passed. Jericho arrived at his Baltimore apartment and lay on his green living room couch. The apartment was almost empty except for the couch, a TV, and a few dishes in the kitchen. The only other room that had furniture was his bedroom, which had a bed and a lamp on a nightstand.

Jericho dug in between the couch cushions and found the remote control and turned the TV on. It was already on his favorite channel, BNNN, the Baltimore National News Network. Most of his cases came from watching the channel because it reported on strange occurrences across the nation. The channel showed a documentary about Area 51, so Jericho muted the sound and placed the remote back under a seat cushion. He got up and went into his bedroom, in which the entire room and its contents were all black.

Jericho cut on his lamp, walked over and slipped open the closet door. Only two pairs of black cargo jeans and matching shirts hung from hangers. He reached down and pulled up two loose wooden boards in the floor. He pulled out a small green lockbox and walked back to sit on his bed. He pulled out a silver key that hung from a necklace around his neck. *Good thing Comet and those vamps didn't find this, or they probably would have tried to kill me.*

Jericho opened the lockbox. Considering the contents was

a rotting severed hand, it didn't smell. He picked up the hand and studied the ruby ring on the middle finger. *Comet wants this ring or the Book of the Dead…or both. Hangoctuforre needs either one of the two to break down the wall between the underworld and Earth. I can't let him have the ring. It's too powerful. And we can't give him the book. It's too important. I'll go back to New York. I'm sure Tom has a plan by now. I've only got one more day until that clown-posse comes gunning for me. But this time, I'll have the Sword of Caine.*

Jericho tried to pull the ring off the finger. It didn't budge. He threw the hand against the wall in hopes of jarring the ring loose. Still nothing. *Dammit, Hangy. What in the hell is up with this ring?* Jericho let out a smile. The mentioning of his nickname for the Hangman was amusing. Jericho tried one last time to pull the ring off the finger with the same result. He decided to put the ring back in the lockbox and take it with him. He went back to his living room, cut off the TV and picked up his over-sized duffle bag. It housed the Sword of Caine. Now, the bag was also home to his sword, the Hangman's severed hand, and the Hellfire Ring. Jericho left the apartment and went down to the parking garage where his stolen black pickup truck was parked. He got in and had to hotwire it again before he drove off.

Sampson, Maine

It was around midnight in the small town, and the pub called Thirst Quencher was the only business still opened in the downtown area. It was on the corner right next to a lumber store, and the aroma of fresh chopped wood remained in the air. The blue neon lights that bared the Thirst Quencher's name lit up the area. A green beam of light blew the door off its hinges. Kente waited for the smoke and splintered wood

to settle. He walked in the pub and looked around at the surprised patrons, who were all stood in anticipation. The huge
white and bald bartender, wearing a white t-shirt, black leather vest and blue jeans, pulled out a shotgun from behind the
bar. He had a goatee and looped earrings in his ear.

"Who the hell are you?" the bartender asked. "That's my
fucking door!"

"So, this is your place?" Kent kicked wooden shrapnel out
of the way. "That's all I needed to know."

Kente pointed the ring at the bartender and fired a green
beam of light. It struck the bartender in the chest. He fell
backward and crashed into the wall of bottles of liquor behind
him. The bartender stood, and before he could speak, he burst
into ashes. The other patrons tried to run toward the back, but
Kente shot a beam of light toward the ceiling in the back, col-
lapsing it to block the exit. The vampires, about five of them,
all dressed in blue jeans, t-shirts, and black boots, stood ready
to fight. A couple wore blue-jean vests, and the other wore
leather jackets. They belong to a vampire biker gang. They all
exposed their vampire faces. They were lumpy and disfigured.
Their fangs were also exposed. The humans, also numbering
five, cowered in the corner next to the rubble.

Kente crept toward the center of the bar. "I'm going to
give you guys one chance and one chance only to tell me what
I want to know. If I don't like the answers I get, I'll start dis-
secting your limbs one by one."

The vampires all stared at each other then back at Kente.
The taller vampire in the front with long white hair leaped
into the air and launched at Kente. Kente shot a beam of light
and hit the vampire in the face. He turned to dust in midair.

"Anybody else?" Kente asked. "No? Good. Now tell me where I can find the sorcerer Damian Red?"

There was a long silence as the vampires stared at Kente and the ring he held out, pointing at them. They hissed and huffed. Their chests moved in and out. Saliva dripped from their mouths.

"Fine." Kente pointed the ring at the nearest vampire. "Suit yourselves."

Kente shot a beam of light at the vampire's leg, and the leg exploded into ashes. The vampire fell to the floor on his side. Kente then shot another beam and struck the vampire in the arm. The arm turned to ashes as well. Kente smiled. *I'm starting to enjoy this.*

"One last time, bloodsuckers." Kente pointed the ring at the vampire's head. "Tell me what I want to know."

"G-Go screw y-yourself, Cromwell," the vampire managed to say.

Kente fired and hit the vampire in the forehead. The vampire's head exploded, and soon, the rest of his body turned to ashes.

Kente turned to the other vampires. "Ok. Who's next?"

Another vampire, younger and portly, held up his hand. "But they'll kill us."

Kente smiled. "And what do you think I'm here to do to you? I said I'd dissect you if you didn't give me any info. I never said I'd let you live."

The vampire shrugged and attacked. Kente shot a beam of light and struck him in the chest. He burst into ashes.

"You know what?" Kente looked at the two remaining vampires. "Screw it."

Kent shot two beams of light and knocked the vampires to the floor. Once they tried to get up, they turned to ash. Kente turned his attention to the scared humans in the back. He shook his head as most were still bleeding from vampire bites on their necks or forearms. Kente's eyes glowed green. He and the ring were becoming one. He pointed the ring at the humans.

"You all are just as bad as those vamps." He sighed. "Say goodbye."

Kente shot a green beam of light, and it hit a young male human in the back as he tried to turn away. The man staggered forward and bumped into the other humans. He looked down at his hands and saw they were glowing green.

The man looked back at Kente and held out his hands. "B-But why?"

He fell forward to the floor, and his body turned to red liquid. Kente pointed the ring at a female. He turned to the side as he heard thunder from outside. His eyes flickered back and forth from neon green to their regular brown color. Lightning struck the ground just outside the open door. When the smoke cleared, a tall, long-haired brunette stood in its place. He wore sunglasses and a white trench coat. His skin was pale, and he had to duck to step inside the opening through the rubble.

"That's enough, Kente," he said. "These are humans. Yes, they're flawed, but they're humans nonetheless."

"Wait a minute." Kente cocked his head to the side. "I remember you. You're that angel that fought my dad."

BA, the Bad Angel, standing at almost seven feet, put his hands on his hips. "Yes, that was me. And now I'm here stop you before you make another mistake."

Kente's eyes watered. "They killed my mother."

BA held out his hands. "Look, I'm sorry about what happened to your mother. I truly am. But this is not the way."

"Step aside, angel." Kente waved his hand across his body. "I'll leave and leave the rest of this trash alone. But *I will* be leaving."

"I can't let you do that without confiscating the ring. It's too dangerous."

Kente smiled. "So, you really want the ring, do you?"

"Kente, do n—"

Kente raised his hand and shot a green beam of light at BA, who dove to the side, and the beam blew a hole in the wall. BA stood and pointed at his own ring, the white marbled Peace Ring, at Kente. He fired a white beam of light. Kent just as quickly fired a beam of light from the Ring of Light. The two beams collided in the middle. A blinding light exploded from the impact. However, Kente knew his ring had no equal. He fired a constant beam of light at BA. BA countered with a constant beam of light from his ring. The two beams collided again in the middle of the room. Kente's beam began to overtake BA's and forced the angel backward. As the green beam got closer to BA, the angel began to slide back. The vein his forehead began to thicken, and he began to sweat.

BA pulled away and jumped through the shattered door to the street. He looked to the sky. His eyes lit up, and he summoned his battle armor. It was black metal, the kind knights wore in the medieval days, with a red cape. Before BA could adjust to wearing his armor, a green beam of light struck him in the chest. The shot made him collapse to the ground on his back. The rings were known to be lethal. But BA's armor absorbed the brunt of the blow. His chest plate was dented, and with Kente approaching, there was no time for the armor to regenerate from the damage. It was known to do so after a day or two, depending on what caused the damage.

Kente stood over BA and prepared to shoot another beam at BA's head. But the angel sprouted his wings and took off.

"Just like I thought." Kente looked to the sky and watched BA disappear into the night air. "No one can stop me."

Kente turned around back to the pub. BA was standing behind him and punched Kente in the face. Kente fell to the ground and back-peddled away from BA. Once he was far enough away, he stood and wiped the blood from his lip. He was groggy. Even with the ring, he was still human, and the punch from the angel discombobulated him. He tried to focus, but his eyesight was blurry. He held his fist up toward the sky. BA prepared for another attack. But a green forcefield engulfed Kente's entire body. BA ran over and threw another punch, but the forcefield was too strong to be penetrated.

BA's eyes tightened. "Whoa. He's really getting the hang of things."

BA raised his hand to fire a beam from the Peace Ring. However, Kente winked at the angel and disappeared in a fog of green mist.

New York

It was early in the morning as Jericho sat on the church steps. He didn't know where Tom lived. It was one of their rules so that no one else would eventually find out where they resided. But he'd paged Tom with their special code that meant for them to meet at the church. Jericho continued to look in all directions. He wanted to make sure he wasn't followed. The streets were almost empty except for the few people that worked early.

Jericho looked to his left and saw Tom walking toward the church. *He loves walking. I'll never get over that. It must be one of the reasons he hates the fact that I commandeer pickup trucks.* Jericho stood and folded his arms. He looked down at Tom's shoes and laughed. They were black tennis shoes that were dusty and tattered.

"Now what?" Tom asked as he stood in front of Jericho. "I feel like you're always laughing at me."

Jericho shook his head. "Those shoes are screaming out in pain, my friend."

"Screw you, Jericho." Tom smiled and pushed his way past the slayer. "Everyone can't just take what they want, including shoes. Now, why have you dragged me out here this early?"

Jericho looked in all directions again. "I think it'll be better if we talked inside."

Tom used a large silver skeleton key to open one of the double brown church doors. He led the way as Jericho followed. They walked down the center aisle of the church and nodded at the nuns, who were up early as well, placing programs in the pews.

When they arrived at Tom's back office, he fished around for his keys in his front pocket. When he opened the door, he put on the lamp on the nearby desk, and Jericho pushed past Tom. He threw his duffle bag on the floor and rushed over to the cot on the other side of the room. Jericho lay down on the green blanket on the cot, crossed his legs, and interlocked his hands behind his head on the pillow.

"You sure do have a way of making yourself comfortable, big guy." Tom closed the door and leaned up against it with his arms folded. "Some people might consider that to be rude."

"Yeah, yeah, yeah," Jericho said as he shook his head and sank deeper into the cot. "Where's the Book of the Dead?"

"Hidden."

"Shouldn't I know where it is as well?" Jericho asked. "After all, it is part of the prophecy of the Death Brothers. The last time I checked, I was one, and you were the other."

Tom shook his head. "You need to let that go, Jericho. You're the vampire slayer, and I hunt demons. End of story."

"We're considered the second coming of some badass dudes, Tom. You need to accept it."

Tom waved his hand at Jericho. "Whatever. Why do you want to know where the book is?"

"I had a visit from our fallen angel friend the other day." Jericho sat up and supported himself by resting on his elbows. "He was with a nest of vampires."

"Comet?"

"That's the one," Jericho said. "They turned my assistant, and I was forced to dust him."

"Whoa!" Tom put his hand over his heart. "John's dead?"

"Unfortunately."

"Wow. Makes you wonder if we're dooming these people to sure death."

"My conscience is clear, priest," Jericho said. "I don't force anyone to join me."

"You're a cold man, Jericho." Tom sighed. "But they came after you for the book?" Tom asked, "That's weird. They've probably known I've had it for a while."

"Well," Jericho sat up on the edge of the cot and placed his feet on the floor, "they also want Hangy's Hellfire Ring."

"And what makes them think you have it?"

"Because I do." Jericho nodded toward his duffle bag. "I kinda scooped it up after BA cut off the Hangman's hand."

"Really? Let me see it."

Jericho got up and walked over to get his duffle bag. He placed it on the cot and unzipped it. Tom walked over and peered down into the bag. Jericho pulled out the green lockbox, opened it, and placed it on the cot. The decayed hand still did not smell like a rotting piece of flesh.

"Jeez, Jericho," Tom said. "You could have at least taken the ring off that disgusting thing."

"You go right on ahead and try to pull it off." Jericho held out his hand toward the lockbox. "If you can, I'll give you a thousand dollars."

Tom burst into laughter. "You don't have a thousand dollars, big guy. It's why you're always stealing stuff. But I'll take your word for it. So why do they want the ring and the book?"

Jericho shrugged. "I'm assuming they accomplish the same thing and that's to allow that bastard, Hangoc—"

The lamp flickered and thunder sounded.

"Jericho!" Tom pushed Jericho's shoulder. "You know better than to say his name."

"Dammit, Tom. We're in a church, for crying out loud. Aren't we protected in here?"

Tom sighed. "Never mind that for now. What do we do about Comet?"

"Well, he gave me three days to hand over the ring." Jericho rubbed his chin. "That was two and a half days ago. They'll be back and we need to be ready for a fight. So, before it's too late, go ahead and drop to your knees and do what has to be done."

Tom jerked his head to the side and stared at Jericho. "Man. What in the hell are you talking about? We're best friends but—"

"Not that, you perv and moron." Jericho laughed. "I'm saying that we need some backup and to call your angel friend."

"Ha. Ha. Ha." Tom's face turned red and held up his finger. "But wait. So now the big badass vampire slayer suddenly needs back up? This is funny."

"Hey, man." Jericho walked toward the far wall and leaned against it. "We are up against a fallen angel, vampires, probably demons, and I'm sure that sorcerer won't be far behind."

"Wow! You know what? You're right." Tom bent down to his knees. "Those are tough odds, even for us."

"Indeed. That extra firepower will come in handy."

Tom bowed his head and clasped his hand together over the cot. "Artherial, the Bad Angel. This is Tom Padilla, and we need your help. Please come as quickly as you can."

Jericho looked around the room and then at Tom. "Was that it?"

"That's it. All we have to do is pray to him."

Suddenly the light began to flicker and then went off. The room was dark, and Jericho backed up against the wall again.

"Here we go with this crap again," Jericho said.

When the lamp came back on, the six-foot-ten angel stood in front of the door. He had his hair in a ponytail and had on his dark sunglasses. He moved his head from side to side to crack the neck.

"Ahh, Thomas," BA began. "It's so nice to see you again. Same to you, Jericho," he said dryly.

"Still the leader of my fan club, I see, angel." Jericho used his foot to push himself away from the wall. "It's too bad that only people with souls get my sense of humor."

"Is that what you call it, slayer?" BA smiled and ground his teeth. "Because I think your humor is quite juvenile at best."

Jericho threw his head back and laughed. "Oh, really? Sounds like to me that when you left Purgatory, you kept that stick stuck up your ass."

"You know what, slayer?" BA took a few steps toward Jericho. "I'm already getting tired of your mouth."

Jericho walked toward BA. "Do something about it."

BA's eyes glowed white, and the Peace Ring on his finger did as well. Jericho's eyes glowed white well. The Sword of Caine glowed and shook inside the duffle bag.

BA balled up his fist. "You don't really think that your feeble slayer skills are a match for me, do you?"

Jericho balled up his fist as well as he peered up at the taller angel. "I've faced off with tougher guys than you, my friend."

"Ok." Tom stepped in between the two and pressed his hands up against their chests. "That's enough. We're on the same side here. We have a literal end of days around the corner. We don't have time for this."

Jericho and BA both turned and walked away from each other. Jericho went back to his corner, and BA leaned against the door again. They both gave each other intense stares, but each knew Tom was right.

Jericho wiped his hands on his pants leg and walked over to BA. "He's got a point, Pale Ale. We have bigger fish to fry."

BA extended his hand and shook Jericho's. "I agree. Now, what's going on?"

"That demon dispatched Comet to go after Jericho and the Hellfire Ring," Tom said.

BA turned to Jericho. "Slayer…you didn't."

"I did." Jericho dropped his head. "I went back and found it. Sorry."

"After Nevada," BA began. "I looked all over for that thing."

"Well, at least we know it was in good hands." Tom held up his finger. "But now they know Jericho has it. They've always known I've had the book. It's only a matter of time before they come looking for both."

"And they're not alone," Jericho said. "They're running with packs of vampires, probably demons, and that sorcerer is lurking about as well, I'll assume."

BA pounded his fist in his other hand. "Sounds like Nevada all over again."

"Yeah," Tom cut in. "But now we're dealing with a fallen angel, a sorcerer, and that demon. The stakes are a little higher this time, especially if they get their hands on the book or the ring."

"We need some help, man." Jericho put his hand on BA's shoulder. "And we need it now."

"Well, I'm here, aren't I?" BA asked.

"Not just you." Tom sat on the cot. "We need the wizard."

"Ha. Ha. Ha." Jericho clapped once. "Even after he got his ass handed to him the last time him, and the sorcerer faced off. But who are we kidding here? You guys know that's not who I was talking about. We need the Hangman."

"You're kidding, right?" BA asked. "He only has a little

time left in Purgatory. He may not even want to help. But then again—"

"What?" Tom stood again. "What is it?"

"Someone killed his wife, Dorothy." BA dropped his head and shook it. "And his son, Junior, is running around like a loose cannon, killing everyone in his path…including humans."

There was a long silence as they all stared at each other. Jericho sighed and shook his head as well. As much as he wanted to reunite with the Hangman, he didn't want to have to deal with a vengeful Hangman. They'd seen that story play out before. *And of what of Kente Jr? If I'm reading the angel correctly, there's no way he lets the kid walk away from this.*

"How is Junior doing this?" Jericho asked. "He's just a kid."

"He's a kid with the Ring of Light," BA said. "And he's learning to master it as each day passes."

"Wow!" Tom paced the middle of the room. "That ring is more powerful than the Peace Ring and Hellfire Ring combined, right?"

BA sighed. "Exactly."

"Then what more of reason do we need to bust out Hangy from Purgatory?" Jericho threw his hands in the air. "We just can't sit around and let the fight come to us on several fronts. We need to be proactive."

"Darn!" BA dropped his head and put his hands on his hips. "Ok. Give me the ring. But if this blows up in our face, I'm blaming you, slayer."

"I wouldn't expect anything else, coming from you." Jericho smiled. "Now, Tom, it's your job to go get the wizard. He's about to be a new father, so he might be a little reluctant to come…especially after that last ass whooping the sorcerer gave him."

Tom shrugged. "And what will you be doing?"

"I'll be out west." Jericho walked over and zipped his duffle bag. "I'll go and retrieve Ms. Taki."

"Ms. Taki?" BA asked.

Jericho walked up to the angel, gave him the lockbox, and patted him on the back. "Don't worry, angel. She's adorable. You'll like her. It'll make Tom jealous, but he'll get over it."

Tom followed Jericho out of the office. "Very funny, Jericho...you jerk."

BA followed as well. "My God. What have I gotten myself mixed up in with these humans?"

They walked out the front doors of the church. BA sprouted his wings and took off. Jericho and Tom stared at each other. Tom sighed, while Jericho had a smile on his face. They then looked up and watched as BA was barely visible.

"Well, there he goes." Jericho turned and spat on the ground. "The great white Bad Angel, himself. Damn, he's so anal. Guess that's why you like him."

"At least he's not a homicidal half-demon."

"Don't worry about Hangy." Jericho nodded. "He likes me."

"That's what I'm afraid of."

Part 4

THE HANGMAN RETURNS

Kente Cromwell Sr. sat on the front porch of his log cabin in Purgatory. As always, the sky was clear and blue. The weather was warm, and a gentle breeze brushed off his face. Besides sitting on the porch, most of his days consisted of chopping wood and thinking about what led him to his unearthly confinement. He didn't want to fight his situation anymore, and just serve his time. He knew he was wrong for his actions in his life on Earth. He'd committed adultery and betrayed the love and trust of his family. But until then, he lived a peaceful and righteous life. He knew it was why he was serving time in Purgatory and not punished in a more tortuous place.

He thought about how he'd made a deal with Hangoctuffore to become the Hangman. How he escaped Purgatory by getting the better of BA. And how he killed many people, including his son's girlfriend, to get his revenge. His daily reflection was part of his punishment.

Cromwell looked up and saw what he thought was a bird headed in his direction. He cocked his head to the side and his eyes squinted as the object became larger as it got closer. He then realized what it was and who it was. *BA. Why can't this guy leave me alone?*

BA landed in front of Cromwell's cabin. His wings

disappeared as he walked closer to the porch. Cromwell stood and placed his hands behind his back. He leaned up against a diagonal wooden log, which helped support the canopy covering the porch.

"I'm going to start thinking that you're sweet on me, angel." Cromwell smiled. "You finally got your freedom from this place, and here you are again."

"Don't flatter yourself, Cromwell." BA put a foot on the bottom step. "I'm here on official business."

"What business could you possibly have with me?" Cromwell asked. "You don't have anything to do with this place anymore."

"This is about your son."

"Kente?"

"He's lost it." BA twirled his finger around his temple. "Against my better judgement, we figured you were the only one who could reach him."

"What's he doing?" Cromwell asked. "And who is 'we'?"

"Your buddy, the slayer, and Padilla."

"Wow. It's that bad?"

"Yes." BA nodded. "He's killed humans…with the Ring of Light. You remember that thing, right? After all, you're the one that left it in his possession."

Cromwell laughed. "I do. Is this something else you're going to blame on me?"

"I'm not here to argue. You've done your time."

"Well, let's go inside, angel." Cromwell gestured toward the front door. "I'm tired of sitting out here."

San Diego

The red and black, sleek, and modern motorcycle whizzed by all the cars in traffic on a regular street. There were several cars in the street but enough room for the rider to drive by them. The sun was bright at midday and at its peak. The rider wore a black helmet with a tinted visor, black leather pants, a red leather jacket, and black tennis shoes. It was Susan Taki. Right behind her were three of the same style motorcycles with men all wearing black suits and black helmets. She looked back and saw one pulling up on the right side. One pulled up on her left. The other stayed behind her. She was surrounded, so she got on an on-ramp and got on the highway, which had less traffic. The other bikes followed.

A blue pickup truck drove up smashed into the bike at her rear. The bike flipped forward and over Susan's head. The rider crashed to the ground. Susan and the other riders dodged the wrecked bike and passed it. When he stood up, the pickup truck pulled up beside him. Jericho swung the Sword of Caine out the window and chopped off the rider's head. Jericho pushed the gas pedal to the floor. The wheels of the truck made a streaking noise. Smoke emitted from them as Jericho sped off in Susan's direction.

As Jericho pulled up behind Susan, she turned and recognized the slayer. He pointed to her right, which meant he'd take the rider on the right. She nodded. Jericho then sped up and got next to the rider on the right. Susan slammed on the brakes and stopped. The rider on her left stopped as well. The rider that Jericho engaged only slowed down once he recognized the slayer next to him.

Jericho tried to ram him with the truck. The rider swerved

and sped up, and Jericho watched as Susan and the other rider did U-turns and drove the other way. Jericho sped up as well to catch the other rider. When there was a small break in the median, the driver cut through it in hopes of losing Jericho. But Jericho turned the wheel to make the hard left and almost turned over the truck. He kept his pursuit of the rider.

The traffic on the other side of the highway had stopped from all the damaged cars. Susie and the rider chasing her continued going in the opposite direction. Jericho smiled. It was what he would have done. He didn't know if the pickup truck could catch the motorcycle, but he pressed the gas pedal to the floor. The truck began to shake as it reached the speed of one hundred and twenty miles per hour. Neither he nor the rider could go as fast as they wanted because they still had to maneuver through traffic.

As they reached an overhead bridge, Jericho was surprised as he began to slow down because the rider slowed. When the rider stopped, Jericho looked across to the other side of the highway and saw Susie with her hand on top of a young Asian man's head. Their bikes were crashed in the middle of the highway. Jericho watched as blue electricity flowed from the man's body to Susie's body. *Wow! So that's what her gift looks like. Impressive.*

The rider Jericho pursued got off his bike and let it fall the ground. He jumped over the median to attack Susie. She looked just in time, with her eyes still glowing blue, and backflipped about five feet. She landed in a fight stance and stared at Jericho.

Jericho shrugged. "You don't need my help."

The rider pulled out two knives from his back pocket and

held them in both hands. Susie moved her head from side to side to crack her neck. She lifted her jacket and pulled out her nun-chucks from the small of her back. She whipped them around. They made a whistling sound against the wind.

The rider didn't remove his helmet and launched at Susie. She slid her hips backward to avoid being stabbed in the gut. She jumped in the hair, and with a spinning heel kick, knocked the rider backward. It gave Susie the time to study the rider more for weak points. They charged each other. She flipped over his head and kicked him in the back. He fell forward. Before he could recover, Susie jumped on his back and wrapped the chain of the nun-chucks around the rider's neck. He attempted to stab her, but with the strength she acquired from the other demon-possessed man, she was able to lift the rider up in the air and slam him back to the ground.

His helmet cracked and then popped off his head, exposing another Asian demon-possessed man with dyed blonde hair. He got up to run away, but Jericho threw the Sword of Caine, and it lodged itself in the ground in front of the demon to stop his get-away. The demon turned back to Susie and gripped his knives tighter. He let out a battle yell and attacked again. She kicked him in the stomach, and he doubled over. She stepped back and swung her nun-chucks from side to side and smacked him in the face several times. The electric currents from each hit seemed to semi-paralyze the demon. He dropped the knives and tried to punch her. She ducked and came back up with an uppercut, knocking the demon backward, and his head bounced off the concrete. Susie jumped down with her knees on his chest and then sat. He shook his head violently to avoid her placing her hand on him.

Susie placed her hand on his forehead. "Sit back and take it, you son-of-a-bitch!"

The demon's yellow essence, a smoky vapor, tried to escape through his ears, but Susie's grip was already too tight. The vapor was sucked back inside the body, causing the demon's body to jerk. Finally, the blue electricity flowed from the demon's body and into Susie's. He hemorrhaged. Susie smiled as it dawned on her that the human was still alive. She could feel it.

"Oh, thank God." She stood and offered her hand to the Asian man. "Are you ok?"

He grabbed Susie's hand and pulled himself up. "What happened? The last thing I remember was I was at a birthday party in China Town."

"It's a long story," Susie said.

"Is that Nahn Ho over there?" He pointed to the other rider a few feet away who lay dead on the ground. "He was at the same party."

"I'm sorry." Susie picked up her nun-chucks. "I couldn't save him. Now, go home. I'm sure it'll all come back to you one day."

The man slowly walked away, staring back and forth at Susie and the dead Asian. He grabbed his forehead and tears ran down his eyes.

"Nice work, young lady," Jericho said as he approached Susie, and they watched the man walk away. "You know what? You would make a good assistant."

"Nice work?" Susie punched Jericho on the arm. "You were almost no help, Caine. I could have been killed."

"But you weren't."

"Is that how you get your rocks off?" she asked. "Because it's obvious you're not interested in women that are attracted to you."

Jericho raised his eyebrows as he stared down at Susie. "Listen. I came here to ask for your help."

"My help?" Susie stepped backward and put her hand across her chest. "Wow! Me and the slayer, side by side, kicking butt."

Jericho laughed. "Well, not exactly. It's me, you, Tom, a wizard, an angel, and hopefully a half-demon."

"Holy crap!" Susie's eyes bulged. "This is it, isn't it? What you guys told me about?"

"We think so," Jericho said as he pulled his sword out of pavement and stuck it in the sheath. "And we need all the help we can get. Are you in?"

She slapped Jericho on the butt. "You bet your sweet ass."

Jericho dropped his head and chuckled to himself. "Oh, Lord."

Purgatory

Cromwell and BA sat in the log cabin's living area and sipped tea. Neither person trusted the other, so neither took their eyes off the other. Cromwell stood from his brown cloth chair and walked over to the fireplace. He used two mittens to raise the tea kettle resting over the fire. He poured another cup of tea and returned to his chair.

"Wow," BA began. "You need mittens to lift that? Given who you are, I'm surprised."

"I don't have any powers here, BA. You made sure of that." Cromwell held up his cup and gestured to BA. "Another one?"

"Cut the crap, Cromwell," BA said. "We're not friends or

some old buddies. I came to ask for your help. If you don't want to give it, then I'll deal with Junior myself."

"You wouldn't dare touch my son after you put me in here, angel."

"Oh, wouldn't I?"

"Let's just say, things would get a little uncomfortable in this world...for everyone."

"Is that a threat...Hangman?" BA put his cup down and stood. "This place was supposed to purge you of all those kinds of thoughts."

Cromwell stood as well and put up his hand. "Calm yourself, BA. But you're talking about hurting my kid. It's a natural fatherly instinct."

"You mean like how you murdered his girlfriend and her whole family."

"Why are you bringing up old stuff?"

The two supernatural beings breathed in and out deeply, then sat again. BA leaned over his chair and picked up the green lockbox he'd brought with him. The sun disappeared behind a patch of clouds that had formed over Cromwell's cabin. They turned to look out the window. They'd seen a dark and cloudy day only once in the mythical place. It was day Kente Cromwell Sr. became the Hangman and escaped.

BA waved it off and got back to what he was doing. He opened the lockbox, and lightning struck the front porch of the cabin. A fire ignited where the lighting struck. BA and Cromwell stared at each other. Cromwell walked over to the door, and another bolt of lightning crashed in front of him and forced him to back up.

Cromwell turned to BA. "What do you have in there, angel?"

"This."

BA pulled out Cromwell's rotting hand with the Hellfire Ring attached. The Ring was glowing red and pulsating.

"Where'd you get that?" Cromwell asked.

"The slayer." BA backed up as the front wall of the cabin caught fire. "He and the demon hunter believe you are the only one that can take the ring off and use it."

"The hell you say?"

"Exactly."

The fire dissipated, and a bright white figure stood in its wake. He was tall, bald, pale, wore a brown trench coat and sunglasses. He had a goatee, and his hands were huge as he balled his fist. He stretched out his hand, and with an invisible force, picked up Cromwell and tossed him into the far wall. The same force kept Cromwell from stuck to the wall.

"What are you doing, Artherial?" the stranger asked

"How's it going, Haniel?" BA put the lockbox on the table. "I was wondering if I'd run into you. Now, please. Release the human."

"What's going on here, Artherial? How dare you bring that thing here to Purgatory? It's forbidden."

"It and he are a part of a mission I'm on." BA took a step backward toward Cromwell, who was still pressed against the wall. "I need you to release him."

"You know, when they gave you my job years ago as the guardian of this place, I felt bad for you." Haniel moved closer to BA and Cromwell. "When you got stuck with the name, Bad Angel, I felt bad for you. But right now, brother, I can't think of any reason not to turn you in and not have you punished again."

"The fate of the world, brother," BA said.

Haniel looked at Cromwell and then at BA. "Has nothing to do with Heaven or Purgatory."

BA tossed the lockbox, and it landed below Cromwell. "Fine."

The two angels rushed across the room and collided. Neither backed up as they grabbed each other's hands and pressed their chest against one another. Both then sprouted their wings. They took off and exploded through the roof of the cabin. Cromwell fell to the floor just as the cabin collapsed.

A pile of wooden rubble slammed down onto Cromwell, trapping him underneath. He tried moving his legs first but couldn't. He tried moving his arms next, and only one could barely move. As he tried to push up from the floor, a shooting pain ran through his side. He felt a sharp pain in his ribs. He figured at least two were broken or cracked. He then saw the red glow from the opened lockbox he'd landed on. It was the cause of his damaged ribs, and at the same time, it was his salvation if he could reach inside.

Cromwell came up with a plan. He had to maneuver his trapped body into a fetal position. He used all his strength in his legs to move them up to his stomach to the point where he was kneeling. He pulled his arms in to place his hands flat on the floor. He then pressed upward with his back again. The pain in his ribs trickled through his entire body. He stopped as the collapsed house pressed down harder on his back. He heard the two angels grappling on top of the wreckage. *Dammit BA. You left the ring, so I could retrieve it. Now, go fight that angel away from here.*

Once he heard them fly off again, he tried to press up the

wooden logs once more. He only needed a little space to put his hand on the lockbox. He pushed up again, and that's when the pressure caused his ribs to crack even more. He screamed out in pain.

Cromwell lowered his back. There was no way out. He'd have to wait until the angels were finished and hope BA was the victor. He thought about his wife Dorothy and their son Kente Jr. Then, an uneasy feeling rushed through his head. *The angel isn't telling me everything. Why would Junior be running around killing people? Where's Dorothy in all this? Junior loves his mother. Surely, she would be able to stop him. Something's amiss.*

Cromwell took a deep breath. "Ahhh!"

He arched his back and pressed his arms and knees to the ground. Through the pain, he was able to lift the wooden logs just slightly enough to stick his hand underneath his body and was able to slide out the severed hand under his body. He latched on to the Hellfire Ring and pulled it off. It was just as BA had said. Cromwell was the only one who could have. However, putting on the ring would prove just as difficult as Cromwell had to allow the collapsed logs to come crashing down again

He cuffed hands over the ring and allowed the ruble to crush his body. He maneuvered his right hand underneath the left and slipped on the ring. He took a deep breath as the weight of the fallen cabin and the lack of air made his eyes roll. He almost passed out.

But then a red glow lit up the rubble underneath the house. Thunder and lightning echoed overhead. Finally, an explosion sent wooden logs flying in each direction. When the smoke cleared, a tall man, wearing a black robe with a hooked staff, burned flesh, and glowing red eyes stood where the log cabin once sat. His hooked staff was a dark metal pole with a large sharpened hook on top and a half sword at the bottom. It was made of the famed black steel, which was able to cut through anything. The Hangman was back. He reached behind his back and pulled the hood over his head to where only his fiery red eyes, a burned nose, and mouth were seen.

The Hangman looked up just in time to see a silver sword headed his way. He raised his hooked staff and blocked it to the ground. The owner of the sword, Haniel, was right behind the sword, with BA trailing him. Haniel landed a few feet in front of the Hangman and reached out to call his sword back to his hand. BA landed a few feet behind Haniel.

"And where do you think you're going, demon?" Haniel asked. "You're not leaving here again. I won't allow it."

"Ahh," the Hangman began. "Purgatory's new watchdog. Turn around and ask the old one what happens when I make up my mind that I want to leave."

BA jumped over Haniel's head and landed between the angel and Hangman. "Listen, guys. This doesn't have to go this way. This is not what I came back for."

Haniel got in his fighting stance. "You know very well that this is exactly how this has to happen, brother. He's not going anywhere."

San Diego

Jericho and Susie drove in the pickup truck and headed east. It was about midnight and Jericho's favorite time to drive. Besides, with his size, it was uncomfortable to take a plane. Susie, visibly upset about driving all the way to New York, pouted the entire way until they reached the edge of California.

"How have you survived this long driving around the country?" Susie broke the silence. "This is kinda stupid, slayer."

"I've been doing this for a very long time and I've only died once."

Susie cocked her head to the side. "Once? Are you serious? Tell me about it."

"It's a long story." Jericho turned slightly but did not take his eyes off the road. "Tom and I ran into three old-school demons. One of them named Pick managed to stick two icepicks in my back. I died. And because Tom and I are the so-called reincarnations of the famed Death Brothers, he was able to bring me back."

"Tom Padilla?"

"Yeah."

"What is it with you and that guy?" Susie glared out the window. "You guys act like lovers, brothers, and enemies, all rolled into one."

"Hey." Jericho raised his finger. "Enough of that crap. I love Tom Padilla. I'd give my life for that guy."

"I know. Others have too."

"Are you still on that?"

"You guys haven't done or said anything yet to change my mind about that guy."

"Tom's father, his great grandfather, and great grand-uncle were all men of God." Jericho thumbed the steering wheel. "He'll go down as a saint when he finally bites it, albeit a tainted one. Hahaha."

Susie's head turned as far as it could to look out the window. "Hold on. Did you see that?"

"What?"

"Oh, my God." She punched the air with her fists. "I say again. How have you survived this long?"

"I'm an ass-kicker."

"Ok, *ass-kicker*. Turn around. Two vampires are mauling someone on the side of the road back there."

The long two-lane highway was empty, so Jericho executed a U-turn with no problem. He sped back to the scene where two male vampires were dragging an older man into a wheat field.

Jericho's nostrils flared open. "I don't go around telling you how to catch and kill demons. Vampires are my specialty."

"Well maybe somebody *should* tell you something," Susie countered. "Jeez, I might have to take you up on that assistant thing."

Jericho turned off the road and stopped at the edge of the wheat-field. They got out of the truck. Susie already had her nun-chucks in hand as Jericho pulled out the Sword of Caine from his duffle bag.

Jericho brought the sword up to his eyes. "You didn't warn me, ole buddy. What's that about?"

"You talk to it too?" Susie walked past the truck and glanced at Caine. "No wonder you're alone."

"Don't worry about me, young lady." Jericho sheathed the sword, which was strapped to his back. "I've bagged my fair share of women."

"Shame." Susie picked up the pace. "Maybe that's why you only have love for another man. It's because you've never loved or received real love from a woman."

Jericho ran past Susie. "Shut up, and let's go dust those vamps."

Susie pulled out a small flashlight and tracked the blood drops through the wheat-field.

"Why don't you just tell them where we're at with that thing?" Jericho said sarcastically. "It'll save us a lot of time."

"How else are we going to find them?"

"Pish!" Jericho twisted his lips. "I'm the slayer. This is what I do."

They walked until they came upon the old man lying face-down in the dirt. He was dead, with several bloody fang punctures covering his neck.

Jericho put his finger over his lips. "Shh. They're close by."

Susie stopped and looked around. "How close?"

"Right here, darling." A tall, gray-haired vampire leaped out from the wheat and crashed into Susie.

They fell to the ground. As Jericho ran over to help, the other, larger vampire jumped onto his back. Jericho fell face-first to the ground. He turned over, and the vampire allowed Jericho to stand and get into a fight stance.

"Wrong move, suck-head," Jericho said.

"I believe in a fair fight," the bulky bald and pale vampire replied. "Besides, I'm not the one who made the mistake of trying to play the hero."

Jericho pulled out the Sword of Caine. "Oh yeah?"

"Holy crap, Lester!" the vampire turned to the other and yelled out. "It's the slayer."

"Ok." Jericho gripped the sword tighter. "He's Lester. So, what do I call you, my huge friend?"

"The name's Hugo." The vampire pounded his fist into

his hand. "And how lucky am I? I get to feast on slayer blood tonight."

Jericho saw a blue spark across the way. It was obvious that Susie had dispatched Lester. He knew he had to get rid of Hugo just as quickly.

Jericho looked up and pointed to the sky. "Wow! Is that the moon?"

Hugo looked up and quickly looked back at Jericho upon realizing that he'd just made a mistake. A *swoosh* sound later, and Hugo's head rolled across the ground. The decapitated head and body turned to ashes a second later.

"I can't believe that worked." Jericho sheathed his sword. "That idiot had more brawn than brains, I guess."

"Again." Susie made her way through the wheat. "How are you still alive, slayer? That was the oldest trick in the book."

Jericho laughed. "It was."

She walked off. "What a shame. Some woman needs to domesticate you...and quick."

Jericho cuffed his hand around his ear. "Excuse me. I didn't quite catch that."

"Nothing," she said as her voice trailed off.

Purgatory

The Hangman extended his hand and swung his hooked staff, knowing BA would duck. He was aiming for Haniel. Surprisingly, BA didn't duck, though, and blocked the staff with his battle-ax. Haniel pushed BA aside and launched at the Hangman. He made several stabbing motions and all either missed, or the Hangman ducked or blocked them.

"It's funny how you're fighting with everything you've got,

angel, when I have this." The Hangman extended his fist with the Hellfire Ring and shot a red beam of light. "Like taking candy from a baby."

The beam of light struck Haniel in the chest and catapulted him backward. He smashed into a huge tree and fell lifeless to the ground. The Hangman moved closer with the ring, pointing at Haniel's body.

"Goodbye, angel," the Hagman said.

"No, Cromwell. I can't let you do that," BA said from behind the Hangman. "You will not kill my brother for doing his job."

"And who's gonna stop me?" Acid saliva dripped from the corner of the Hangman's mouth. "You, BA?"

"Yes…I am."

The Hangman spun around and fired a red beam of light from the Hellfire Ring just in time to collide with a white beam of light from the Peace Ring. Because the beam of light from the BA's ring was almost upon the Hangman when the half-demon blocked it, the force of the impact forced the Hangman to back up. They stood about ten feet away from each other as continuous beams of light met in the center.

"I-Is this what you really wanna do, angel?" the Hangman asked.

"I haven't had a good tussle in a while." BA planted his feet further into the ground. "So, yes, it is."

"Screw the ring, then. Let's do it hand-to-hand."

Both beings stopped the energy from their rings and prepared their weapons. The Hangman attacked first with his hooked staff. He lunged and swung wildly. He was out of practice. But he knew that the black steel of his staff only had to make slight contact with the angel to cause damage. BA blocked most of the Hangman's aggression with his battle-ax. Finally, the Hangman swung his staff, and BA ducked. The angel kicked the Hangman in the chest, sending him backward. Haniel recovered and kicked the Hangman in the back of the head. The half-demon stumbled forward. He was trapped between the two angels. One had the Peace Ring and a battle-ax. The other had vengeance in his heart and a sword.

The Hangman knew with the rings involved; he was on the same level as BA. He turned to the side to keep both angels in sight. The Hangman decided to attack Haniel. The angel was a superb swordsman, though, and matched every move the Hangman made with one of his own. He even punched the Hangman in the face. That was a mistake. The Hangman's acid-like saliva burned Haniel's hand. The angel drew his hand back and studied it. That's when a red beam of light struck him in the chest again. He flew backward and landed on his back.

The Hangman walked up to Haniel and prepared to fire again, but his non-ring shoulder was slashed from the back by BA's ax.

The Hangman dropped to one knee and held his shoulder. It bled too much for him to continue to fight. He knew his regenerative abilities didn't work fast enough to take on two angels even though Haniel was down.

"Damn you, BA." The Hangman got back to his feet. "I'm not sure I can help you now."

"What are you saying, Cromwell?" BA spread his arms out to the side. "I could have killed you if I wanted."

"I'm saying, see you around." The Hangman held up the ring in the air, and a red electricity consumed his body. "Bye, bye."

The Hangman disappeared.

Part 5

ORIGINS 2: MERLIN AND THE GRAND LIBRARIAN

Chicago, Illinois

Tom arrived at Alexander's apartment. He'd called ahead to make sure he was welcomed to visit the wizard and his new wife. Once inside the small apartment, he shook Alexander's hand and looked around for Emma.

"She's in the bedroom." Alexander pointed to the room as he realized Tom was looking for her. "She's stuffing her face as usual."

Tom laughed. "I'd hate to be your wife."

Alexander put his hands on his hips, dropped his head, and chuckled. "Yeah, sorry about that. Either she's eating, or she's cranky. But tell me. What do you think of the name Octus?"

"Do I even wanna know how you guys came up with that name?"

"My daughter's name was Octavia." Alexander's smile disappeared. "It was the least we could do to honor her."

Tom's eyes squinted. "You mean the daughter that tried to kill you and Emma?"

"That's the one."

"Wow!" Tom shook his head. "You guys are weird."

Alexander let out a deep sigh. "So, what brings you here, Father Padilla, marital lessons?"

"Three things, if we're going to be friends, Alexander." Tom sat on the couch. "First, I'm not a priest. Second, I'm not married. And third, I save all my lessons for an over-grown vampire slayer."

Alexander laughed and sat in his favorite recliner black leather chair next to the couch. "So, what's this about, Tom?"

"We're calling all of our allies." Tom leaned forward and clasped his hands together. "Jericho has already been attacked by Comet, who is looking for the Hellfire Ring and the Book and the Dead. Dorothy Cromwell, the Hangman's wife, has been killed by Damian Red as he attempted to take the Ring of Light. And now Kente, Dorothy's son, is on the loose with the ring, destroying everything and everyone on his way to get vengeance."

"Holy crap," Alexander said as he leaned back in his chair.

"That's not all."

"There's more?"

Tom nodded. "BA has gone Purgatory to convince the Hangman to return to earth and help rein in his son…and help us."

"Whoa!"

Alexander stood and held up his finger. He walked to the kitchen and opened the top cupboard. He pulled out a bottle of whiskey and grabbed two small glasses.

Alexander returned and put the glasses on the coffee table. "This calls for something stronger than just mere water or coffee."

"Indeed, it does." Tom watched as Alexander poured

whiskey into both glasses. "I see you've hidden your stress reliever well, wizard."

Alexander put his finger over his lips. "Shhh. Em doesn't know I have this."

Tom lowered his voice. "Here's to the escape from a pregnant wife."

"Ha. Ha. Ha. Indeed."

The two men clanked their glasses together in a silent toast. They continued to talk. Tom told Alexander about Susie and how Jericho had traveled to California to seek her help. Tom waited until Alexander poured another drink and drank from the glass.

"Your job, Alexander, is what it's always been."

"Oh yeah?" Alexander asked. "And what's that?"

"Damian Red."

Alexander swallowed hard. "That guy's tough, mate. I've only ever battled one other wizard as skilled as he."

Tom settled back on the couch. "And who was that?"

Alexander's Story

His name was Tobin Drake, also known as the Grand Master Wizard. He was like me and my master Merlin, a Suma wizard. That meant that he could have used light and dark magic without suffering the consequences of having his lifeforce drained. Tobin had ten soldiers that traveled with him wherever he went. They were all wizards, but none were Suma wizards. They all were skilled in hand-to-hand combat as well.

They'd just sacked the town of Santee in Alexandria, which allowed Merlin to pick up their trail. He didn't have time to gather an army of wizards, so he came by the Grand Library and asked for my help. At the time, I didn't know I was a Suma wizard and wanted nothing to do with it. I barely knew anything about being a wizard, which is why I gladly accepted the post as the Grand Librarian.

Merlin arrived at the Grand Library at five o'clock in the morning. The sun was almost out but not quite. He pounded on the front wooden door with his staff, and I rushed from my room in the back to greet him. I tied my brown wizard's robe with a rope around my waist as I hurried toward the door. When I opened the door, I sensed the tension in his face. His eyes bulged and were bloodshot. His right cheek pulsated even though he hadn't spoken. His long white beard, which was in a ponytail and tied together by a string under his chin, seemed dirtier than usual.

"Merlin?" I finally spoke. "What's this all about?"

"It's time, Alexander," Merlin said as he took off his pointy wizard's hat and placed it on a nearby library table. "Time for you to fulfill your destiny. No more hiding."

"But I'm not ready. I can barely conjure and sustain a simple spell."

"That's why I chose you." Merlin leaned forward and rested his foot on the library chair. "You're humble and modest—everything a wizard needs."

"Are you sure, Master Merlin?" I sat in the seat across the table from him. "There's gotta be more wizards that can be of more help than I."

Merlin raked his fingers through his long gray hair, which reached his shoulders. He stared at me. He'd become known for his stare that either meant he wanted to cast a spell on you, or he was disappointed with you. I knew it was the latter in my case.

"Listen, Master—"

"Hold on." Merlin held up his hand. "When we go on this mission, and you are definitely coming, Alexander, you will simply call me Merlin, as we will be colleagues."

I dropped my head and sighed. "Ok. What will I need?"

"Call your library and apprentice, tell him we are leaving, and don't know when we'll be back." Merlin stared up into the air. "Or leave your daughter Octavia in charge. How old is she now, twenty?"

"I don't think either of them are ready for this job," I said.

"Good. This will get them ready."

Merlin put his hat back on and grabbed his staff. He began walking toward the front entrance but glanced at the books.

He turned around to talk to me. "By the way, Alexander. Where is the Book of the Dead?"

"In the chamber."

"We may need it." Merlin stopped at the entrance. "I don't want to, but we're dealing with some pretty dangerous characters."

With that, Merlin exited the library and headed back to my home. Our intent was to leave at dawn to track down Tobin and his ruthless pack of wizards. It then dawned on me that the reason Merlin couldn't get any other wizards to join him is because none wanted to face Tobin. There were very few Suma wizards in the world. To face one, a Suma wizard would need at least another Suma by his side. Plus, Tobin had the back up of other wizards. Right then, there was only Merlin and me. Not good.

The Underworld

Hangoctuforre paced in his chamber, wearing his black hooded robe and sandals. Only a fireplace, a burned leather couch in front of it, and a small round table were in the room. However, the chamber was huge. He needed it. He always paced. As time went by, he stared at the two oversized metal doors that led to his chamber. He was expecting news, good news but didn't know when it was coming.

His fireplace was lit. It was his way of communicating with demons and allies on earth. He continuously glanced at the fireplace and his chamber doors in hopes that someone, anyone, would deliver the good news to him.

Someone rapped at the metal doors with the metal ring on the other side. He sucked in air and let it out slowly. It was the moment he'd been waiting for.

"Enter," he said.

His number three henchman, Argos, entered the room, wearing an all-black suit. Argos had possessed a tall white man with greying hair. He was medium build with a scar on the right side of his face. He walked with a slight limp. He had a limp that he obtained from a run-in with Tom Padilla. Argos had since become a sort of secretary for Hangoctuforre. He handled the daily briefings for the demon lord.

"Bad news, boss," Argo said with his deep voice. "Damian and Comet have both failed in their respective missions."

"Stop." Hangoctuforre held up his hand. "I don't even want to know the reasons. Failure is becoming too common around here lately. Where are they now?"

"We've lost contact with Damian," Argos said. "Comet is in New York and still in search of the ring."

"That leaves the Book of the Dead then. We must have at least one of them, Argos. If not both."

"I'm sure we will, sir. But your soldiers have gathered in the meeting room." Argos pointed at the hallway. "They are eager to hear your plan, boss."

Hangoctuforre followed Argos out of the room and headed to the chamber down the hall. He walked in the brown, stone room. A huge oval table sat in the middle with twenty chairs around it. Torches were mounted on the walls. Several chairs were placed against the wall. Once Argos sat, the only empty seats were the main throne chair at the head of the table and two slightly smaller chairs on the right and left of it. It was how Hangoctuforre liked to operate.

Everyone stood while Hangoctuforre made his way to his seat. The guest included vampires and demons alike. The three most powerful vampire leaders, who represented their clans, were in attendance. They included Kofee, leader of the Dekayers clan or DK's, Alfred Thompson, leader of the Thompson clan out of New York, and Boyd Kelly, leader of the Murphy clan out of Ireland. Each vampire leader was accompanied by two of their top henchmen. Papa Rango, the witch doctor, and sworn enemy of BA was also on hand.

Three demon lords that were locked away for centuries for attempting to overthrow the underworld were present as well. They were: Econdro, the Evil Genius; Zade, the Mad Demon; and Blaelock, leader of the Immortal Destructors. Hangoctuforre knew the three demons despised him, but with another chance to roam and wreak havoc on the earth, their hatred was subdued.

Four more seats, which included one for Argos, were demon generals that were handpicked by Hangoctuforre to lead other demons into battle.

"Sit back and relax, my friends," Hangoctuforre said. "We will give Damian Red and Comet a few more minutes before we begin."

Zade shook his head. "Are you sure we need a sorcerer and fallen angel on our side? It's bad enough we have to entertain these half-breed vampires."

Kofee jumped to his feet. "Who are you calling a half breed, you has-been demon? Does anyone know you even exist anymore, outside of the demons in this room?"

Hangoctuforre slammed his scorched fist on the table. "Knock it off! This is the most powerful group of demons I've ever assembled. We can't be stopped this time. And from what I understand, we've already failed to kill Susan Taki. Now, bring in the witch."

Argos rushed over to the metal door and pulled it open. Ahmya Taki was pushed in from behind by a demon. Her hands were shackled. She hissed at all the demons but bowed to one knee once she stood next to Hangoctuforre's throne.

Hangoctuforre put his hands together to form a triangle. "Ahmya Taki. You are another human I've allowed to join our quest to rule the earth. Why is it that your niece is not with us or dead right now?"

"I tried, master." Ahmya clasped her hands together and brought them up to her forehead. "But that damn vampire slayer showed up to help her."

Hangoctuforre's eyes squinted. "Your former mentor, Natasha, leader of the Fallen Sorcerers, was loyal to my one of my favorite pupils, Desoto. She earned the title of the Scourge of the East. I was hoping you would become the Scourge of the West. But you have failed me."

Hangoctuforre eyes lit up, and he held out his hand as if he were clutching Ahmya's throat. An invisible force began to choke her as she started coughing.

"I-I'm s-s-s-sorry, my m-master," she said.

Hangoctuforre released the hold, and Ahmya grabbed her throat and massaged her neck.

"Please give me one more chance," she begged.

"You will have another chance Ms. Taki." Hangoctuforre leaned forward. "Not because I'm merciful. But because Susan has grown in power and is using them to aide our enemies. I need someone she trusts to get close and destroy her."

"I will, my master," she said.

"Now rise and take a seat." He gestured to one of the chairs against the wall. "Let this gathering begin."

Alexander's Story

I went back to my house and waited for Merlin to finish taking a bath. He came out in my favorite bathrobe. But it was Merlin. I dared not say anything to one of the most powerful wizards ever known. He sat at the wooden dinner table and prepared to eat the soup I'd made while he bathed. Our dining area was small. I was rarely home as I spent most of my days and nights at the library. I sat out two wooden bowls and spoons before I turned to the furnace to fetch the soup.

My daughter, Octavia, entered the room as well. She had long, dark hair like her mother that reached her buttocks. She wore a white wool gown and was barefoot. She pulled up a chair, put out another bowl, and sat next to Merlin.

"Can you show me how to cast a basic spell, Lord Merlin?" she asked.

Merlin pulled at whiskers of his beard. "I'm sorry, my dear, but magic isn't a plaything. Only real wizards should use it."

"Is that why you're taking my father on this mission?" She placed her chin in her cuffed hands as she stared into Merlin's face. "Is he a real wizard now?"

Merlin glared at me as I stood anxiously awaiting his answer.

"Your father is sufficient for this mission. Yes, it will test him. But I believe he will make it through this as a better wizard."

His answer brought a smile to my face and erected more confidence in me. If we were facing Tobin and the other wizards that night, I think I would have been ready. Unfortunately, we had to find them first, which, according to Merlin, would take another day.

The next morning, after I left instructions for the library with Octavia, Merlin and I mounted our horses and set off to track down Tobin. We arrived at Santee, the last town that he'd left in ruins. The town had two main stone buildings for meetings, the school and the small government that existed. The rest of the structures were wooden cottages. Some of the cottages were still in flames, while others emitted black smoke. A line of refugees walked from the far side of the town and headed back to Alexandria. Tobin and his wizards knew Merlin guarded Alexandria and didn't want to face off with the wizard just yet. Everyone knew of Merlin's exploits when he destroyed King Midas years before.

"Let's ride, Alexander." Merlin didn't bother to get off his horse. "They can't be that far ahead."

"Should we try to help these people?" I asked.

"They have a mayor," Merlin said. "We have a more important mission, or other towns will end up like this one."

"Yes, Mas—I mean Merlin."

We sped off. I had a wizard's wand that I'd made from a tree branch as my weapon, while Merlin had a sword and his long white wooden staff with a ruby mounted in the center of a crucifix at the top. They were strapped to his horse. Was I merely a decoy? How was I supposed to do battle with a Suma wizard and ten other more skilled wizards? My doubts returned—fear actually. Merlin sensed it, pulled up the reins on his horse, and stopped.

Merlin turned his horse to face me. "You cannot doubt your abilities, Alexander. It is a surefire way to end up dead. You have enough skills to do battle with any wizard. You've just got to have faith in yourself."

I shook my head. "But how, Merlin?"

"I've made a ton of mistakes as a wizard, Alexander. Finding you and choosing you for this mission was not one of them."

"But ten accomplished wizards, and a Suma wizard?"

"Alexander." *Merlin pressed his hand against the air.* "You're thinking about the numbers instead of the quality of a wizard. I have had a small glimpse of our future. I think we'll be ok."

"Ok."

"You sure you're ok now?"

"Yes."

"Well, let's ride."

We entered the nearby massive Willow Forrest. We slowed our pace to a trot. It was the perfect place for an ambush, which is exactly what happened. A dark stream of smoke headed our way. It was so fast that it knocked Merlin from his horse. I jumped off my horse and pulled my wand from my belt. Merlin stood and had to calm his horse, so he could retrieve his staff and sword. We stood back-to-back and waited. The stream of smoke headed our way again.

Merlin held up his staff. "Revelare (reveal)."

The smoke stopped, floated to the ground, and a man appeared in its place. The man was averaged sized, long black hair, brown sandals, short beard, and wearing a brown wizard's robe.

"Well, well, well," *the man began.* "Merlin and his. . .assistant?"

"Tobin Drake," *Merlin said.* "I've been looking for you. Where's the rest of your brood?"

Tobin looked around. "They're around, waiting on my word. But you can make sure that they don't have to show themselves by letting us leave without incident."

"I have no idea what your plans are, Tobin." Merlin scanned the trees. "But I can't let your reign of terror continue."

Tobin giggled. "Merlin, Merlin, Merlin. We're the most powerful people on earth. How come we're not its rulers? I'm just trying to rectify that."

"We are meant to be servants of the King, Tobin," Merlin said. "It's in our mandate at wizards."

"Servants?" Tobin laughed. "That's where you're wrong, Merlin. I serve only myself."

Tobin held out his and his staff, a metal silver pole with a triangle attached at the top, and pointed it at us.

"Cicer (pulse)." A slightly visible pulse shot out of the staff.

Merlin twirled his staff around. "Deflectere (deflect)."

The pulse bounced off Merlin's staff and hit the ground.

Tobin pointed at us and looked around the forest. "Kill them!"

The ten wizards ascended on the area. Each wore the brown wizard's robes with their hoods on their heads. They had identical staffs; the way Tobin wanted it. The staffs were simple long brown wooden sticks, about the length of the wizard, with a triangle at the top, which was Tobin's wizard symbol. They surrounded us, twirling their staffs and inched closer to us.

"Ok, Alexander," Merlin said as there wasn't any space in between our backs. "This is where you become the wizard that I knew you'd always be. Follow my lead."

"Yes, sir," I replied.

Merlin raised his staff toward the sky and his free hand. "Ventus (wind)."

I did the same. Through the trees, I could see the sky had darkened and the wind picked up. A tornado funnel surrounded Merlin and me.

"Call down the lightning, Alexander!" Merlin shouted over the wind. "Send them all to the underworld."

"How can I?" My forehead wrinkled as I turned to stare at Merlin. "I will pay the consequences for using the magic in that way."

Merlin continued twirling his staff and blocking multiple pulses from the wizards.

"Alexander. I didn't want to tell you unless I had to, but you are a Suma wizard."

"What?" I asked

"Yes." Merlin returned my gaze. "Every Suma wizard I've trained turned evil and perverted their gifts. I didn't want the same thing to happen to you. It's why I graciously accepted your recommendation to become the next Grand Librarian. Now, bring down the damn lightning!"

I was stunned at what I'd just heard. My eyes squinted as I looked out the tornado funnel. The wizards whose faces were slightly visible frowned as they couldn't break through the funnel. They continued firing pulses in their vain attempts.

I stopped concentrating on the wind, and it lessened. I saw the strenuous expression in Merlin's face had he had to keep the tornado flowing by himself.

I raised my arms and looked to the sky. "Fulgur (lightning)."

A lightning bolt erupted from the sky and slammed down onto one of the ten wizards. He was electrocuted and fell dead to the ground. The other wizards saw their colleague fall but continued their pulse attack on the tornado funnel.

Merlin's arms slowly lowered. He'd begun to get tired. I saw the panic in his face and the sweat forming on his forehead. The funnel lessened more.

"Again, Alexander!" Merlin shouted. "Our lives depend on it."

I raised my arms again. "Fulgur (lightning)!"

This time two lightning bolts came crashing down and eliminated two more wizards. The rest of them stopped using pulse blasts against the tornado funnel. Merlin dropped to one knee, and the funnel disappeared. I grabbed his arm and helped him back to his feet. Tobin levitated from a branch in the overhead tree.

"That's impossible," Tobin said. "Another Suma wizard right under my nose. You must join me, Alexander. Look at your mentor. He's finished."

Merlin coughed. "Tune him out, Alexander. He corrupted ten others to gain his power. Don't listen to him."

"Silence!" Tobin gestured his staff at Merlin. "Flagellum (whip)."

An almost invisible whip snapped through the air and across Merlin's chest, sending him crashing to the ground.

Tobin turned his attention to me. "Flagellum (whip)."

Almost immediately, I countered. "Clipeum (shield)."

A shield appeared in my hand, and Tobin's whip smacked into it. He continued to try to use his whip against me but only could get me to move backward from the force.

"No!" Merlin got back to his feet. "This is my fight, Alexander. Keep the rest of them at bay. I'll deal with Mr. Drake."

"Fine with me," I said. "He's all yours."

Tobin laughed. "Merlin, it's time to go back to school."

"Yes, it is." Merlin pointed at Tobin. "But I'll be the one handing out the lessons."

I pointed my staff at the wizards, who all looked on as if they didn't know what to do. I could sense that their allegiance to Tobin was one of fear and going to war with two Suma wizards as not what they'd wanted to do.

"Hangoctuforre (hanging noose)!" Merlin pointed his staff at Tobin and looked to the sky.

Nothing happened. It was as if Merlin had forgotten the consequences of mentioning the demon's name aloud.

"Hangoctuforre (hanging noose)!" Merlin said again.

The sky darkened again. I looked up and saw a dark cloud
hovering above us with lightning pulsating within it. Two bolts of
lightning shot out from it. The first formed an electric noose and
grabbed Tobin by the neck. It strung him up in the nearby tree. The
second bolt went for Merlin because he was the one who summoned
the lightning by mentioning the demon's name. I threw my shield
toward Merlin just as the lightning bolt was about to strike. The bolt
hit the shield, but the shield still struck Merlin in the face. He fell
to the ground. The other wizards glanced up at Tobin and then back
at Merlin. They scattered.

"C-Cowards!" Tobin yelled out. "C-Come back and s-save your
master."

None returned. Again, I helped Merlin to his feet. He was even
weaker. He leaned on my shoulder more as we stared up at Tobin, who
had begun to squirm as the noose tightened.

Tobin held out his arms to the side. "Solvo (release)."

The electric noose snapped away from the tree, and Tobin crashed
to the ground. Merlin pushed away from me and held his staff up in a
defensive position. He said something I'd never heard another wizard
say.

Merlin held his staff to his head, and it began to glow. "Tactu
mortem (death touch)."

Merlin charged Tobin and swung the staff at his head, but Tobin
ducked and pulled out a small knife from a pouch on his belt. He
stabbed Merlin in the side. Merlin turned and looked at me. He knew
he'd made a mistake as he began to take slower steps back in my
direction.

Tobin held out his staff to the side. "Goodbye, Merlin. Tactu mortem (death touch)."

Tobin's staff glowed red as he raised it and prepared to jam the triangle into Merlin's back. Merlin stumbled toward me. He could barely lift his hands. The death touch spell was powerful and draining, especially if the wizard failed. Merlin had just failed. Tobin reared back to plunge his staff back down to kill Merlin.

"Cicer (pulse)!" I yelled out

My small wand shot out an invisible pulse and knocked Tobin off balance. He didn't fall. He was determined to kill my teacher. And killing Merlin would assure him he had no equal.

"No!" Tobin said as he charged Merlin again. "No one will deny me this."

I ran toward Merlin as well. "Tactu mortem (death touch)."

My wand started to glow red as I thrust it over Merlin's shoulder and jammed it into Tobin's neck. I ripped it out just as quickly. Tobin stopped. He covered the wound on his neck. It didn't bleed. He then looked at me. He fell to both knees. Merlin fell face-first to the ground.

"I can't believe this," Tobin said as he stared up at me. "Defeated by an apprentice."

Tobin fell to his back. His skin turned pale, and his body hemorrhaged. He died. I ran over to pick up Merlin yet again. His shoulder was badly injured. We walked a few feet until we reached our horses. They were dead. The remaining wizards, in one last cowardly act, had killed them.

Merlin collapsed to the ground. "We must get to Niviane. She's probably the only one who can help."

"Who's Niviane, Lord Merlin?" *I asked.* "I've never heard of her."

"She a nurse in the town of Cantor." *Merlin began shivering.* "F-fly m-me to h-her."

"Fly you?" I looked around and almost laughed. "I'm a wizard. Not a fictional genie with a flying carpet."

He pushed his staff in my direction. "I must u-use the last of my p-powers to slow the effects of the injury."

"Why?"

Merlin pulled down his shirt and touched his wound. "W-we are not gods, Alexander. To attempt to cheat d-death will drain me. Desierunt (subside)."

Merlin's wound closed. The wound glowed white along with Merlin's eyes.

Merlin's hand shook as he reached up to me with his staff. "Y-you must l-leave now, A-Alexan-d-der. T-Take o-off."

Merlin passed out. I didn't know what to do. He said I could fly, but that was impossible even for a Suma wizard. I wondered if he was delirious. Then I thought, wait a minute. His staff. He was trying to give me his staff for a reason. My wand was considered a joke in the world of magic. It was also why I had to be careful. I looked around to see if the other wizards still lurked about. Any one of them would love to get ahold of Merlin's staff.

I picked up the staff. I could feel the energy flowing through it. Merlin's life essence had probably passed to it as well. I sat next to Merlin to think. I didn't know what to do. Even with his staff, I was positive that I still couldn't fly. But then I thought.What if he wasn't talking about me but was talking about the staff.

I held the staff over my head. "Volent (fly)."

I could feel the staff wanting to move as it jerked slightly. Maybe I wasn't using the correct spell. I wasn't a GrandWizard or even a Suma wizard for long, so I never studied the magic beyond parlor tricks or some of the menial spells Merlin had taught me.

I rested my forehead on the staff and sighed and then raised it over my head again. "Tolle fuga (take flight)."

The staff almost shot out of my hand. I held it tightly and reached down to pick up Merlin's body and put him over my shoulder. Luckily, he was a thin man, and I easily picked him up. I then let the staff whisk us up in the air and take off. We weren't moving fast, but just as fast as a horse would carry us. I had to cast another spell to make sure my grip didn't slip away from the staff

We landed later in the evening in the town of Cantor. My body ached from holding on to the staff and holding on to Merlin's body. It was a small village. There were maybe ten small cottages perfectly surrounded by the forest. Three nurses, all dressed in white with white bonnets, greeted us as the town's edge. Two of them wore a red cross on their bonnets, the universal sign for medical. They unwrapped a mesh stretcher from two wooden poles, placed it on the ground, and I lay Merlin's body on top of it. The women were strong as they lifted both ends of the wooden poles and carried Merlin's body back to the medi-cal cottage.

The last woman, who had a pink cross on her bonnet, was in charge. She was Lady Niviane. She was a tall redheaded woman with green eyes. She seemed genuinely concerned for Merlin.

"My lord in heaven," she said as she watched them take Merlin away. "He's only ever come here when other's needed medical attention. I never thought I'd be tending to him. And who are you?"

"My name is Alexander from Alexandria," I said. "I'm the Grand Librarian and Merlin's last pupil."

She cocked her head to the side. "That's odd. He never told me he had another pupil or anything about you."

I returned her uneasy expression with my own. "Was he supposed to tell you?"

"No," she said. "Forget I said anything. Let's just go see to his well-being."

The Present

"Wow!" Tom said. "Great story."

"Yes, it was." Emma pushed away from the wall she'd been leaning on. "I've never heard it before."

"Sorry, honey." Alexander turned around to Emma with a surprised expression on his face. "I didn't think you'd want to hear those things."

She folded her arms. "But you just told the story to this man I've never met before."

"Oh, excuse my manners." Tom rose and extended his hand to Emma. "My name is Father Tom Padilla."

Emma laughed. "A priest? That's rich. What is a priest doing hanging around with Alex?"

Tom smiled. "I'm an exorcist."

"Figures." Emma shook her head and grabbed her pregnant belly. "Ok. What do you need Alex to do? I mean, *that is* why you're here, right? You need him to get involved in something crazy?"

Alexander held up his hand. "Hold on now, dear. I—"

"Ma'am," Tom cut in. "If I didn't think we were gonna return him back to you before little Octus was born, I wouldn't be here."

"Well, I don't like this one-damn-bit." Emma glared at Alexander. "How many times must this peaceful old man get involved with your supernatural crap?"

Alexander held up his hands. "It's not like that, honey."

"Isn't it, Alex?" Emma put her hands on her hips. "You're a married man and soon will be a family man."

Tom studied Emma's face. She didn't want Alexander to go off and fight in a conflict that no one else even knew about. But just like everyone on the team, Tom knew it was Alexander's duty. As much as he just wanted to get up and leave the Merryweather's alone, he knew they needed Alexander's help, especially to deal with Damian Red.

"I don't like to make promises," Tom said. "But I can promise you this, Mrs. Merryweather. I will bring your man back home safely."

Emma sighed as she walked over to hug Alexander. "I will take you at your word, priest. You bring him back to me. But I have one condition."

"Name it," Tom replied.

Emma rubbed her stomach again. "Please wait until after the baby is born. Can your war wait until then?"

Tom shot a quick look at Alexander and dropped his head. "The war can wait. But we'll need to at least barrow him before then to do some planning."

"Thank you, father." Emma clasped her hands together. "Thank you very much. He's all I have."

"Will do." Tom grimaced but smiled because he usually didn't pass himself off as a priest. "And so, you know, I don't break promises to lovely young women."

"Are you sure you're a priest?" Emma asked while smiling. "Sounds like you're hitting on me."

Alexander laughed. "He's not hitting on you, Em. But no, he's not a real priest. He's a demon hunter."

Emma slapped her forehead. "Jesus!"

Alexander nodded in agreement. "Indeed."

Part 6

THE REUNION

Harvey, Illinois

It was still dark at dawn when Kente Jr. arrived back to his deserted home on Delaware Street. The entire street had been deserted for years, but none of the houses had been torn down or even touched since they were last inhabited. Only a few streetlights were functional. The city had basically segregated the street and left it alone. The deaths from the Hangman's murderous spree would forever be remembered but only on Delaware Street.

Kente walked up to the front porch. He looked around to make sure he was alone. He wasn't. The Ring of Light began to glow bright green. He kicked open the door and ran inside. He backed away from the front door and sat on the stairs.

"Is that any way to greet your old man?" The Hangman's voice echoed throughout the house. "I've been treated better by strangers."

Kente held up his fist with the ring. "Show yourself, demon. So, I can send you back to the underworld."

"Now why would you go and do a thing like that, Junior. I've come back to help you avenge your mother."

Kente Jr. stood and turned his head in all directions. "We'll start with you then. You're the reason that guy showed up and killed her."

The Hangman's dark ghostly figure appeared at the top of

the stairs. Kente Jr. turned and fired a green beam of light from his ring. The Hangman moved to the side, and the beam hit the wall behind him, creating a huge hole.

Red electricity overtook the Hangman's body, and he disappeared. "Come on, Junior. You can do better than that. How have you killed anyone with that aim? Now, who killed your mother?"

"You did, you bastard." Kente whipped his head around to find his father's voice. "I'm going to make sure you, and others like you, pay for her death."

"Others like me?"

"Supernaturals."

"A supernatural killed your mother? What was it?"

"He said his name was Damian Red…a sorcerer."

A gust of wind flung opened the front door. Kente Jr. fired and a shot from his ring. The shot hit a tree in the front lawn. The tree split down the middle and fell to the street. Kente grunted and stomped his foot.

"Why are you so angry with me, Junior?"

"Because you deserted us," Kente said. "You left me and Mom alone because you were selfish and couldn't be faithful."

"I'm sorry, Junior. But there's not a day that goes by that I don't think about you guys and my mistakes. But killing me won't put our family back together or bring your mother back."

"Oh yeah. But it will *bring me* closure."

"Junior, you've got to stop this. BA wants you dead or alive. Trust me, that guy won't stop until he gets his way."

"So, this is what your visit is about, the angel?" Kente smiled. "Well, I'm not afraid of him…or you."

"Well, you should be."

An invisible fist smashed into Kente's face. He fell backward to the steps. His eyes rolled back. He attempted to get back up but couldn't. He shook his head rapidly to shake off the effects of the punch. He wobbled back to his feet and stood upright.

"Is that all you've got?" Kente wiped his hand across his face where the punch landed. "I'm not some little kid anymore, *Hangman*."

The Underworld

Damian prepared to knock on one of the huge metal double doors. However, the door opened just as he cocked his fist back.

"Enter, my son," Hangoctuforre said. "We've been expecting you."

"We?" Damian asked.

Once the door was opened, Damian walked into the room and looked around. He saw Hangoctuforre sitting in his favorite chair, a loveseat in front of the oversized fireplace. Comet, the fallen angel, stepped out from the shadows in the room.

"You both missed my meeting." Hangoctuforre drank from a gold goblet that smoked from the liquid inside of it. "Now, report."

Sweat formed on Damian's head. "The ring can't be claimed, sir. The Hangman is back and looking for his son, who has mastered the Ring of Light."

"Padilla still has the book," Comet cut in. "I can still get it with enough time."

"So, you both have failed me," Hangoctuforre said without

looking at either. "Why have I put you above any of the other members of my army?"

"Because you trust us." Comet walked over to Hangoctuforre. "Look. I want to see these humans bow to you as well. But combined, Padilla and Caine will be a handful. Plus, I understand they've recruited Susan Taki. She could make things uncomfortable for all of us."

"She'll be taken care of." Hangoctuforre finally stood and faced his two main henchmen. "But I need the Hellfire Ring or the Book of the Dead. Now, which one of you shall acquire them for me? Huh?"

Damian dropped to one knee and bowed. "I will, my master, or I'll die trying."

"Don't look at me," Comet said as he returned Hangoctuforre's cold gaze. "I've told you once before. I don't work for you, demon. I work with you. I will do my part. But I'm not dying for you."

With the sound of the fluttering of wings, Comet was gone. Damian rose and stared at Hangoctuforre.

"I like him," the demon lord said. "But he's just assured me that we will have to destroy him when we conquer the earth. I can't have someone still roaming the earth that won't serve me."

"Should I do it now, my master?" Damian asked. "He's already defied you twice."

"Not yet. His time will come. Now, go and get the ring or the book."

New York

Jericho and Susie arrived at the church Tom used for his

office. They were met by Bishop Scott, who ushered them to Tom's back office. Jericho had the key, so he opened the door, and they entered. When they got inside and turned on the lights, they were surprised to find BA meditating and sitting on Tom's cot in the dark.

"Whoa." Jericho took and step back and stepped on Susie's foot. "Angel. What in the hell are you doing here?"

"Jesus, Caine." Susie pushed Jericho in the back. "Get off my foot, and this is a church for Christ's sake. Watch your mouth."

BA opened his eyes and stood. "You must not know this heathen very well, Miss. His soul is uncleansed."

"Oh, excuse my manners." Jericho held out his hand towards BA. "This big clumsy, pale-looking guy is the Bad Angel or BA for short."

"Wow!" Susie's eyes opened wider. "I've heard stories about you."

Jericho turned to Susie. "If you heard he was a jerk, then the stories were true."

"Watch it, Caine." BA took off his sunglasses and exposed his glowing white eyes. "I've had just about enough of your mouth already."

"Your attitude isn't helping, BA," Jericho replied.

Both huge men stared at each other. But Jericho tried to stay calm. He remembered when BA helped him during his fight with Dakota, the vampire angel, a werewolf, and Caden Murphy, leader of the Murphy vampire clan from Ireland. To date, those battles were the toughest Jericho has had as a slayer. After it was over, Jericho realized that BA didn't really do as much as Jericho had given the angel credit for. *But he did help,*

I guess. Even a little.

"You two need to take it down a notch." Susie stood in the middle of them. "We're not here to fight each other. There are much bigger things out there to obsess about."

"You should only be talking to him." BA pointed at Jericho. "He's the one that wants to test his new abilities against his allies."

Jericho waved his hand at BA and walked over to the far corner and sat in a wooden chair. He crossed his legs and stared at BA for a few more seconds and then opened his duffle bag. He pulled out a magazine about monster trucks and pretended to read. He knew the angel was right. He did want to test his skills against the angel but didn't want it to seem like he was the one attempting to break the peace.

Jericho also wanted to groom Susie. He knew she looked up to him, and he was setting a bad example for the young warrior. After all, he's the one that travelled across the country to bring her into the conflict.

The door swung open. BA, Susie, and Jericho jumped into their fighting stances. Even though it was a church, they knew their enemies knew it was Tom's sanctuary. However, it was Tom and Alexander, who walked through the door. They held their hands up to assure their friends they weren't a threat.

"Calm down, everybody," Tom said as he glanced nonchalantly at Susie. "It's just us."

"That's how you end up with the business end of the Sword of Caine sticking out of the side of your neck," Jericho said. "You should know better than that, Tom."

"Don't mind him." BA walked over to shake Tom and Alexander's hands. "He just wants to fight anybody."

"Good." Tom nodded. "Because we're going to need it. Where's the Hangman?"

"He took the ring and disappeared," BA said. "I think he might be going after his kid."

"Then why are we wasting time here?" Tom asked. "We should be wherever he is. That's all we need is for the Hangman to become one of our enemies."

"Don't worry." BA waved his finger. "The younger Cromwell wants nothing to do with his father. He'll come back to us...if they don't kill each other first."

Harvey, Illinois

Kente went outside to the sidewalk. He shot green beams of light and moved all the abandoned cars out of the way.

"More space?" The Hangman's voice rang out. "It doesn't matter where we do this, Junior. I want that ring, and I'll avenge your mother for the both of us. But I need you to stand down."

"No way!" Kente looked up and around at the trees. "Now, stop hiding, demon. Come out and take your beating like the man you used to be."

"All that power attached to your little finger, and you still don't know how to use it. Give it to me, son. Let me take that burden off your hands."

"Screw you!" Kente Jr. backed up against a tree. "And don't call me son. My father died years ago."

Suddenly, the wind picked up and blew Kente into the street. He fell face-first and pressed himself back to his feet. An invisible fist punched him in the stomach again, and an invisible foot kicked him in the chest, knocking him to the ground.

He lay on the ground for a few seconds. His face frowning. He balled up his fist. He slapped himself repeatedly. He stood again and fired green beams of light into the sky. It exploded like fireworks. When it sparks came down, a few bounced off an invisible space.

"Gotcha!" Kente said as he fired from the Ring of Light.

The beam hit the Hangman in the shoulder, and he was forced to reappear. He dropped to the middle of the street on one knee and clutched his shoulder. Kente began firing continuous beams of light in the Hangman's direction. The Hangman held his own ring in the air, and a red force field surrounded him. Knowing he probably couldn't survive another shot from the Ring of Light, the Hangman knew it was time to stop joking around with his son. The green beams of light didn't penetrate the forcefield, so Kente stopped. That's when the Hangman jumped to his feet and shot a red beam of light over Kente's head. A fireball hovered over Kente and long strands of fire ascended around Kente. They formed a cage with fiery bars.

Kente appeared confused at first as he shot beams of light at the fiery bars. The bars flashed but for only a moment. It wasn't enough for Kente to escape. He glanced at the Hangman, who had begun to move closer to his captive son. Kente then looked up at the fireball still hanging over his head, which was the source of the cage. He shot a beam of light into the fireball. The fireball pulsated a few times and then exploded.

"If you want this ring." Kente pointed to the ring on his finger. "You're gonna have to take it from my cold, dead hands."

The Hangman's hooked staff appeared in his hand. "That's not what I wanted, son, but if it's what I have to do to get it, then so be it."

Kente fired from the Ring of Light. The Hangman put up his staff almost too late to block it. He shot sent him sailing backward. He cracked the back of his head on the concrete. He rubbed the back of his head and stared up at Kente, who approached with the ring, pointing at the Hangman.

"What's wrong, old man?" Kente asked. "Which is it? Getting old or slow?"

The insult energized the Hangman. He jumped in the air, twirled around, and kicked Kente in the face. Kente rocked backward. He held his ring fist up. A green force field glowed around his body. The Hangman did the same and his red force field appeared again. They charged each other and collided in the middle of the street. The impact knocked both to the ground, and their forcefields disappeared. The Hangman, being the bigger and stronger of the two, got back to his feet first. He pointed his ring at Kente. *Dorothy, forgive me for what I'm about to do.*

Suddenly, a lightning bolt crashed down on the street between Kente and the Hangman. White smoke filled the air. When the smoke disappeared, BA, Jericho, Tom, Alexander, and Susie stood in its place.

BA put his hands on his hips. "Looks like you didn't need any help after all, Cromwell."

"What are you doing here, angel?" the Hangman asked. "After our last encounter, surely you don't think everything is copacetic."

"Wait," Jericho cut in. "You didn't mention anything about an encounter."

"I didn't think I had to report anything to you, slayer," BA said. "Least of all, anything regarding *him*."

The Hangman held out his hand, and his fallen hooked staffed floated over to him. BA held out his hand, and his battle-ax appeared in it. Susie pulled out her nunchucks, and Alexander's staff appeared in his hand.

Jericho unsheathed the Sword of Caine and walked over and stood next to the Hangman. "Don't worry, Hangy. I've got your back."

"Don't start this again, Jericho," Tom said. "We're not here to fight. But *he did* pull out a weapon first."

The Hangman pointed behind them. "And while you idiots were busy preparing to fight me, Kente got away."

They all turned around and looked at the ground. Kente had fled.

"I see you've got backup this time around, BA." The Hangman nodded toward Alexander. "Who are these two?"

"This young lady is Susan Taki," Tom cut in. "She's a gifted Kung Fu artist, amongst her other gifts. And this is Alexander Merryweather. He's a wizard from the past when Merlin walked the earth."

"A wizard?" The Hangman cocked his head to the side. "What can you tell me about Damian Red?"

"He's a powerful sorcerer," Alexander responded. "Maybe even more powerful than me."

The Hangman looked around the group and noticed Jericho and Tom's quick glance at BA.

"BA?" The Hangman also turned his gaze to the angel. "You know anything about this guy?"

"Is this a game show, Cromwell?" BA answered. "I just know we need to stop these guys before they raise the demon again."

"Hey, jackass." The Hangman's voice raised. "This guy killed my wife. It's why Kente Jr. is hellbent on finding and destroying him. I have made it my mission to do the same. That's still my family, no matter what you say."

Tom put a hand out in front of the Hangman and on in front of BA. "Ok. Ok. Ok. This is getting us nowhere. Let's just find the bastard, and we'll get to the bottom of it later."

"That's fine," the Hangman said. "But if I find out there's something else going on, my wrath will not just stop at the sorcerer."

Susie stepped in as well next to Tom to change the subject. "Well, they can't just take Kente's ring. That's obvious. And you both have yours. What else do they need?"

Jericho snapped his fingers. "The book. The Book of the Dead. Tom, they'll raise your church to the ground if they think it's there."

"I hate to say it, big guy." Tom nodded. "But you're right. Let's back get to the church in New York. It's unguarded. They only have the demon alarms to warn then of trouble."

Alexander bounced the tip of his staff off the ground. "Aperta portal (open portal)."

Thunder sounded, and a bright white portal opened next to Alexander. He waited until Jericho, Tom, and Susie stepped through, and then he followed. BA looked to the sky and spread his wings. He leaped into the air and flew away. The Hangman raised his arms into the air, and red lightning covered his body. He disappeared.

When the street was empty, a teenager walked out and stood on the front steps of the Cromwell house. *Hmm, Dad really does care about me and mom. Maybe I'm wrong and was too hard on him.* Then a stinging sensation struck Kente in the back. He tumbled down the four steps and landed on his knees. He put his hand to head and felt the lump, which was quickly growing on the side of his head.

He turned around. "You. How dare you enter my house?"

"You had your fun, boy." Damian slowly walked toward Kente with his double-headed snake staff pointed at the youngster. "I underestimated you before, just as the angel and your father did. I won't make that same mistake twice."

Kente raised his fist and pointed the ring at Damian, but Damian shot another invisible pulse at Kente, which struck him in the chest. Kente fell backward, and his body began to convulse.

Damian put his foot on Kente's chest. "I'm gonna take your ring, young Cromwell, and that will be just the beginning. By the time those fools get back to New York, it'll be just in time for them to find out that we have the Book of the Dead already." Damian bent down closer to Kente's face. "There's nothing that anyone can do to stop us now. My master will destroy your father and anyone else that gets in his way. Say goodbye, young Cromwell."

Kente couldn't move. The pulse had paralyzed him. He tried to telepathically connect to the ring. The only thing he did was allow the ring to glow green. Damian looked down at the ring and then back up to Kente's face. The sorcerer laughed.

Damian then jammed the pointy end of his snake staff into Kente's shoulder. "Tactu mortem (death touch). I can't take the ring while you're still alive, but I can take it off your dead body."

Kente screamed out in pain from the stab wound, but he knew that wasn't the end. He understood that Damian used the same spell when the sorcerer killed Dorothy. Kente knew it was the inevitable result for him as well. He began to cough as he watched Damian's sinister expression while staring down at him. The sorcerer's smile was cold. It let Kente know that Damian had done it for years. There was no remorse in Damian's cold black eyes. Finally, Kente's eyes began to roll back and forth. His body became colder. He focused on Damian's face one last time and then closed his eyes for good.

New York

It was the early part of the afternoon when Jericho, Tom, Susie, and Alexander stepped out of the portal across the street from the church. They all looked to the sky as BA landed beside them. They waited for the Hangman to appear as well, but he didn't.

"This is not good," Jericho said. "Now, where could he have gone?"

"That's the least of our concerns, big guy." Tom pointed across the street as black smoke emitted from a church's windows. "Let's go!"

They all ran across the street. BA kicked open the door, and a blast of fire burst out. BA wasn't fazed, but the others were blown backwards and back down the steps.

"Slick move, angel." Jericho punched the ground as he got back to his feet. "Anybody ever tell you what happens when you open the door of a burning building?"

"I'm not a firefighter, Caine," BA said. "Cut me some slack."

The entire church soon burst into flames, and the inside

was consumed. BA clapped his hands together, and a huge pulse of wind blew through the church. It wasn't enough and so BA repeated the act. The flames finally blew out. They all entered the church and saw that the damage wasn't as bad as imagined. Only a few pews were smoking, and parts of the walls were scorched. A couple of the pane glass windows were shattered.

Fire trucks arrived on the scene a few minutes later. However, they were too late as Jericho and BA carried out the dead bodies of two nuns and Bishop Scott. They placed the bodies on the concrete in front of Tom, who dropped to his knees and wept. He said a prayer for the victims. It was the second time in a couple of years that someone had entered the church, and either killed someone, or someone was taken hostage.

"Damn demons are gonna pay." Tom pounded his fist in his hand. "This is happening all too often."

Jericho put his hand on Tom's shoulder. "It couldn't have been a demon, buddy. The alarm would have alerted the Bishop and nuns. They know what you do. They would have known to arm themselves with crucifixes and holy water. This had to be a human or something else."

"An angel, maybe." BA ran his hands through his hair. "A fallen angel wouldn't have set off the alarm."

"Comet," Alexander said. "I was wondering when he'd show up again."

"What about the book?" Susie asked.

"Gone," Tom replied. "While they were pulling out the bodies, I checked the place I'd hid it. It's gone."

"So, what does that mean?" she asked.

Tom glanced around the scorched church once more. "It means prepare yourselves for war."

Springfield, Connecticut

A couple of days had passed. The bar door flung open. It had been two weeks since Kente Cromwell Jr. had been there and terrorized the place. The bar had since reopened, and patrons had returned. They were assured that security had been tightened, and they were safe. Of course, it was the afternoon, and the only people present were the new vampire bartender and human conscribes.

The humans were making themselves ready by placing razor blades and other metal cutlery around bar tables. Around six p.m., vampires started entering the establishment. The new bartender kept an electric whip and shield underneath the bar.

As the humans prepared, they sat and drank either wine, beer, or liquor. The vampires liked drinking blood with wine infused in it the most, so there was more wine in stock than most other bars.

A tall, long-haired brunette female conscribe stepped outside the bar. She was pale from years of having her blood drained, but not enough to kill her. She'd gone out to smoke and for fresh air even though she could smoke inside. She felt a bit of dust hit her in the head. When she looked up, she didn't see anything. However, when she looked back at the street, a fiery noose materialized around her neck. She dropped her cigarette as the noose tightened and burned her neck. She looked up to see where the noose hung from. It was just suspended out of nowhere. She was pulled up. She kicked her legs. She flailed her arms. Nothing worked. She tried to scream. The only sound she made was a choking noise.

The Hangman appeared at her knees. "Don't worry. You're about to have plenty of company."

Red lightning appeared around the Hangman's body, and he disappeared. He reappeared inside the bar. He wore his new suit. It was more snug than his hooded robe. It was a black leather jacket and matching pants. His wide hood only partially exposed his burned flesh in the shadow of the hood. Only his burning red eyes, like embers, could be seen.

"Who owns this shithole?" The Hangman stood at the front door. "Looks like you fixed it up a little too soon."

The bartender, a medium-sized man with short blond hair, reached down and grabbed a shield and his tomahawk. He leaped across the bar in front of the Hangman.

"Who are you, Mister?" the bartender asked.

"I have many names," the Hangman said. "But I like the Hangman the best."

The bartender swallowed hard. "Holy crap! We have no problems with you, man. It was your son."

The Hangman laughed. "I know. And now I'm here to finish what he started."

"Please." The bartender shook his head. "Don't do this. We didn't have anything to do with what happened to your son."

The Hangman cocked his head to the side. "My son? What happened to my son?"

"You don't know?" the bartender asked. "He's dead."

"That's a lie," the Hangman said. "I just saw him a couple days ago."

The bartender took a step back. "It's true."

The Hangman looked off to the distance. The patrons were running and pushing each other, trying to escape out the back door. The ring on his finger lit up, and the back door closed. Some of the male patrons tried to open it but couldn't. They took turns ramming their shoulders into the door, but it didn't budge. The Hangman then raised his arms, and seven nooses appeared from the ceiling and ensnared the seven patrons. The Hangman twirled his two fingers toward the ceiling, and the humans were lifted off the ground as the nooses tightened.

The bartender attacked the Hangman with his tomahawk. He swung. The Hangman caught his wrist, bent his hand back until the vampire dropped the weapon.

"Now, give me the shield." The Hagman nodded toward the shield the bartender still held. "I might need this."

"Sure thing, Mr. Hangman, sir." The bartender held out the shield. "It's all yours."

"I know," the Hangman said as he called his hooked staff to his hand.

The Hangman pushed the bartender backward and swung the sword end of his hooked staff. He chopped off the vampire's head. The body and the head fell to the ground and turned to ashes. The Hangman walked over to the humans that were hanging in the back. They were still alive and struggling to get free. He sighed and with seven quick strokes, decapitated them all with the hooked staff. *Serves them right. If that vampire was right, it means my entire family has died because of me. And because of that. There will be hell to pay.*

The Underworld

Hangoctuforre sat at the head of his long oval table again.

This time Damian sat to his right and Comet to his left. He stared around the table at all his guests, who were eager to hear what the demon lord had to say.

Hangoctuforre gestured to Comet. "Show them, my friend."

Comet stood and picked up a huge, thick, leather-bound book from the floor. "I give you the Book of the Dead. Soon, the dark lord will walk the earth again."

Hangoctuforre turned to Damian. "And you?"

"It wasn't as difficult as we thought." Damian reached into his jacket pocket and pulled out a ring. "But we now have the Ring of Light in our possession."

Hangoctuforre stood and spread his arms out to the side. "My brothers, friends, and allies; we are ready. We have come from miles, all over the globe and all over the underworld to be here today. We are uniting to enslave human-kind and destroy all those that either stand in our way or refuse to be enslaved. It's time for demons, half breeds or not; vampires, purebloods or not, to come together under one banner. And we will make the earth our playground once more. We will seal the entry to heaven, have all the blood, bodies, and souls to ourselves. Now, are you with me?"

A loud chorus of cheers erupted. Most clapped, and others whistled. Even the demons that weren't fond of Hangoctuforre knew it was the greatest collection of power the underworld had assembled to wage war on the earth. Hangoctuforre knew he'd have to deal with the malcontents once the war was over. But he figured he'd conquer the earth and worry about it later.

Part 7

ORIGINS 3:
THE POWER RINGS

Thebes, Egypt 1057 BC

It was the time of Orack, the sorcerer. He had a hand in placing a king on the throne for over one hundred years. Only a few people in Thebes knew of his existence. Fewer knew of his role in being a king maker. In those days, only a small group of men could claim to be a wizard or a sorcerer, but they never opposed Orack. Because in his possession were the three rings of power. When connected, as they always were, melded together by magic, they were known as the Power Ring. Separated, they had their own names as well.

The center and most powerful ring, encased in silver, was the green emerald ring: The Ring of Light. It gives its bearer extra strength and the ability to disappear and appear over short distances. It is the only ring that can kill instantly when only a single beam of light is shot from it. It is the only ring that can combine with the other two rings.

The Peace ring is a round-shaped and marble ring. It can only be wielded by someone with a pure heart. However, when combined with the other two rings, anyone can use it. The Peace Ring has the same lethal capability as the Ring of Light, except it usually takes two shots from it to kill a supernatural being. Depending on the person, it can also cleanse a person's soul.

The Hellfire Ring emits fire beams of light. Its only purpose is destruction. Only a person with evil intentions is able to wield the Hellfire ring.

Orack was the first to ever hold the Ring of Light, and he used it to claim the other two. He successfully mastered its power and took over the lands His native language was Hebrew, but Latin was spoken to cast spells.

However, two wizards, Malak and Gosham, joined forces on a mission to take the Power Rings and separate them. They also recruited a Shaman, Mateo, and two twins, Eli and Enok. Mateo was considered an enemy of the crown. He was caught several times for attempting a coup but escaped. He then realized that it was Orack who had helped keep the king in power, so he knew he had to try something else.

Eli and Enok were tall, well-built men that once served as the king's personal guards. However, they witnessed him forcing himself on a young girl and swore to quit. They vowed to never let it happen again, and the only way to do it was to help overthrow the king. When Mateo was arrested for the last time, it was the same day they resigned their commission. They pretended to say their farewells and went down to the dungeon. They found Mateo being tortured by two guards.

"Are you guys going to continue torturing a bum?" Eli asked. "Or are you going to say farewell to the men who trained you?"

The two guards smiled and dropped Mateo to the ground, which was covered in straw. They dropped the knives and whips they were holding as well. They walked over and grabbed Enok and Eli's forearms, and the two twins did the same. It was a greeting and a farewell.

Enok glanced behind the guards to nod at Mateo. "You guys are the king's best guards now. Sure would be nice if we had a faster way out of here than to walk back up and out of this dungeon."

Mateo rose to his feet. The white glow in his eyes flickered. "Umi, shumi, shumi."

Both the guards grabbed their guts and bent over. They vomited, and Eli and Enok punched them in the face, knocking them unconscious.

"Who are you two?" Mateo asked. "And why are you doing this?"

"We want what you want." Eli walked over and put his hand on Mateo's shoulder. "And that's to put an end to King Morlock's reign. But we weren't kidding. We need to find a way out of here. There are one hundred guards standing between us and freedom."

Just as the words left Eli's mouth, an explosion blew a hole in the wall. All three men dove to the ground. When they looked up, two men in brown robes stood in the rubble from the hole.

Malak motioned toward the hole. "Are you guys just going to lay there, or is this an escape?"

Gosham twirled his hand. "Let's go. Let's go. Let's go. The guards will surely have heard that. We have little time to waste."

Mateo, Eli, and Enok got back to their feet and hurried through the hole in the wall. Gosham held up his wizard's staff with a crucifix at the top.

"Illustrant (illuminate)." He waved his hand in front of the crucifix, and it resembled a torch. "Now let's make haste."

All five men ran down the tunnel that Gosham and Malak had created. Mateo, the older of the men began to fall behind. Gosham, always the sentimental wizard, stopped and pointed his staff at Mateo.

"Plaustra (wagon). Let's see if this helps," Gosham said.

A brown wooden wagon with wooden wheels appeared next to Mateo.

Mateo stopped and pointed his thumb to his chest. "For me?"

Gosham reached down, grabbed a rope, and instructed Enok to do the same. "It's gonna be bumpy, but this way, we won't lose track of you."

Mateo got in the wagon and Gosham and Enok, turned, put the ropes over their shoulders and took off running again. The wagon ride was bumpy as Gosham said, but they were able to keep up with Malak and Eli. Once they reached the end of the tunnel, Malak had to put his arm out to stop Eli from going further. The tunnel led to a twenty-foot drop, not directly to the river, but they had to jump over about five feet of tall trees to get there. They'd need a running start, and it was dark so they couldn't see much. They only heard the roar of the flowing river.

However, the escape plan depended on Mateo being able to jump over the trees. The mission would be for nothing if he couldn't, so they waited for Mateo to go first. He stepped back about twenty-five feet and took off running toward the hole. That's when they heard the palace guards running towards them. Mateo jumped. He hit a tree skinned his buttocks, but he landed in the water.

"You all go ahead." Gosham pointed to the end of the tunnel. "I'll deal with them if I have to."

"Are you sure, Gosham?" Malak asked. "We didn't come here to free a prisoner, just to leave someone behind."

Gosham clapped his hands twice. "Go, my friend. Leave this to me."

Eli, Enok, and Malak ran as well. They built up enough speed to clear the trees and land in the water. They tried to float and look back up toward the tunnel, but the current was too strong and quickly carried them downstream.

Meanwhile, back in the tunnel, as Gosham prepared to run, a spear landed near his foot. The guards had arrived and were about ten feet away. Another spear would surely hit him.

Gosham raised his staff and in the air. "Vis ager. (force field)."

A white glow surrounded his body. Even though it was dark in the tunnel, several spears bounced off the force field. The guards stopped about five feet in front of Gosham. They pulled out their swords and prepared to attack.

Gosham raised his staff in the air again. "Luto (mud)."

The ground became softer and eventually turned to mud. The guards ran toward Gosham and either began to slip or sink.

Gosham smiled. "Ad normalis (return to normal)."

The ground became solid again, leaving the guards submerged in the hardened ground. Gosham turned back toward the hole in the wall and ran for it. He leaped across the trees and dove into the water. He allowed the current to the rest.

Devlin, North Dakota

The Hangman materialized walking down a dark street toward the local high school. It was the only one in the small town. It was about seven o'clock at night, and he was surprisingly the only person on the streets. Under his hood, a constant frown appeared on his face after learning of Kente Jr's demise. He pushed open the front doors, which weren't locked. He walked down the hall until he heard what he was searching for: a group of men in an Alcoholics Anonymous meeting. He stood outside and stared through a small rectangular glass window outside the classroom. There were about ten men in total, sitting in three rows of chairs. An overweight bald white man had just spoken and sat back in his seat.

The Hangman's hooked staffed appeared in his hand. He looked down at the Hellfire Ring, which had begun to glow red. He put his burned hand up to the window and closed his eyes. Inside, a tall, slender Native American had just stood to talk. A noose lassoed around the man's neck. His long black hair, which was in a ponytail, was caught in with the rope. The Hangman raised his hand in the air, and the man was lifted off the ground. The men in the room all jumped to their feet and looked above him to see where the rope came from. It just hung from out of nowhere.

The Hangman swung open the door. His anger drowned out his sense of humor. He dove into action. The man sitting next to the door and known as the Master-at-Arm's head was cut off first. He slumped over and fell out of the chair at the same time his head hit the floor. The Hangman pointed his ring and fired off three beams of red light and struck three men. They died almost instantly upon hitting the floor. The other men tried to run toward the windows, but the Hangman disappeared and reappeared in front of windows to block their escape. With three strokes from his hooked staff, three heads rolled across the floor.

Two men remained. One grabbed a small wooden chair and hit the Hangman in the back of the head with it. He didn't budge. He turned to face the man and punched his fist through the man's face. Blood splattered across the other man's face, and he turned to run. But the Hangman grabbed him by his shirt collar and put the Hellfire Ring against the man's temple. The Hellfire Ring began to glow. The man's head began to smoke, and his eyes popped out of his head, the Hangman dropped the body and began to walk out of the classroom. He turned and looked at the ceiling, where the Native American man still hung and was dead. The Hangman gestured his hand to the ground, and the noose disappeared, dropping the body to the floor. *Hmm. Now, that's how you get things back to normal around here.*

The Hangman walked back outside the school. He looked to the sky. Red electricity covered his body, and he disappeared.

The Underworld

Hangoctuforre sat on his throne-like chair in the meeting room. It was empty, and he waited for his guest to arrive. He tapped his fingers on his new sword. It had the same power and was almost equal to Jericho's. The one difference; the slayer and the Sword of Caine had become one. He looked at this newly acquired ring, the Ring of Light. He knew because of the way he'd gotten it, he'd have to deal with an irate Hangman. But at that moment, he had business to tend to.

His guest entered the room. He was a thin man with glasses. He looked more like a banker than a cold-blooded demon. He had a bald spot in the back of his head and wore a black suit with a white shirt. It was an unusual look for the demon-possessed man as he rarely ventured from the underworld to possess a new body. He usually wore a ragged leather trench coat with a tattered shirt and pants. He did have his silver dagger roped around his waist in a knife holder.

"You called for me?" the demon said.

"Yes," Hangoctuforre replied. "Come in, Zade. We have much to discuss. Have a seat."

The demon known as the Mad Demon slid slowly into the chair at the other end of the table. "Well, spit it out."

"You know what, Zade? You've always been too smart or crazy for your own good."

"Meaning?"

Hangoctuforre straightened himself. "Meaning I understand that you have planned a coup once we've taken back the earth."

Zade stood. "You know what—"

"Sit down!" Hangoctuforre thundered. "Or I'll make you wish I had destroyed you years ago instead of imprisoning you."

"Without that ring, you're nothing."

Hangoctuforre looked down at the ring on his finger. "Oh, you mean this ring?"

Hangoctuforre shot a green beam of light from the ring and struck Zade in the chest. The demon flailed backward and crashed into the wall behind him. He grabbed his chest and reached out for the table to pull himself up to his feet. He pulled the dagger from his pouch.

"You bastard!" Zade coughed. "How dare you break the truce we agreed to? Wait until my brothers hear about this."

Hangoctuforre stood and began to inch toward Zade. "What makes you think they will hear anything about this?"

Zade began to back up and reached backward for the door. "You son-of-a whore. You won't get away with this."

Hangoctuforre smiled. "I already have."

Hangoctuforre pointed the ring and shot another beam of light at Zade. Hangoctuforre knew he didn't need to shoot another beam at Zade. Because he knew, in time, Zade would fall like many others that had been struck with the Ring of Light. The beam struck Zade in his chest again. He tried to raise his dagger, but he didn't have the strength. He collapsed to the floor and clutched his chest. His body began to liquefy and dissolve. Only Zade's demon yellow demon essence hovered over a pile of white liquid and then evaporated.

Springfield, Connecticut

BA, Susie, and Tom entered the old warehouse in a deserted part of town. It was dark, almost midnight, but one overhead light was on inside the two-story building. They were following a tip about Kente Jr. being spotted in the area. BA wanted another shot at Kent Jr. He didn't like feeling as though he'd lost the last time they'd faced off. To make matters worse, he'd betrayed himself and freed the Hangman. The thought constantly rushed through BA's head like glass. He had two Power Rings in his possession, and because he'd listened to a human, one was back in the hands of what he considered to be a murderer.

BA held out his hand to stop Tom and Susie, who were behind him. "Hold up. Something's wrong."

"What is it, angel?" Tom asked.

"Stay alert," BA said. "We're not alone."

BA sensed a nervousness in the air. It wasn't coming from

whatever was out of place. It sensed it coming from Susie. BA knew she was tough, with a unique gift, but she hadn't faced off with anything like Hangoctuforre and his demons.

"Calm yourself, Susan." BA put his hand on her shoulder. "I'm sure whatever's out there can sense your nerves too."

"Gotcha," she replied. "But this is all new to me."

BA also sensed something he hadn't felt in a while—infatuation. It was radiating off Tom for Susie. BA smiled and glanced at Tom.

"What?" Tom asked.

"Noting, demon hunter." BA smiled again. "You humans are funny though. And are we sure it was a good idea to send Caine and the wizard after Cromwell?"

"Jericho is the only person the Hangman trusts." Tom slipped on his brass knuckles. "Besides, Merryweather is with him. It'll be ok."

"Jericho's the best," Susie cut in. "Even compared to a badass like the Hangman."

BA sighed and brushed off Susie's compliment. Jericho had become an irritation for the angel. He felt the uneasiness every time he and Jericho were in the same vicinity.

Those thoughts were quickly erased by three barrels being tossed in the hero's direction. BA knocked one to the side, and Susie and Tom sidestepped the others. Three huge gargoyle-like creatures stepped out of the shadows. Their odor was unmistakable. It smelled like burnt animal fur. Their skin was gray, eyes black with noses shaped like a pig. They had three massive fingers and toes with sharp claws on each. They also had tails.

BA looked up to the ceiling and then all around. "Midnight Scavengers. Now, where is their master?"

"What are Midnight Scavengers?" Tom asked.

"They do the bidding of a witch doctor, named Papa Rango." BA held out his hand, and his battle-ax appeared. "This is not good. I almost lost the wizard in our last encounter with them."

The Midnight Scavengers surrounded them. One appeared from behind Susie and attempted to bite her.

"Watch out Taki." BA turned toward Susie. "Their bite and claws are lethal if they can release their toxins."

Tom had never encountered a Scavenger before, but he ran to aid Susie. He jumped on the Scavenger's back and began punching the beast in the side with the brass knuckles. The Scavenger flipped Tom off his back and turned his attention to the demon hunter. Before Tom could recover, the Scavenger dove on top of Tom and bit him in the shoulder. BA knew he had to act before the Scavenger's toxin was released into Tom's shoulder, so BA blasted the Scavenger with a white beam of light from the Peace Ring. The Scavenger, being a supernatural creature wobbled to his feet and took his place alongside the other Scavengers.

BA expected his powers to diminish like the last time he faced off with Scavengers and Papa Rango. BA's eyes glowed white, and he held up his battle-ax. White electricity covered his body until he was wearing his angelic battle armor. It was a black steel armored suit from head-to-toe with a black steel grate across his face. Only his eyes could be seen through the grate. However, he didn't feel the weak sensation overcome him. His armor didn't disappear like before.

"These guys have just screwed up," BA said. "Without Rango and his spells, I can deal with them myself."

BA took off his helmet and held up his fist. The Peace Ring lit up the warehouse and a pulse erupted throughout. When the light died down, the three Scavengers were in piles of dust. *Hmm, this must be how Jericho feels when he dispatches a vampire. I could get used to this. But where is their master, and why did he only send three knowing I'd be at full strength? Something's not right here.*

Susie put Tom's arm over her shoulder. "Let's go, priest. You've done your part for today."

"What about me?" BA asked.

"Oh, yeah." Susie nodded at BA. "Thanks, angel."

Tom looked back at BA and then smiled. He grimaced and leaned closer onto Susie's shoulder.

"Oh, God," BA said. "That's just great."

Thebes, Egypt 1057 BC

Gosham was the last of the five men to pull himself onto the riverbank. The others were sitting on boulders, waiting for him. They hugged and patted each other on the back. It was time to do what they'd come together to do, and that was to stop Orack, confiscate the Power Ring, and dethrone King Lotus.

"We have to separate Orack from the Power Ring." Malak paced on the riverbank. "And that won't be easy."

"I can come up with a spell," Gosham said. "But it can only be accomplished once because the ingredients are so rare. And we'll need a dead shot with an arrow or sling-rocket."

"I can do that." Enok stood. "I'm gifted with a slingshot. As long as your spell works, wizard, I'll hit any target you need."

Eli nodded in agreement. "He speaks the truth."

"Good," Gosham said. "But just a word of caution: if anyone is hit with a beam of light from the Power Ring, it's over.

And that includes Malak and me. The combined ring is *just that* powerful."

"And what is my role in all of this?" Mateo also stood. "I'd hate to think I was freed for nothing."

"You're not a wizard, but you're useful." Malak put his hand on Mateo's shoulder. "We need your abilities to disable Orack's guards. They're human and should be no problem for a shaman."

Mateo smiled. "Indeed."

Gosham and Malak gave each man a list of ingredients so they could create a spell that would temporarily disable the Power Ring.

As the night fell on Egypt, the five men emerged outside of Orack's pyramid in the middle of the desert. The moon was full and provided the light they needed. There were no visible guards, but he didn't need any. However, they knew there would be some inside of the huge structure. Armed with the Power Ring, Orack was the most powerful sorcerer on earth. And even without the ring, he still was a skilled wizard.

The only visible opening to the pyramid was a rectangular opening near the top. Orack floated in and out of the pyramid through it and forced his guards to use ropes to gain access.

"Give us your ropes." Gosham pointed up. "We'll secure them to the top once we get there."

Gosham and Malak raised their hands and staffs. "Supernatet (float)."

They floated to almost the top of the pyramid and into the clouds with three thick ropes. They forced steel pikes in the stone and allowed the ropes to fall.

As they floated, Malak turned to Gosham. "There's no way Mateo makes it up here on his own. One of us is going to have to go back down and get him."

"And let me guess." Gosham shook his head. "The 'one of us' is me."

"I'm not as strong as you. He'd drag us both down."

"Do we really need him then?"

Malak thought for a second. "Yes, we do. Someone has to deal with the guards when we get inside."

Gosham shook his head again. "Descendentes (descend)."

Gosham levitated back down the pyramid. On the way down, a few feet from the bottom, he nodded at Eli and Enok, who were making their way up the ropes. As he reached the bottom, Gosham didn't know what the plan was, but he witnessed Mateo tying the rope around his waist.

Mateo straightened as he was startled. "Oh, you guys finally figured out that I can't make that climb, did you?"

"Yeah, it finally dawned on us," Gosham said. "What were you planning on doing, letting the twins pull you up?"

"Exactly."

"Well, I've come to retrieve you myself."

Gosham walked over, grabbed Mateo by the hips, and placed the shaman over the wizard's shoulders.

Gosham looked to the sky. "Supernatet (float)."

Going slower than before, the two men began to hover toward the top of the pyramid. They passed the twins, who simply shook their heads and laughed.

"Hey," Mateo said. "Don't blame me for this. This is as uncomfortable for me as it is for you two climbing up this thing."

"Yeah. Yeah. Yeah," Eli replied.

As they reached the top, Gosham lowered Mateo into the rectangular opening. Torches were already lit, so they didn't have to bring their own or use magic.

"Well, shaman," Gosham began. "This is what we brought you here for. Now, go find and eliminate the guards. We'll be right behind you when the twins arrive."

Mateo ran his hand through his beard. "It will be my pleasure."

Gosham stood in the entrance while Malak continued to float as they waited on the twins. Once the twins reached the top, they all entered the pyramid together. As they made their way down the passageway, they were just in time to witness Mateo whip out his knife to engage the guards. There were five guards in total and dressed in gold armor from head to toe. They carried golden spears. Their faces were painted gold as well.

Mateo's eyes rolled back until only the whites were showing. He held his gold medallion necklace and rotated his knife in a circle toward the guards. Two of the guards fell to their knees, clutching their stomachs. They began to vomit. The other guards bent down to assist their fellow guards.

"Eli," Gosham began. "Go help the shaman. We need Enok with us to complete the plan."

"Are you sure?" Eli asked. "Seems like you'll need my help with Orack. Mateo appears to have this covered."

"He's not a young shaman anymore," Malak cut in. "He's capable of being surprised even if it seems like he's in control."

"Alright," Eli said. "I'll go help, but I think you'll need me with you guys."

Eli drew his sword and ran to attack the guards. Mateo's

eyes returned to normal, and he joined in the fight with the remaining three guards. Gosham, Malak, and Enok took one last look at their friends and headed down another passageway. Torches were lit along the walls. They crept as Malak and Gosham had their wizard's staffs in hand, and Enok carried his sword. He had his slingshot and metal pellets in a pouch attached to his waist.

"Shhh." Gosham put his finger over his lips. "You feel that, Malak?"

"Yes," Malak replied. "I can feel the energy from his power pulsating through my body."

Gosham turned and put this hand and Enok's shoulder. "When we get in there, you need to take cover and take the shot when you have it. You probably won't get more than one."

"I want to fight him too," Enok said.

Malak shook his head. "We don't have time to argue. He can vaporize you into nothingness."

"Fine," Enok agreed. "But I don't like this."

The three men walked into the lighted room. Torches were lit on two levels, which brightened it even more than the hall. As they stood at the entrance, they saw a bald man with gold-hooped earrings and white toga sitting at a desk with his back turned to them. He had a red-painted stripe going from the back of his head to the front. A round bed took up most of the room and ancient weaponry was scattered throughout the walls as well. Enok walked over to a large trunk and stooped behind it.

"Ahh," Orack began. "Come in, my former pupils. And tell your friend to come out from hiding. We are all friends here."

Gosham glanced over at Enok, who had a confused

expression on his face. It was obvious that Orack, being their former mentor, surprised the twin.

"We're not here to parlay with you, Orack." Gosham pointed at the wizard. "We're here to take the Power Ring and restore order to this kingdom."

Orack turned to face his former pupils and smiled. "You always were the funny one, Gosham. But even you're not so out of touch with reality to believe that you'll relieve me of the ring. Besides, two wizards against one wizard and a man is surely not a fair situation."

Gosham looked around. He didn't see another wizard in the chamber, and, by his count, he was in the company of the other wizard and a man. But then Malak walked over and kneeled in front of Orack.

"My lord, Orack." Malak kissed Orack's hand. "I have delivered the traitor as you wished."

Gosham squinted and cocked his head to the side. "Malak... no!"

"You're an idiot, Gosham." Malak stood to face Gosham. "You didn't really think we could defeat Lord Orack, did you?"

Gosham held out his staff. "Cicer (pulse)."

The invisible force knocked Malak across the bed and into the table with silverware on it. However, when Gosham turned back to Orack, Orack was standing with his eyes glowing dark pink.

"Extraho (extract)." Orack held out his hand, and Gosham's staff whipped across the room and into Orack's possession. "Too easy. You were always my favorite student, Gosham. Join me again as I plan to take this kingdom for myself."

Malak stood with his arms out. "But, master, what about me?"

"For you," Orack said as he raised the Power Ring. "All I have is this."

A dark pink beam of light blasted out of the power ring and struck Malak in the chest. He crashed up against the wall and sunk back to the floor.

Malak's eyes opened wide, and his brow ruffled as he glared at Orack. "B-B-But why, m-master. I've been n-nothing b-but loyal to you."

Malak's body went limp as he leaned against the wall. He began to shake, and the dark pink glow consumed his body. His body evaporated.

Orack pointed the ring at Gosham. "Now, are you going to join me...or join *him?*"

Gosham looked over at the spot where Malak once lay. He'd never seen the Power Ring in action before. A painful tingle ran through his spine. He was afraid. He'd never felt it before, but he knew he was face-to-face with death.

Suddenly, as if both wizards had forgotten about him, Enok popped up from behind the trunk with his slingshot ready. Without hesitation, he fired. The magical silver pellet, as it grew closer to the Power Ring on Orack's hand, began to glow white. It smashed into the Power Ring, and Orack withdrew his fist. He shook his hand and raised his fist again. This time he pointed it at Enok and fired. Enok attempted to dive out of the way, but he wasn't fast enough. He was struck in the side and disintegrated before his body hit the ground.

Orack laughed as he turned back to Gosham. "You didn't really think he could knock the Power Ring from my finger, did you?"

Gosham shook his head. "Nope. That was just the beginning. What I wanted to happen, will happen at any moment."

The Power Ring began to glow dark pink and Gosham took a step backward. Orack looked down at his hand.

Orack violently shook his head from side to side. "This can't be."

Orack frowned and pointed the ring at Gosham again. However, when he attempted to fire a beam of light from the ring, the ring exploded into three pieces. They all slid off Orack's fingers and landed on the floor. He stooped down to pick them up. The grabbed the Hellfire Ring first. As he went to pick up the Ring of Light, Gosham's hand was there first. Both wizards looked at each other and then scrambled to get to the Peace Ring. But Mateo beat them to it.

Mateo put on the ring and pointed it at Orack. He attempted to fire, but the ring didn't work.

"You, shaman moron." Orack smiled. "You're not pure of heart. The ring won't work for you."

"Give it to me." Eli walked into the room. "Where is Enok?"

"I'm sorry, Eli.", Gosham said. But he's with your ancestors now."

Eli dropped his head and squeezed his eyes with his fingers. Orack, sensing the ring would work for Eli, shot a red beam of light from the Hellfire Ring and blasted Mateo in the chest. The shaman was sent flying backward and crashed into Eli. They hit the floor. Mateo's hand shook as he pulled off the ring and handed it to Eli before vanishing.

"Give me the ring, human," Orack said. "Or suffer the same fate."

"No, Eli bring it to m—"

Orack waved his hand across the air. "Silentium (silence)."

Gosham grabbed his mouth as he couldn't speak. He shook

his head and glanced back at Orack, who was laughing. Gosham held up the Peace Ring and fired a white beam of light at Orack. Orack fired a red beam of light from his ring. The two beams collided in midair. They both fired a continuous beam of light at each other. Neither backed up nor relented. That was until a green beam of light struck Orack in the shoulder.

"That was for my brother," Eli said. "And this is for Mateo."

Orack turned and blasted a hole in the wall. He began to run toward it. He almost entered the other side when white and green beams of light struck him in the back. He fell forward through the hole. The other side was dark. Suddenly, two red beams of light came out of the hole. Eli and Gosham stepped to the side and let the beams explode against the wall behind them.

They slowly walked toward the hole with their rings out in front. But no more beams shot out the hole. Gosham reached up and took a torch off the wall. He tossed it into the hole. Nothing was there, only the Hellfire Ring, still glowing red, lay in a pile of dirt.

"Phew!" Gosham wiped the sweat from his brow and turned to put his hand on Eli's shoulder. "I'm sorry about your brother, my friend. If its consequence, he died bravely."

"Thank you," Elie said. "It's the only way he knew. But what now?"

"We keep the rings separate." Gosham bent and picked up the Hellfire Ring. "This may have seemed simple, but these rings were responsible for keeping Orack in power, and in turn, creating multiple corrupt kingdoms."

"Do you want my ring, wizard?" Eli asked as he held out the Ring of Light.

"No. The Peace Ring can only be wielded by the pure of heart. We shall keep it in the realm of men. I will bury the other rings and hope they will never be unearthed again. But I know that will never happen. The power they radiate is too great to ignore."

Eli put the ring in the satchel around his waist. "So, is this the last we'll ever see of each other."

"Probably."

"Well, I could use a ride back out of the pyramid, if you don't mind."

Gosham laughed. "It's the least I could do, my friend."

Part 8

PAIRED UP

The Underworld

At dawn, Hangoctuforre, dressed in his brown hooded robe, and Comet made it to the edge of the underworld followed by three other demons. They'd left Damian behind with the Book of the Dead just in case something went wrong and they had to get back to the underworld. A huge invisible forcefield awaited them, leading to the Nevada desert. The other side was brighter than the underworld and they stopped a few feet in front of the barrier.

Hangoctuforre pointed the ring at the barrier and shot a green beam of light. When the beam impacted the forcefield, Hangoctuforre and Comet stepped back as the field began to glow bright green.

An oval opening opened, just large enough for the Hangoctuforre's and Comet's massive bodies to enter. As they exited the other side, Hangoctuforre waved his hand for the other demons to follow.

"Hurry." Hangoctuforre waved on his fellow demons. "We don't have much time."

However, when the other demons tried to enter, the doorway closed. The demon in front smashed into the barrier, and his body was scorched and burst into fiery ashes. His yellow demon essence floated in the air and evaporated. The other demons simply turned and walked away.

"Well," Comet began as he surveyed the desert. "That's that."

"Dammit." Hangoctuforre pounded his fist in his hand. "I feared that would happen. We'll just have to bring them through with a spell from the book. That Damn Padilla."

Comet laughed. "Let's not dwell on that. Let's go and have some fun. It's your first time back in a while."

"Indeed."

The desert was cold, but the sun was rising. Hangoctuforre looked over the hills and saw the lights from the Las Vegas strip. The last time he was there, he'd lost a battle with BA and the Hangman. He'd always wanted a rematch. He knew if he could fight them one-on-one, his chances would be even better. It's why he enlisted the help of Comet. The fallen angel didn't talk about it much, but he wanted revenge against BA from the Great War. And Hangoctuforre wanted the Hangman. He was incensed that he had to share his powers with the half-demon.

The fallen angel and the demon lord set out across the desert for the lights leading to the Las Vegas strip. *The humans won't know what hit them.*

Calgary, Canada

The nervous couple sat across from each other at their dining room table, staring at their visitor. They'd entertained him for two days and didn't know what to do as they weren't allowed to leave. They couldn't call in to work, nor go out for food. They held each other hands and teared up as they looked each other in the eyes.

"Don't start that crap again," the Hangman said. "I don't eat anymore, but you're making me want to puke my guts out with that sentimental stuff."

"P-Please, sir." The man stood, still wearing his three-piece suit since coming from work to a surprise two days earlier. "Let my wife go. She won't tell anyone. She can't hurt you."

The Hangman laughed. "You can't hurt me either, so why let her off the hook, when neither of you can do anything to me."

"My name is David Hire, sir." David held up his finger. "It's weird that you've come here because I am a Psycho Supernatural Therapist. I deal with people who claim to either have seen or are supernatural beings. I know who you are… Hangman."

The Hangman tapped his bottom lip with his finger. "Hmm. That *is* interesting, David. Now, sit your ass down. I didn't say you could stand. But tell me more."

David eased back into his chair. "I've followed your story for many years after you went missing. Slowly, information started disappearing about you, so I gathered all I could. Your name is Kente Cromwell Sr. and you are in possession of a demon's powers from the underworld."

"Well, now." The Hangman nodded. "Are you a fan of mine then, David? Come on. Be honest."

David turned his head to the side. "No."

"And why not?" the Hangman asked.

"Because you killed everyone on your street back in Harvey, Illinois." David pulled on his jacket collar. "You're a murderer."

The Hangman clapped. "So…you think you know me, Dave? Well, do you know that my wife and son were killed recently? Do you know that I was asked to come back to help that wretched angel and the other do-gooders fight a battle that I want no part of? Well, do you!"

The Hangman's voice echoed off the walls. Dave's wife Sarah flinched.

"I'm sorry for your loss, Mr. Hangman, sir," Dave continued. "But what possible purpose does it serve for you to hold us captive? You could destroy this entire city if you wanted."

"Just waiting, David," the Hangman said. "I needed a place off the grid and now I'm waiting for something else."

"For what?" Dave asked.

Thunder sounded, and the fluttering of wings sent a breeze through the dining area.

The Hangman smiled. "For that."

"Cromwell," BA said as he appeared sitting in a chair opposite The Hangman. "A new stomping ground?"

"One place is as good as another," the Hangman said.

BA glanced at David and Sarah. "At least I know now why Caine and the wizard couldn't find you. Well, I'm here to ask you to release these people and return with me to the States. Or, there's always back to Purgatory."

"Is that a threat, angel?" the Hangman asked.

"I said, I was here to 'ask' you to release these people." BA pounded the table. "Besides, why are you here?"

The Hangman glanced at BA's hands. "I came here hoping Heaven's greatest tracker would find me, and you did. I wanted to see if you had the Ring of Light. Someone killed my boy and said it was a demon. I'm just covering all my bases."

"And you think I would kill your son just to take back the ring." BA shook his head. "That tells me what you think of me."

"Come on, BA." The Hangman stood. "You're called the Bad Angel for a reason. You've fought my son before for the ring. And you hate the thought of the most powerful ring of the three, ending up in my hands."

BA dropped his head. "Yes. All those things are true. But I was merely trying to stop him before he made a grave mistake, of which he did. Then, I brought you back to help, or don't you remember? Now, let these people go."

The Hangman put his hands on his hips and took a quick glance at the couple. The Hellfire Ring began to glow red. BA jumped to his feet. However, red electricity overtook the Hangman's body, and he disappeared.

New York

The restaurant was fancy, fancier than either of the two had been in. All the tables were covered with white silk tablecloths and golden silverware. The plates were all the highest quality. A huge marble fireplace was lit on the far wall with a moose's head mounted over it. And as fancy as the place was, it was empty. Shut down as a favor to Tom from the owner, whose daughter Tom saved from possession. Tom and Susie sat at the center table and stared into each other's eyes. Susie reached across the table for Tom to place his hand in hers. He gladly did.

Tom was dressed in his usual black suit and a gray tie. Susie wore a blue dress with her shoulders exposed.

"I've saved a lot of people doing what we do," Susan began. "But no one has ever saved my life. Not even Jericho when he had the chance. But I understood that."

"Yeah, Jericho does have his own unique style." Tom smiled. "It's who he—"

"No, Thomas." She waved her hand across the air. "I didn't

say that to start a conversation about Jericho. I said it to say that you jumped on that beast to save my life. I will never forget that."

"Oh." Tom's face turned red. "Well, you're very welcome. You're part of the team, Susie."

"It's more than that." She squeezed his hand tighter. "I came to New York to kill you based on faulty information. You're nothing like I was led to believe."

Susie got up and pulled her chair around to Tom's side of the table. He almost stood, but he was nervous and didn't know how to react. She poured two glasses of red wine and passed one to Tom. He took it, and they clinked glasses for a toast.

"To us," she said. "Hopefully, this is the start of something great."

"To us," Tom responded. "My thoughts, exactly."

Tom's last encounter with a demon made him to want more out of life. He died saving the world, and now, he wanted a romantic partner. He wanted kids. He knew it was time to pursue those other things besides demon hunting. And as he stared into Susie's eyes, he knew she was the one.

"I hate to ask, but is this relationship doomed from the start?" Susie said with a smile. "I mean, I fell for you because you saved my life."

"Don't worry about that." Tom shook his head. "I fell for you when I first met you. If I see things start to slip, I'll pull us back."

Susie giggled and blushed. "Wow, Tom. You're amazing."

The smile disappeared from Tom's face. "Well, I'm glad you think that, but we're both gonna have to be at our amazing best right now. Three demons just walked in the front door."

Susie and Tom jumped to their feet. Tom had recognized the stench of dead flesh when the wind blew through the restaurant. The men's faces were also pale and scarred. Tom's smile returned as he watched Susie pull nun-chucks from the small of her back even though she was wearing a dress. *I love that woman.* Tom reached into his inner jacket and pulled out his brass knuckles and put them on. He stood side by side with Susie and waited for the demon-possessed men to make their move.

Chicago, Illinois

Alexander was stuck in traffic. He knew he should have just used magic to teleport to the hospital, but he always obeyed the rules. Using magic for personal use was forbidden by Merlin. Emma was at the hospital already. She was a few weeks early, but she was in labor. He knew she didn't like the idea of him going off to fight, so he wanted to make sure he didn't miss the birth of their child. They didn't get an ultrasound done so they didn't know the sex of the baby. They wanted it to be a surprise.

Alexander arrived at the hospital and was directed to the delivery room. He put on green hospital scrubs and a mask. As he approached, he could hear Emma screaming in pain. He stood at the door and breathed deeply. He was from a different time, and he hadn't seen childbirth in the current century. So, he had to get himself prepared for what he was about to witness.

Alexander walked into the room. Emma lay in on a hospital bed surrounded by two nurses and an Asian female doctor. The doctor had long black hair and was thin.

The nurses were two black women wearing masks and hairnets. Alexander rushed over to the right side of the bed and grabbed Emma's hand. He hadn't been to any child birthing classes, but he knew he had to show support even though he didn't know what to do.

"Alex, you made it," Emma said and then screamed.

"I'm here, Em." Alexander squeezed her hand tighter and looked at the doctor. "You have to breathe, right, doc?"

Doctor Nguyen nodded at Emma. "Yes, Emma, keep breathing steadily. The baby is crowning."

Alexander bent over and looked to see under the cover at Emma's legs. He saw the top of the baby's head and a patch of its hair. His eyes rolled back, and he fainted.

About twenty minutes passed when a nurse revived Alexander as he sat on a nearby couch. He sat up, massaged his temple, and then looked around the room. Emma was surprisingly still in labor. However, when he looked across the room, he saw a nurse cleaning a newborn baby. He stood. *My word. Twins. I can't believe this.* Alexander walked across to room to see the baby that was being cleaned. It was a boy. He had light brown skin and curly hair.

Alexander turned his attention back to Emma, who had just let out another scream. He rushed over to the side he was on before. He decided that he wasn't going to look under the sheet again as he grabbed Emma's hand. She was sweating, and tears ran down her cheeks.

"Keep pushing, honey," Alexander said. "You're almost there."

Emma glared at Alexander. "And how would you know, Alex? You were busy taking a nap."

"I'm so sorry about that, Em." Alexander put his hand on her forehead. "But I'm here now. Just keep doing what you're doing. You're so strong."

"It's almost here, Emma." Dr. Nguyen reached under the sheet. "Just one more big push."

Emma yelled out again and pushed one last time. She was spent and lay back on the bed.

"It's a girl," Dr. Nguyen said. "You have a baby girl."

Alexander started crying. The nurse gave him a pair of scissors to cut the baby's umbilical cord. He was hesitant at first, but then cut the thin cord from the baby's naval. The nurse took the baby and placed her on the counter to clean her up. They also began working on cleaning up Emma. A nurse then gave the baby to Alexander. He sat in a recliner chair next to the bed and held out his other hand. He wanted to hold the boy as well.

Alexander looked over at Emma. "Look, honey. There's two of them."

However, Emma was exhausted and asleep. Alexander turned his attention back to the children and smiled. He rocked back and forth in the chair. He continued to cry. It was the second chance he'd been waiting for.

"You, my dear daughter, shall be named Octavia after your auntie." Alexander bent down and kissed the girl on the forehead. "And you, you my son, I fought with your mother over this name, but you will be named Octus."

Las Vegas, Nevada

Hangoctuforre and Comet arrived at the front steps of city hall around noon. Hangoctuforre wanted to make a statement.

He pointed his ring at the white stone building and fired a green beam of light from his ring. The beam blew a hole in the side of the building. Hangoctuforre fired another shot and brought down two of the huge stone pillars in the front of the building. Employees began running out the back doors. People screamed and yelled as they ran, while others were crushed underneath the rubble.

Hangoctuforre laughed. "That's right, run, you filthy vermin. Run for your lives. Scream to the heavens so they'll send your so-called heroes to save you."

A bright light appeared in Comets hand as he stretched it out. And when it disappeared, a sword was in its place. "My turn."

"No." Hangoctuforre held up his hand. "Save your energy, my friend, for the fight that's yet to come. We're only here to announce our arrival."

"And what about them?" Comet pointed to the four police cars that arrived.

"Fine." Hangoctuforre nodded. "Go have some fun."

With the words barely out of Hangoctuforre's mouth, Comet launched his sword through the air. It crashed through the windshield of the lead police car and penetrated the driver's chest. The car swerved and rammed into a parked car on the street. The officer in the passenger side, who didn't have on his seatbelt, smashed through what remained of the windshield and landed face-first on the pavement. He lay unconscious.

Comet reached out his hand, and his sword tore away from the officer's chest and sped back into Comet's hand. The officer died. Comet then sprouted his wings and jumped into the air. He came down on the hood of another police car and caved it in. The car stopped, and Comet shoved his sword through windshield twice, stabbing both the driver and the passenger. They died instantly. The two other police cars stopped before reaching Comet and Hangoctuforre. All four officers got out and opened fire. The bullets bounced off Comet's body. Hangoctuforre made himself almost invisible, and the bullets passed through his body. The officers stopped firing and stared at each other.

"Enough of this," Hangoctuforre said as he pointed his ring at the officers. "These humans bore me."

Hangoctuforre shot a continuous green beam of light until he'd struck all four officers. They glowed at first and then evaporated. Hangoctuforre and Comet glared at each other with smiles on their faces. Hangoctuforre then started shooting green beams of light at terrified and running passersby. Comet threw his sword as well and called it back to his hand each time it struck someone. They stood in the middle of the street and marveled at their work.

"This seems easy enough," Comet said as he looked at the dead bodies on the street and sidewalks. "Our victory will be a cinch."

"Not quite." Hangoctuforre held up his finger. "These humans are mere appetizers. It'll get interesting when the heroes arrive."

Comet nodded. "I can't wait."

New York

Susan went on the attack first. She whipped her nunchucks around, popping two of men in the face. The other demon-possessed man stood in the doorway and watched. Neither he nor Tom interfered. Susie took care of it by herself. That was until the demon standing at the door, eyes turned black and he balled his fist. Susie was lifted off the ground and flung into the nearby wall. The demon pointed at Tom, twisted his hand, and an invisible force sent Tom sailing backward until he crashed into the table behind him.

Tom struggled back to his feet and located Susie across the room. "He's the leader. We've got to take him first."

Susie wiped off her shirt. "Tell me something I don't know, Thomas."

Tom and Susie stood next to each other once again with their weapons ready to fight. The lead demon waved his hand toward Tom and Susie, and the two other demons attacked.

"Not the date we wanted," Tom said. "So, let's make this quick."

Susan nodded. "Agreed."

Las Vegas

Hangoctuforre and Comet walked down the middle of the abandoned strip. Dead bodies littered the street and abandoned cars were scattered throughout, some still running.

"Are you ready, Comet?" Hangoctuforre turned slightly and glanced at the fallen angel. "It'll be nothing but a test, but a necessary one."

Comet nodded and dropped to his knees. Hangoctuforre walked a few feet away and looked to the sky. His eyes glowed red. He gripped his sword handle with both hands and leaned his forehead against it. Red electricity crackled as it covered his body.

Hangoctuforre repeated, "Hangman. I summon you. I summon you to me and this place."

A few feet away, Comet prayed, "Artherial, my brother, I pray to you in hopes that you will join me."

The sky darkened. Clouds formed over the area. The wind picked up and began blowing trash down the street. A bolt of lightning struck the ground a few feet in front of Hangoctuforre. When the smoke and debris cleared, the Hangman stood, wearing his black robe and hood. He had he hooked staff in one hand, and the Hellfire glowed on the other.

"Who dares summon me?" he asked in a thunderous voice. "No one summons me."

"Well, apparently, someone can." Hangoctuforre pulled his hood back on his robe, exposing his red demon face and two horns on each side of his head. His skin was charred, and his eyes were yellow. "It's time for the rematch."

The Hangman threw his head back and laughed. "Rematch? You're implying that the first fight was something special. We kicked your ass."

"Things are a little different this time," Hangoctuforre said as he gestured to Comet. "No two-on-one this time."

Comet stepped forward. "We're just waiting on our other special guest."

The sounds of wings flapping ushered in BA, who stood to the right of the Hangman. "I'll assume that's me?"

"You've got it, brother," Comet responded.

The Hangman looked over to BA. "Angel. I thought I'd lost you in Canada."

"Funny how we keep running into each other." BA smiled. "Tells me that we're supposed to be doing this together."

"Maybe," the Hangman responded.

Hangoctuforre didn't waste any more time. He fired a green beam of light from his ring. The Hangman just as quickly raised his staff and blocked it. He returned a red beam of light from the Hellfire Ring, and Hangoctuforre blocked it with his sword. BA then fired a white beam of light from the Peace Ring, and again, Hangoctuforre blocked it with his sword. Finally, the Hangman and BA fired steady beams of light from their rings, prompting Hangoctuforre to create a green force-field around himself with his ring.

Hangoctuforre then turned to Comet. "Anytime you want to join in would be fine with me."

"Oh…yeah." Comet held out his hand and called on his sword.

"Wait a minute." The Hangman turned to BA. "How'd he get the Ring of Light? "Kente had it last?"

BA shrugged. "I have no clue, but there's no time to think about that now."

Comet threw his sword toward BA and the Hangman. They stopped firing their beams of light and ducked. The sword acted as a boomerang and returned to Comet's hand. BA looked and then reached his hand to the sky. It was as if Comet knew what was happening as he did the same. Two bolts of light rained down and struck each angel. Their armor started forming around their bodies. BA's was all black with a metal face grate across his helmet. Comet's was gray with angel wings on the chest plate. His face was completely covered by a gray metal mask. BA held out his hand and called his battle-ax to it. He and Comet charged each other and engaged in a sword versus ax confrontation.

"Just you and I this time, Cromwell," Hangoctuforre said. "You power stealing, second rate, wanna-be demon."

"What's wrong?" The Hangman smiled. "The big bad demon lord can't take a half-demon without his full powers?"

Hangoctuforre and the Hangman charged each other. Hangoctuforre avoided being struck by the famed hooked staff—made of black steel. Hangoctuforre had the sword he'd created with the same abilities as the Sword of Caine. Neither the Hangman nor Hangoctuforre knew which weapon was greater, but they were about to find out. They both had the equivalent demonic powers, they both were in possession of a power ring, and they both had the same intensity and obsession for destruction.

The Hangman leaped into the air and came down with his hooked staff. Hangoctuforre blocked it with his sword, but the impact forced him to drop to one knee. The Hangman attempted to drive the engaged weapons back into Hangoctuforre's face, but the demon blew black smoke from his mouth and blinded the Hangman. The Hangman staggered backward, wiping his eyes. Hangoctuforre recovered to his feet and charged. He swung his sword like a baseball bat and knocked the hooked staff from the Hangman's hands. The vibrations from the impact caused the Hangman to look down at his hands as they shook. When he looked back up, a green beam of light struck him in the chest and caused the half-demon to be catapulted backward for half the block. The Hangman crashed to the ground, creating a small crater. He struggled to get up and couldn't.

Hangoctuforre, seeing the Hangman was temporarily down, turned his attention to BA and Comet. They swung their weapons at each other, with each one blocking the other and not backing away. Suddenly, BA held up his arm to block an attempted strike from Hangoctuforre's sword. The sword cut a gash into BA armor, causing black blood to drip out. The armor was tough. If it had been any other metal, BA's limb would have been severed. BA jumped backward to get both Comet and Hangoctuforre in his sight. He looked over and saw the Hangman on the ground, struggling to get back into the action.

Hangoctuforre held out his sword to stop Comet from advancing. "You see, BA. As much as I'd like to finish off you two right now, this was just a little exercise."

"Let's end this now, demon." Comet tried to push Hangoctuforre's blade aside. "We've got them on the ropes."

"NO!" Hangoctuforre thundered as he took a quick glance at the sky. "It's not time. I'll explain later. But back to you, BA. I want all of you heroes to die at the same time. I want the rings. I want the Hangman's hooked staff. I want the Sword of Caine. I want it all. And when we see each other again…I *will* have it all."

Hangoctuforre eyes glowed, and a green force field surrounded him and Comet just a red beam of light from the Hellfire Ring arrived. The beam of light bounced off the forcefield. The Hangman, breathing heavily, walked over and stood next to BA as Hangoctuforre and Comet began to back away. They smiled and waved as a portal opened behind them. They stepped through it and the portal closed almost immediately.

"Better late than never, Cromwell." BA's armor disappeared.

"I see you still fight the same—like crap. I can't believe you let him get the jump on you."

"Do you want some, angel?" The Hangman's eyes glowed red. "I'll show you just how much I've improved."

"Shut up, demon." BA looked around at the carnage. "We can't let this happen again."

"We? For the last time, there's no *we*."

"I brought you back for a reason, Cromwell."

"And I'll thank you....one day. But for now, we're done, bird brains."

"So, you're just going to walk away?"

"Yes."

BA sighed. "He's never going to stop hunting you for his powers, your weapon, or your ring. You know that, right?"

"He got lucky today." The Hangman turned to walk away and then slightly back to BA. "That won't happen again."

The Hangman held up his fist, and the Hellfire Ring glowed red. Red electricity surrounded him, and the half-demon was gone.

Part 9

POSSESSION

New York

Jericho entered the darkened alley behind the bar he'd just left. *Damn slayer powers. Can even get drunk like I want.* Only one streetlight blinked in the alley, and rats ran in between garbage cans. Jericho was angry. He was angry and wanted answers. *I'm a freaking Death Brother, and where's the priest? He's out trying to date while there's evil lurking about. I should have just let the girl kill him.*

Jericho stopped walking and turned his head to the side. He heard footsteps, several of them. *Somebody's gotta either be crazy or stupid for following me.* He turned around a saw four men coming his way. All four men were pale, but only three exposed their vampire faces, which consisted of pultruding fangs, deformed faces, and bloodshot eyes. Jericho then figured the other man had to be a demon. He'd possessed a young man's body. Jericho recognized him from the bar. He assumed the demon had seen him and alerted the vampires. After all, Hangoctuforre had gathered all the creatures of the night and demons.

The vampire standing in front was a well-built, bald black man with a Jerry Curl. He had a spider tattoo on the center of his forehead. The other two were both blond, except one had a tattoo of a spider covering his entire face. The other one had on a tank-top and had spider tattoos on both of his huge biceps. All three vampires wore blue jeans, black combat boots with black shirts.

"Well, well, well," the lead vampire said. "If it isn't the vampire slayer and all alone."

"And who might you be?" Jericho asked. "My own personal welcoming committee? I'm touched."

"The name's Chaco," the curly-haired man said. "The big guy is Saben, and the other one is Spider Face, for obvious reasons. We represent the Spider Vamps. Demon, you can go. We've got this."

"Are you sure?" The demon frowned. "I'm here to help."

"We owe this guy." Chaco waved his hand toward the demon. "He belongs to us."

The demon slowly began to walk backwards before turning around and leaving. He stopped and took one last look and then finally disappeared around the corner. Jericho smiled. It had been a while since he'd been in a fight. He was about five inches taller than Saben and more muscular as well. He wanted to save the huge vampire for last.

"Should have told the demon to stay." Jericho pointed to the spot the demon once stood. "Somebody's gotta bear witness to the dusting of...Chaco, was it?"

Chaco laughed. "You've taken down some pretty tough clans in your time, slayer. But that all ends tonight."

"So, what are you waiting for then?" Jericho dropped his duffle bag. "A bell to ring?"

Spider Face was the first to attack. He ran toward Jericho and leaped into the air. Jericho reached up and grabbed Spider Face by the neck. He ripped Spider Face's throat out and dropped the vampire on the ground. The vampire crawled around on the ground holding his throat. He had to get away until his regenerative powers kicked in.

When Jericho looked back up, Saben's huge fist connected to Jericho's jaw. Jericho fell against a wall. He wiped the saliva from his mouth. *Now that's what I'm talking about.* Jericho pushed himself from against the wall and kicked Saben in the chest. The vampire sailed across the alley and slammed against a brick wall.

Chaco pulled out a long knife from the small of his back. Saben recovered and pulled out a similar knife from his boot. Spider Face struggled to his feet as his throat began to heal. He maneuvered around Jericho to rejoin the other vampires. He pulled out a knife as well.

"Bringing a knife to a sword fight?" Jericho smirked. "That's really stupid."

Jericho reached down, unzipped his duffle bag, and pulled out the Sword of Caine. He joined the vampires in a fight stance. He studied all three vampires. *Now, who is it going to be? Who's going to have the guts to get froggy and jump first?*

Jericho knew which one he wanted first. He wanted to take out Spider Face, who was coughing up dust. Black blood dripped down the vampire's shirt as his neck continued to heal. Jericho charged the vampires, spun around and swiped at Spider Face's head. However, Chaco and Spider Face raised their knives and blocked Jericho's sword. Saben then punched Jericho in the face again. Jericho teetered to the side, holding his jaw. Jericho massaged his jaw and then let a smile escape. He jumped into the air and drop-kicked Saben. Once Jericho hit the ground, on his knees, he whipped around and swept Chaco's legs from under him. Chaco fell and rolled out of the way. Spider Face attempted to plunge his knife down into the top of Jericho's head. Jericho moved to the side and stabbed Spider Face in the ribs. While the vampire clutched his wound, Jericho spun around and chopped off Spider Face's head. The vampire's head and body turned to ashes before his body hit the ground.

"He was just getting in the way of things," Jericho said. "Now we can have some fun."

Chaco looked down at Spider Face's ashes. "You son-of-bitch, slayer. You dusted Spider Face."

"And you're next, Chocolate." Jericho smiled and winked.

"So, you do know who we are?" Chaco turned quickly to Jericho. "But how?"

"I'm the slayer, you idiot," Jericho said. "I wasn't planning on seeing your little piss-ant clan for at least a few more years. You're small potatoes right now."

"I'll show you small potatoes." Chaco raised his knife and moved forward in Jericho's directions. "Bring it on, Slayer!"

Chaco launched at Jericho, who stepped to the side and slapped Chaco's forehead on his tattoo.

"Ha, ha, ha." Jericho laughed. "I've been wanting to do that since you arrived."

Saben used his vampire speed to run up and punch Jericho in the jaw. Saben followed it up with a quick punch to Jericho's back. Jericho fell to one knee, arched his back and grimaced in pain. He then let out another chuckle even though, this time, he spit out blood as his cheek began to swell.

"See," Jericho began. "This is why I said you guys aren't ready. "You had a free shot at me, and you threw a punch instead of a knife?"

Chaco sighed. "Dammit, Saben. He's right. What in the hell are you doing?"

"Sorry, Chaco," Saben said. "I wasn't thinking."

"Don't be sorry." Chaco rubbed his forehead, where Jericho had left a handprint. "Just kill him."

Both vampires charged Jericho again. Jericho smacked away an attempted stabbing from behind by Saben and then threw his sword in the air. He punched Saben and staggered the huge vampire. Chaco stopped, looked up to see where the sword had gone. When he turned around, Jericho punched Chaco in the face, grabbed his head, and lowered it. The Sword of Caine came down and plunged into the back of the vampire's neck. Chaco pushed away from Jericho, reached back, and pulled the Sword of Caine out of his neck.

Saben's eyes widened. "Good job, boss. You've got his sword."

"You really *are* stupid." Jericho turned to Saben and held out his hand toward Chaco. "Behold."

Chaco dropped the sword, cuffed his neck with both hands, and burst into ashes. Jericho reached down and grabbed his sword. He turned his attention back to Saben, who still had a shocked expression on his face. Jericho then leaned the Sword of Caine up against the building.

Jericho snapped his fingers to break Saben's trance. "Are you ready? You don't really want to do this with weapons, do you?"

Saben swallowed hard and looked at Jericho. "You killed Chocolate." Saben dropped his knife. "I'm gonna kill you with my bare hands for that, slayer."

Saben swung at Jericho, who ducked, but Saben kneed

Jericho in the forehead. The slayer crashed into three trash cans that were behind him. Jericho shook his head rapidly and got back to his feet. A white spark flashed in Jericho's eyes. The knee had caught him by surprise and brought his anger rushing back to his head. *I'm about to teach this moron a lesson that he'll remember for the few painful minutes he has left to live.*

Saben swung again. But instead of ducking, Jericho caught the vampire's fist in his hand. Jericho raised his eyebrows repeatedly as he studied Saben's shocked face. Jericho turned his hand and snapped the bone in Saben's arm. Saben screamed out in pain, and then Jericho punched the vampire in the face. Saben fell to the ground, and his head bounced off the concrete. Jericho jumped and landed on Saben's left leg, breaking it just below the kneecap. Saben struggled to get up but couldn't as he scooted backward and away from Jericho. Jericho walked over, reached down and grabbed Saben's good arm. The slayer ripped Saben's arm out of his shoulder socket and let the arm hang lifeless. Jericho watched as Saben squirmed around on the ground in pain.

"Please, slayer," Saben pleaded. "Let me live, and you'll never see me again."

Jericho shook his head. "No. I don't think I will. You'll just gather the rest of your gang and you'll probably try to ambush me next week."

"Please, slayer. Let me go, and I'll disappear forever."

"Oh, I know you will." Jericho slowly approached. "But it won't because I let you go."

Jericho raised his foot and stomped down on Saben's good leg, snapping the vampire's femur. Again, Saben screeched out in pain. He lay flat on the ground, as all four limbs were incapacitated in some way. Jericho walked over picked up the Sword of Caine. He returned and stood over Saben's body. In a normal circumstance, Jericho would spit out one of his many witty one-liners, but he just wanted to be done for the night. Just as Saben opened his mouth, probably to beg again, Jericho plunged the Sword of Caine into Saben's heart. The vampire turned to ashes almost immediately.

Jericho retrieved his duffle bag and put the Sword of Caine back. He swung the straps of the duffle bag over his shoulder and walked down the alley. Suddenly, a white light hovered over the slayer's head. He dropped the bag again and reached down to pull out the sword. He then hesitated. He'd seen the glowing light before and wondered if it was the same.

Jericho covered his eyes as the light expanded and became brighter. Finally, there was nothing but brightness all around him. When the light subsided, Jericho found himself in his childhood bedroom. It was empty, with one uncovered window.

"Jericho Caine." A voice echoed off the walls. "It seems that I have to come to you again in your time of need."

"Harold." Jericho looked to the ceiling. "Is that you?"

"Yes, my young slayer. It is I, the first slayer and your ancestor."

"But why have you come this time? I'm not in any trouble."

"Because…it is time, Jericho."

"Time for what?"

"Time to stop pretending like you're on a team. Time you decided that you are beyond the Death Brothers. The priest has deserted you. The angel doesn't trust you. And the Hangman is only out for himself."

"But, they need me."

"That may be true. But it doesn't mean they deserve you. You've kept the slayer tradition of having an apprentice even though you haven't found another as of yet. Because you've finally realized the truth, haven't you?

"Oh yeah?" Jericho's forehead crumpled. "And what's that?"

"The truth is, the only true friend that a slayer needs is himself."

"But, Harold, you had assistants."

"I did. And look what happened to me. They let me down. But you are in my bloodline, Jericho. You're a Caine. That means a lot."

"But why?" Jericho spread out his hands and asked. "How are you even here? Are you a ghost or something?"

"Don't be ignorant, Jericho. Ghosts don't exist. But let me fill you in."

Harold's Story

The year was 1893 in Western Europe. My youngest assistant Victor was given information that led us to a pub called The Guilty Pleasure. It was a trap set up by Hangoctuforre and the Sickleby vampire clan. Hangoctuforre had made Warren Sickleby a sword, which was identical to mine. The demons were upset with me because I'd destroyed two demons. And of course, the Sickleby's had become my bitter enemies.

During the fight, I dropped my sword and was overtaken by the vampires. Because I'd killed Warren's son earlier, he relished the idea of killing me. Two vampires held me down, and Warren plunged the sword through my chest. They left me on the ground to die outside of the pub. As my vision blurred, I focused my thoughts on my own sword.

That's when I realized that the sword was still inside the collapsed pub. I reached out to it with my mind. I wiggled the sword loose from under the debris as I strangely sensed my brother-in-law, Victor Trident, approach. Even though I knew I'd be dead by the time he arrived, I knew the sword would find him.

I closed my eyes for the last time. I felt as though I was floating on my back in water and stared at the starless sky at night. I heard a voice. I turned in every direction to find it, but I couldn't.

"Harold Caine," the voice said. "You are with us now."

"With who?" I thought but couldn't speak.

A massive glowing white hand appeared from above and out of the dark. "With us. I am Arellos, an angel. And I am here to escort you to paradise."

"Paradise? But I'm not ready. I still have to help young Victor."

"Your fight is over, Harold. You have fought and died valiantly for a noble cause. Now take my hand and join me."

I stayed floating for a while. I didn't want to believe that I was truly dead—that Warren Sickleby had ended my existence. I knew Victor would be no match for the clan. He needed my help

"Victor, if you don't take my hand, you will stay in this place for all eternity."

"What is this place?"

"It is called the Nether Region. While your soul is safe here, you will never be allowed to leave."

I was conflicted. I didn't want to admit that I was dead. And all I could think about the exacting revenge on the Sickleby's and helping Victor. Not even an angel was going to change my mind. A strange surge shot through my head. It was a vision of Victor possessing the sword. I saw it clearly. The sword had changed in shape and bared Victor's name, Trident. However, I still felt connected to it.

"Do not do this, Victor," Arellos said. "I can sense your thoughts. Even if you joined with the sword, your essence would be trapped in the sword forever. You'd only ever be a witness to the line of slayers throughout history."

"That's better than nothing."

I flipped my body over and turned my back on Arellos. I felt a breeze on the back of my neck as he disappeared. I concentrated and focused my thoughts on the sword again. Surprisingly, I felt my body transition from the Nether Region and into the sword.

Two years had passed, and I'd come back just in time to witness Victor enter the Sickleby clan's lair. Victor fought the young vampire Aubegofu but succumbed to the rest of the clan when Warren showed up with his sword. Victor was executed in the same fashion I was. He was beheaded by Warren. That's when Victor's assistant, Luther, burst into the room on horseback with garlic-laced dynamite. He recovered Victor's body and the Sword of Trident.

Luther was not the next slayer. As a matter of fact, the next slayer wouldn't be found for over eighty years. The sword was hidden, and I was forced into a state of hibernation. When you activated the sword and became the slayer, I awoke and have been with you ever since. When I came to you to help you defeat, Dakota, the vampire angel, I thought that was your greatest challenge. But then you surprised me by dying in the arms of the priest. The sword then took me back in time and helped me understand that the line of slayers has another role in this world. We are a part of the legacy of the Death Brothers. I didn't mind it at first, because it was the Death Brothers power that brought you back to life. But now it is time for you to sever all ties with that destiny and continue to do what you were born to do...destroying vampires as the one true slayer.

"I guess I'm still not understanding why you're here, Harold." Jericho frowned. "Are you here to teach me something else?"

"No, Jericho. I'm here to offer you an ultimatum."

"An ultimatum?"

"Yes. See, you have given yourself completely to this Death Brothers stuff. You've ignored your calling as a result. And it's obvious that there's a showdown looming between you and the angel."

"And?"

"You either forsake this mission with *your friends*. Or I will take your powers and continue the slayer's mission myself."

"How can you do that?" Jericho shook his head. "You're not even alive."

"Do you want to find out?"

"Yes. I'm gonna call your bluff."

Another white light appeared above Jericho and descended as a small ball. The ball of light grew as it came down face-to-face with Jericho. When it disappeared, in its place stood a tall, white, and muscular man. He was as tall a Jericho, but not as bulky. His hair was gray, long, reaching his shoulders. A short gray beard covered his entire face. Jericho didn't hesitate as he reached down for his sword. But Harold reached out with his hand, and the Sword of Caine shot up into it.

Jericho's forehead crumpled. "How?"

"This is the Sword of Caine, my son. And I am Harold Caine."

"You've been planning this for years."

"Ever since you became the slayer, Jericho. You, being of my bloodline, was unexpected, but the final aspect that I needed."

"What are you planning to do?"

"Take over your body. You'll still live as I have in this sword. But for all intents and purposes, Jericho, you will be gone. And I will be the slayer once more."

Jericho punched Harold and sent the one-time slayer sailing backward to the floor. Harold got back to his feet, but still held on to the sword. Jericho knew that was the problem. He'd hoped to jar the sword loose. Harold charged Jericho, swinging and jabbing the sword at Jericho's head. Jericho either ducked or maneuvered around to avoid being struck by the sword. Harold swung wildly one last time, and Jericho ducked. Jericho attempted to uppercut Harold, but Harold had studied Jericho's tactics and weaved to the side. The blow grazed Harold's arm and threw Jericho off balance. Harold then kicked Jericho in the stomach and dropped him to his knees.

"I'm sorry it had to be like this, Jericho." Harold approached and raised the sword to strike. "But you've left me no other choice."

Jericho breathed heavy and clutched his gut. "Stop pretending like this was a difficult choice. You've planned this for years."

"Ha. Ha. Ha. True," Harold said. "But you're of my blood and a fellow slayer. I truly do hate that I have to do this."

Harold brought the sword down in a chopping motion. However, Jericho's eyes glowed white. Harold was right. It was the Sword of Caine, and Jericho was the one true slayer. The sword stopped right as it was about to strike Jericho in the head. Harold's eyes then began to glow as well. He tried to force the sword down even more.

"So, you have made this a battle of wills." Harold grunted as he continued to try to slice Jericho in the head. "But you must understand. I have the fire of a dragon burning inside of me."

"Oh yeah?" Jericho stood and continued to resist. "But I have the power of a Death Brother inside of me."

The glow from Jericho's eyes expanded. He brought his hand up and grabbed the handle of the sword with Harold still holding it as well. They struggled back and forth to gain control of the sword. Both used their legs to knee the other in the stomach. However, each slayer blocked the other's attempted knee with their own knee. Finally, Harold's glow turned red and brighter. He whipped the sword away from Jericho. Harold then reached back and plunged the sword into Jericho's chest.

The glow in Jericho's eyes disappeared, and his eyes widened as he fell back to both knees. Harold ripped the sword from out of Jericho's chest and watched as Jericho fell lifeless on his side to the floor.

"It's over, Jericho." Harold reached down and grabbed the sword's sheath and strapped it to his back. "Just know that the slayer's power continues in you, but through me now. You have represented the Caine's and slayers honorably. There is no shame in passing the mantel back to its original owner."

"S-screw y-you," Jericho managed to say.

Harold threw his head back and laughed. "Defiant till the end, I see. I've enjoyed your wit, all these years. And now you get to sit back and see how I do this job...but better."

Harold disappeared as Jericho continued to lie on the floor. He tried but couldn't move. The scene changed, and he was suddenly in dark space, but a light appeared as if he were watching television. He watched Harold possessing his body and walking down the alley where Jericho fought the vampires. The vision went dark as Harold had sheathed the sword. Jericho was helpless, stuck in darkness, and there was nothing he could do about it.

New York

Tom sat up quickly in his bed in the dimly lit room. He felt a sharp pain run through his chest, and a vision of Jericho rushed through his head. He grabbed his chest. It was the exact same spot where Harold had just stabbed Jericho. Tom surveyed the scene and realized he was in one of the rooms in the back of the church. He'd been staying there and overseeing its reconstruction since the fire.

"Oh my God...Jericho," Tom said. "What's going on?"

Susie's soft hand ran up Tom's back. "Is everything ok, honey?"

"Something's up with Caine." Tom grabbed her hand. "I've never felt this before."

"Jericho's a badass." Susie sat up next to Tom. "He can take care of himself."

"This is different, though." Tom pulled the covers off and swung his feet out to the floor. "I think the big guy's in trouble."

"Ok, Tom. Well, let's go find him."

"Wait." Tom put his finger over his lips. "You sense that? Somethings not right."

BA startled the couple as he stood up out of a chair in the dark corner of the room. "That's not the only problem we have."

Tom frowned and focused on BA. "How long have you been sitting there, Angel?"

"Not long," BA responded. "I didn't see any of your…stuff. But the demon walks the earth again."

"Who?" Susie sat up and covered her naked breasts with the blanket "Hang——"

Tom quickly covered her mouth. "We don't say his name, it's cursed. You can be struck down by lightning, and he will find out where we are if we say his name."

"Well, he's here on Earth and he didn't have the book on his person." BA rapped his fingers on the wall. "But he did have the Ring of Light. He and Comet fought Cromwell and me. That can mean only one thing."

"Kente Jr," Tom said.

"Exactly," BA replied. "He's either being held captive or worse, dead. Either way, this will not sit well with Cromwell."

Tom got up and put on his pants. He kissed Susie on the forehead and handed her, her shirt. He put on the rest of his clothes and made sure his weapons were in his inner pockets. He then pulled a trunk from underneath his bed and opened it. He ran his hands across his twin bamboo sticks with metal knives attached at the ends. He hadn't planned on using them until the war started, but he knew it was near. So, he only grabbed a bottle of Detox and holy water. He put them in his pockets.

"We need to gather our forces." Tom stood. "But first, we need to find out what's going on with Jericho. I fear the worst."

Nether Region

Jericho continued to float on his back in the dark. But then a bright light appeared above him. He didn't bother to cover his eyes. He didn't care if he was blinded. He'd given up. He was fooled and then defeated by something that he never saw coming.

A hand reached down out of the light. "Take my hand, Jericho, and come with me."

"What is this?" Jericho asked. "And who are you?"

"I am the angel Arellos. And I'm here to offer you the same deal as I offered Harold Caine many years ago. I'm here to relieve you of your suffering and allow you to enter paradise. You are basically dead, Jericho. Accept what has happened and come with me."

"What about Harold? So, he just gets to get away with hijacking my body like some petty demon?"

"Harold will answer for is crimes in this world or the next. But this is about you, Jericho. Do not make the same mistake as Harold. Your time as the slayer has afforded you entry into paradise."

"Can I have some time to think about it?"

"No!" Arellos' voice thundered throughout the empty space. "This is a one-time offer, or you can expect to spend eternity trapped in the sword."

Jericho needed more time to think. He didn't turn his back on the angel as Harold had because he was tired of fighting. He'd been a slayer since he was eighteen years old. He often wondered if slaying had cost him living a normal life. *Harold has bested me. It's time to suck it up and move on or…*

"Wait a damn minute!" Jericho finally spoke out to the voice again. "I can't let Harold get away with this. If there is even the slightest chance I will get out of here, I must stick around to make things right."

"Are you sure, Jericho? You have validated your entrance into paradise. You have nothing to be ashamed of."

"If I allowed Harold to get away with this, I will have

brought shame to the Caine name. I will stick around for as long as it takes to see the end of Harold Caine's madness."

There was a long silence as Jericho felt an uncomfortable pain shoot through his back. Once Arellos sighed, Jericho knew he'd disappointed the angel and panicked more. Sweat formed on his brow.

"Come on," Jericho said. "Say *something*."

"Suit yourself, Jericho. And good luck. I was hoping you'd make that choice, but it won't be easy. I can see why you are the chosen one."

Part 10

THE DARK HUNTERS RESURFACE

Cheshire, Massachusetts

Captain Samuel "Sammy" Bloom circled the twenty men standing at attention, dressed in black fatigues, with matching hat and boots. Randy was an average sized man with short, but stringy blond hair and blue eyes. Many people thought he looked too handsome to oversee such an elite group of men. They were the second iteration of the Dark Hunters led by Colonel Randolph Casey.

Sammy sat in his office in the wilderness in Cheshire. The entire compound was built to withstand an assault by an army of vampires. It was out in the open for the sunlight and surrounded by trees to make stakes. Sammy sat with his black combat boots resting on his desk when the phone rang.

"Hello?" he said as he put the phone to his ear.

"Hi, Sammy. It's Randolph."

"Colonel. How's it going?"

"We have a problem."

"Vampires?"

"Of sorts."

"Of sorts, sir?" Sammy pulled the phone from his ear, stared at it, and then placed it back on his ear. "What's going on, Randy?"

"It's the slayer."

"Caine? I thought we didn't have anything to do with him."

There was a long silence as Sammy stared out the window and waited for Randolph to speak again.

"Jericho and I are long-time friends. He was a Dark Hunter with my father, and I've known him for most of my life. I don't agree with all of his methods...or friends, but I trust him."

"Ok, I get that, sir. But what does our current work have to do with him?"

"Unbeknown to anyone, I speak with Caine often. He kind of fed me vampire information that he was too busy to deal with."

"His leftovers?"

"If that's what you want to call it, Sammy. The point is, I've never really stopped working with him. And I haven't heard from him in two weeks."

"That's strange? How?"

"Jericho calls me once a week...religiously. We share information. We talk about life, not just him giving me tips. This is unlike him."

"Wow, Randy. I don't know what you want me to say about this. More importantly, what do you want me to do about it?"

"True enough, our mission is different from the slayer's mission. But we can work together. We need to find him and make sure everything is ok."

"And how do we do that?"

"He was working on a case with his friend in New York, a Father Tom Padilla. He should be able to help you."

"And how many men should I commit to this endeavor?"

"Half for now, including you. But be careful, though,

Sammy. If there's something out there that has detained the slayer, or worse, then we have more to worry about than I think."

"I understand, sir. I'll get right on it."

Sammy hung up the phone and walked over to the window overlooking the training grounds. He stared at his men as they ran in military ranks. He wondered who he'd bring along on the mission. He tapped his fingers on the window ledge. He bit his lip. *I don't want to get involved with the slayer. But I guess that's not my call to make.*

The Underworld

Comet, Damian, and Hangoctuforre set in the meeting room. The other chairs were empty around the huge oval table. As usual, Damian sat on the right side of Hangoctuforre, and Comet sat on the left.

"So, I'll assume you two had fun in my absence," Damian began. "I'm feeling a little left out these days."

Hangoctuforre patted the air with his hand. "Calm down, my old friend. I needed someone to watch over the underworld in my stead. Plus, our little test required only mine and Comet's presence."

"And it was a good test," Comet cut in. "That is until the demon let Artherial and the Hangman walk away."

"You know, I'm surprised by you, Comet." Hangoctuforre pointed at the angel. "You are so fixated on your vengeance against BA that you failed to see what I saw."

"Oh yeah? And what was that?" Comet asked.

Hangoctuforre looked up to the ceiling. "When I gazed into the sky, I noticed that we weren't alone. Angels circled above. I recognized Arellos from one of the last times I invaded the earth and did battle with only angels."

"He's not a warrior angel anymore," Comet said. "He wouldn't have done anything."

"I didn't think you would have wanted to take that chance," Hangoctuforre said. "At least I wasn't."

"So, what now, my master?" Damian asked. "Where do we strike next?"

"Now that we know the heroes are separated," Hangoctuforre clasped his hands together on the table. "We summon the witch to take care of her niece. Then we kill Padilla. He is the only one with the knowledge, who is capable of conjuring a spell from the book of the dead."

"What about Caine?" Comet asked.

"He's the muscle." Hangoctuforre stood and walked around the table. "Once Padilla is dead, we will take out Caine as well. I want my sword back. But the key is to keep them apart. I can't have any Death Brother crap going on."

"And what of the wizard?" Comet stood as well. "He can be quite a pain as well."

Damian pounded the table. "He's mine."

"No," Hangoctuforre said. "I have the feeling that his new role as a father will keep him from this fight. Those other do-gooders just don't know it yet, but the wizard may take a pass on this fight."

"But I owe him, my master." Damian dropped his head and shook it. "I must break him."

Hangoctuforre walked behind Damian and grabbed his shoulder. "You must trust me, Damian. We can't let our thirst for destruction interfere with our plans."

Damian sighed. "As you wish, master."

"Now go." Hangoctuforre sat back in his chair. "Damian, I want you to take the witch and take care of Taki and Padilla. Comet. I'll need you to track down Caine. We'll save Cromwell and BA for last."

Selby, Maine

Harold, in Jericho's body, arrived at the old house on the hill around midday. The house had huge green vines all over it with white tulips growing from them. The house sat alone on the huge property and was surrounded by a brown picket fence. The house had been restored and was livable. Harold looked around before climbing the gate, which was as high as his shoulders. *Ahh, my sister's and Victor Trident's old home. I feel their presence.*

Harold walked up the steps leading to the front door. He looked to his left and saw a white rocking chair in the corner and decided to sit. He'd remembered when he visited his sister and former assistant. He'd sit on the porch and stare out at the horizon before the sun set, and then he'd go out to destroy vampires. He leaned back and stared at the ceiling over the porch. He didn't have a plan, but he knew it would involve vampires. It's why he'd taken Jericho's body. He wanted to prove that he was the one true slayer and that no one could do it better than him. He'd watched Jericho for years and wanted to prove that all the praise Jericho received was because of the groundwork Harold had put down.

"Can I help you, mister?" A little girl walked out the front door. "Who are you, and why are you on our porch?"

"I'm sorry, little person." Harold stood and held up his

hands. "But I once knew someone who lived here a long time ago."

"Mommy doesn't like strange people coming to the house." The little twelve-year-old redhead put her hands on his hips. "She said she likes her privacy."

"I'm not here to disturb your mom. I'll be on my way."

"It's ok for now, I guess. She only comes out at night, along with her other friends and boyfriend. They scare me sometimes."

Harold cocked his head to the side. "How so?"

"Their eyes glow red sometimes, and their faces look weird sometimes too."

"Have you ever seen them in the daytime?"

"No. Mommy says they're like vampires and laughs."

Harold stroked his chin and smiled. "Indeed, they are, little one. Indeed, they are."

Harold walked down the steps and turned back to the girl. He smiled again and waved. As he got further from the house, he turned again and surveyed the place. The windows were painted black, and a rusty metal oversized crucifix lay on the side of the house. Harold remembered it used to stand upright and out in front. *Hmm, sometimes, luck happens even to the best of us. And things just fall right into our laps.*

The Nether Region

It was dark. Only wind brushing up against the Hangman's face let him know that he wasn't alone. *Something or someone is here as well.* He walked a little further, hoping to run into the reason he was in the place. The last thing he'd remembered was disappearing in the middle of the deserted street on the strip in Las Vegas. *It's gotta be the angel. This must be another form of Purgatory. They're pissed because I told them I wouldn't fight in their war.*

As he continued to walk, the Hangman bumped into what he thought was a wall. He stood back, and the object's eyes lit up and glowed white.

"BA," the Hangman said. "I might have known you were behind this."

"I'm trapped here just as you are, Cromwell," BA said. "I was just in New York with the priest trying to formulate a plan. He thinks something is wrong with Caine."

"Well, what's going on? How'd we both get here?"

"I brought you here," a voice echoed in the dark. "This is my domain."

A bright white circular light hovered above them and slowly lowered until BA and the Hangman were visible to each other as well.

"Arellos?" BA asked. "Is that you?"

"Yes, Artherial. It is I who have summoned you both here."

"Cut the crap, angel," the Hangman said. "Get me the hell outta here unless you guys wanna know how truly powerful I've become."

"Calm down, Cromwell." BA put his hand on the Hangman's shoulder, who knocked it away. "I'm sure he's about to tell us why we're here."

"That's right, Artherial. I brought you here for a reason."

"Well, spit it out," the Hangman said.

"The priest is correct. A tragedy *has* befallen the slayer."

"Caine?" BA stared off from the light. "What's going on with him?"

"He's not himself," Arellos said. "His body has been taken over by the essence of Harold Caine. Jericho's soul is trapped in the Sword of Caine."

"Man…What in the hell are you winged clowns talking about?" The Hangman laughed. "That can't happen—can it?"

"Will you shut up, Cromwell, and let him finish?" BA snapped. "That's the problem with you and Caine, everything is a freaking joke…until it's not. Like now."

The Hangman pointed at BA. "You're just pissed because he doesn't like you, BA. Don't take it out on me."

"Silence!" Arellos thundered. "Again, this is my domain. Harold is still a good man. He thinks he's doing the right thing because he thinks Jericho isn't worthy of the powers of the slayer. But Jericho is very much worthy. And the line of slayers won't recover if Harold is allowed to continue to inhabit Jericho's body. If Harold dies while possessing Jericho's body, a paradox will occur within the line. Because Harold is the first slayer, if he were to die again, the line would look for his successor, Victor Trident, who died a long time ago."

"What would happen to the line then?" BA asked.

"The line would disappear, believing there is no more use for a slayer. But vampirism won't end after this war, brother. There will always be a need for a slayer. It's the one thing Harold is right about but going about it the wrong way."

"What if we can convince him he's wrong?" BA asked. "Anything's gotta be better than Jericho."

"Whoa!" The Hangman held up his hand and walked toward BA. "That's just like you angels. Always thinking you can control everything. Jericho's a great ally and probably a better friend than you'll ever be, BA"

BA's eyes glowed white, and the Hangman's eyes glowed red. BA's battle armor and battle-ax appeared on his body and in his hand, respectively. The hooked staff appeared in the Hangman's hand. They walked closer to each other until their noses touched. They breathed heavily and stared into each other's eyes.

An arm reached out of the light and snapped its finger. Both BA's battle-ax and the Hangman's hooked staff disappeared. BA's armor also disappeared.

"I'm gonna be needing that back to kill this bastard," the Hangman snarled.

BA smiled. "That's right, Arellos. Give us our weapons back so we can finally end this for good."

A loud sigh erupted. "You two don't get it, do you? I'm gonna need you to go into the Sword of Caine, together, and rescue Jericho."

BA threw his hands up. "But how?"

"After decades of trying to figure out a way out of the sword, Harold's power grew. He created a door, but the only way he could access the door is through his bloodline. Once Jericho became the slayer, Harold bided his time and waited until Jericho has almost reached his full potential."

"You mean, he can become even more powerful than he is now?" BA asked.

"Is that what you took from that?" The Hangman twisted his lips. "You're worried that the slayer will one day be able to give you a proper tussle?"

BA waved his hand at the Hangman. "Shut up, Cromwell. That's not it at all."

"Anyways," Arellos continued. "Jericho doesn't know the

door exists. Harold and the sword are one, more than Jericho and the sword are. Harold will use all his powers to make sure you don't find that door. That is why I need you to gather Tom Padilla and go into the sword to rescue Jericho's soul."

"Um." The Hangman raised his hand. "That sounds dangerous."

"It is," Arellos said. "If you fail, you all will be trapped in the sword, forever."

BA shook his head and stared at the Hangman. "Wait, why Padilla too? He may be needed here."

"Padilla and Caine share a unique bond. They are the Death Brothers."

BA threw his head back and laughed. "That Death Brothers crap is *true*? Jeez! This just keeps getting weirder by the minute. No descent from you, Cromwell?"

"No," the Hangman said. "I like Caine. I'm in."

"Good." Arellos' light rose. "When you find Padilla and Caine. Call on me. I will give you safe passage into the sword."

Selby, Maine

It was about midnight when Harold arrived at the old house again. He scanned the building once more before reaching inside his duffle bag and pulled out what he needed. He dropped the duffle bag on the ground. It held his stakes, but all he needed was a grappling hook and the Sword of Caine, which was strapped to his back in a sheath.

Harold looked up and launched a grappling hook, with rope to the top of the house. He scaled the side and headed to the only room where a light emanated. As he got to the window, he looked inside and saw the young girl asleep as a lamp on the nightstand lit up the room. The window opened outward like a door. Harold held the rope with one hand and stuck a small pocketknife into the creases in the window. The window popped open, and Harold entered. He unsheathed his sword and crept toward the room door.

"Why are you back, mister?" The girl sat up in her bed. "Mommy won't like this."

"Sounds like your mother is having a party." Harold nodded toward the door. "I'm just attending it."

"Then why did you come through my window?" she asked.

Harold's eyes tightened. "I was hoping to surprise you, but you were asleep."

"Why me?"

"You ask a lot of questions, young lady," Harold said. "Tell you what. I'll answer your questions if you answer mine."

The girl clapped once. "You mean like a game? You can go first."

"How many friends does your mother usually have over?" Harold continuously stared at the door and then back to the girl. "Is it the same friends every night?"

"Sure is, usually around ten. Mommy makes me play outside during the day or stay in my room with the curtains open. She makes me stay in my room at night with the door locked and made me promise to never come out. Why do you want to know so much about Mommy?"

Harold stared at the girl. He was tired of the game already, but he knew it was a delicate situation he needed to handle with care. He walked over and sat on the edge of the girl's bed with a smile on his face. He licked the back of his teeth with his tongue as a metallic taste consumed his mouth. He didn't know what it was, so he continued with his friendly interrogation of the girl.

"I'm going to be as honest as I can be with you, little one," Harold began. "I believe your mother and her friends are monsters—vampires, in fact."

"No." The girl rapidly shook her head. "Mommy is a good person."

"I agree." Harold put his hand on her shoulder. "She has done something that I didn't think vampires could do after they've turned. She showed the capacity to still care for her child. Her rules are meant to protect you, but they are not meant to protect *her*."

"What does that mean?"

"I'm a vampire slayer, my dear." Harold stood. "And it means I must do what I must."

"You're not gonna hurt Mommy, are you?"

Harold sighed. "Lock the door behind me. And no matter what you hear, do not come out of this room."

"Mister, please don't hurt my mommy."

"I can't make that promise, my dear. Besides, as much as it would like to be, that thing down there hasn't been your mother in quite some time."

"That's my mommy." She pounded her fists on the bed. "Don't hurt her!"

Harold unlocked the door with the skeleton key that was sticking out. He opened the door and looked out into the hallway in both directions. The walls were black, and the only chair sat at the nearby steps. Harold gripped his sword tight and eased down the hall toward the stairs. He stopped and waited till the little girl closed and locked the door again. He passed a picture on the wall of the little girl with a woman and a man. Harold assumed they were her parents even though the girl never mentioned her father.

Harold made his way down the steps and saw a vampire sitting on the bottom step, sipping blood from a wine glass. The vampire swayed awkwardly from side to side to the music. Harold could smell the blood mixed with alcohol. Both were fresh. Harold held his sword over the vampire's head and shouted, "boo!" The vampire stood up quickly, and the Sword of Caine was jammed into his head. His eyes opened widely, and the vampire's head slowly turned to ashes, followed by the rest of his body.

Harold let out a grin. It had been years since he dusted a vampire, and it felt good. But then suddenly, a vampire jumped on Harold's back, and they tumbled down the stairs. Harold jumped to his feet, still holding his sword. The vampire stood as well. Two strokes later, the vampire's head fell to the floor and turned to ashes soon after.

The entire group of vampires began to fill in the small space in front of the front door by the steps. Harold stood against the door in his fight stance with his sword gripped tight and out in front. As the vampires got closer, they whispered, "the slayer" to each other, but they weren't scared.

Harold glanced into each vampire's bloodshot and bulging eyes. "Which one of you is the girl's mother?"

"I am." A blonde, balding, but younger woman stepped in front of the other vampires. "What's it to you?"

Harold shook his head as the metallic taste in his mouth grew stronger. "I'm going to give you a head start while I deal with these other guys. I owe the girl that much."

"Oh, really?" She smiled through her fangs. "Well, this is my clan and my nest. Left to me by my late husband after I killed him. So, I'm not going anywhere…and neither are you."

"Suit yourself." Harold gripped his sword tighter. "But don't say I didn't give you a chance."

Harold twirled around, swinging his sword. He chopped off two of the vampire's heads in doing so. The other vampires didn't hesitate, though, as they attacked and grabbed Harold from behind. They pulled at his sword as they knocked him to the ground. Harold was amazed at how strong Jericho's body was. He grabbed a male vampire by the throat and tossed him into the living room. Five vampires remained. Jemma, the little girl's mother, swiped Harold across the face with her claw-like nails. Harold flailed backward and grabbed his face. Blood trickled down from his cheek as he wiped it away and looked at it on his hand.

Harold's eyes glowed white, and he lowered his forehead down to his sword. Two vampires begin to float in the air. Harold looked up at them and flicked his wrist away from his body. The two vampires were launched into the wall. Harold quickly walked over and jabbed each in the chest with his sword. They exploded into ashes soon after. Harold began to turn around because he knew there were three vampires remaining, including their leader Jemma.

"Too late, slayer." Jemma put Harold in a chokehold from behind and pressed one of her long nails against his throat. "So long."

Just as Jemma pressed her nails into Harold's flesh, the front door was blown open, and tiny wooden bits exploded throughout the room. Jemma and Harold were catapulted across the room and crashed into a wall. Wooden stakes were shot from crossbows and struck the remaining vampires in the chest. The vampires turned to ashes almost immediately.

Sammy, dressed in all-black army fatigues, ordered his Dark Hunters to search the rest of the first floor. He helped Harold to his feet while holding his crossbow pointed at Jemma. Jemma cowered in the corner. She hissed and swiped her claws in Sammy's and Harold's direction.

"I figured you'd want to handle this one yourself, sir," Sammy said as he released Harold's arm. "It's the least we could do."

Harold gritted his teeth as he stared in Sammy's eyes. "Thank you, young man. But I think I had this."

"I'm sure you did, Mr. Caine." Sammy motioned for the Dark Hunters to check upstairs. "We were just lending a hand."

Harold turned his attention to Jemma. Even though he didn't know who Sammy was or how the soldiers found out about the house, he knew he had to deal with Jemma before the Dark Hunters brought down the little girl.

"I gave you a chance." Harold nodded at Jemma. "You should have taken it."

"Screw you, slayer," she said.

Jemma launched toward Harold. He jammed his sword through her head. Her eyes rolled back as she turned to ashes. Harold twirled his sword before shoving it over his head and sheathing it.

"And now, back to you, young man." Harold turned to Sammy. "Who are you, and how did you know about this place?"

Sammy raised his eyebrows and sighed. "Your friend

Colonel Casey feared you might be in danger, so he activated your tracking device in your teeth. He would never have betrayed your trust if he didn't believe you were in danger."

Harold glided his tongue across his back teeth. He then realized that the metallic taste in his mouth was a tracking device. He wasn't familiar with Jericho's new technology and didn't know what to think of it. On one hand, the vampires had surprised him, and on the other hand, he didn't want any help. Slayers had an assistant. That was it. Sammy and his soldiers were professionally trained.

"Well, I appreciate your help, um," Harold glanced at Sammy's rank on his shoulder. "Captain, is it? But I'm sure I would have dispatched these vampires on my own."

"Of course, you would have." Sammy nodded. "You're the slayer."

"So, what now?" Harold asked.

"We report back to the colonel that everything is ok, and we go our separate ways." Sammy unhitched the stake from his crossbow and placed it in a pouch on his hip. "We go back to hunting vampires and leave you to do what you do, sir."

"You hunt vampires as well?"

"Yes. We're the new Dark Hunters. But we'll never step on your toes, Mr. Caine, sir. You are the one true slayer. We're just trying to help where we can."

Harold stroked his chin. *Vampire hunters that are only slightly affiliated with Jericho? I'm glad I took over when I did. This is blasphemy!* Harold reluctantly put out his hand, and Sammy shook it. Harold headed for the door. He looked up and saw the other Dark Hunter's leading the little girl down the stairs. Harold stopped.

He dropped to one knee in front of her. "I'm sorry, little one, but your mother is gone."

"Where'd she go?" she asked. "Where's Mommy?"

Harold stood and walked toward the door. "She's gone and never coming back. You'll get a better one now."

The girl began to cry. "What did you do to Mommy? What did you do with Mommy?"

Harold didn't look back as he could sense all eyes were on him as he walked out of the front door. He walked to the side of the house and retrieved his duffle bag. He slung the strap across his shoulders and walked off toward the dirt road in front of the house. His work was done.

Part 11

INTO THE SWORD OF CAINE

New York

BA landed in front of the church on the corner. It was early in the morning, but he still peered in both directions before walking up the stone steps. He stopped at the oversized double wooden doors and used the attached silver medal ring to knock. He waited a few seconds and then knocked again. Finally, and surprisingly, Tom opened one of the doors. He was wearing a brown robe, which reached the floor.

"I didn't expect to see you here, Thomas," BA said. I was actually going to wait until you arrived in a few hours."

"I told you before. I've been sleeping over." Tom stepped to the side and motioned for BA to enter. "Especially since the renovations began."

BA jerked his head back and turned up his nose. "You stink of sex, priest. Don't tell me you soiled the name of this good church and your father's name."

"Hell no, angel!" Tom frowned. "But I did have sex. It just wasn't here. I slept here because it was the closest place to where I had sex. Ha. Ha. Ha."

BA shook his head but smiled. "Boy, I'll never understand you humans. Where's Susan?"

"In the back room." Tom pointed toward the back offices. "We were just going out for some—"

"Coffee," BA clapped and cut in. "Let's go. It seems like I haven't had any in a long time."

BA and Tom walked towards the back room. Susie met them before they could enter the hall that led to the offices. She was fully dressed in black spandex pants and her "I heart San Diego" pink shirt.

"Going somewhere, fellas?" she asked.

"We were just on our way to retrieve you, Ms. Taki," BA said as all three sat in the front pew. "We have a lot to talk about, and it concerns you, Tom. So, let's go get coffee first."

Tom cocked his head to the side. "Well, how important is this, BA?"

"Very," BA replied.

Tom shook his head. "Coffee can wait then. We're at war."

BA groaned and then sighed. "Ok. Ok. Ok. It has to do with Caine."

"Jericho?" Tom asked. "What about Jericho?"

"This won't be easy to hear, priest." BA sat down in the front pew. "But he's been possessed by the essence of the first slayer."

"You're talking about Harold Caine?" Susie raised her finger. "But how? Why?"

"Harold's essence has been trapped in the sword for all this time." BA clasped his hands together. "He's been waiting for his chance to take over Jericho's body. Something recently has given him the opportunity."

Tom walked back down the aisle. He put his hand over his mouth and tapped his lips with his fingers. He began to talk to himself. He kicked pews in anger and cursed himself as well.

"What's wrong, Thomas?" BA asked. "You're the thinker of the Death Brothers. What's going on in that head of yours?"

"This is my fault." Tom returned and glanced at Susie. "I've been...well, I've been preoccupied."

BA stood and placed his hand on Tom's shoulder. "You deserve some happiness, Thomas. No one blames you. Either way, I was told to fetch you. We may need to do an exorcism or something."

"On my best friend and brother?" Tom snatched away from BA. "That's not going to happen."

BA slammed his fist into his hand. "The slayer line will implode if we don't save Caine. He needs you."

Tom rested his forehead in his hands. "I can't believe this. But wait. Technically, he's not possessed," Tom mused. "Harold's essence has taken over Jericho's body, while Jericho's own essence is trapped in whatever item he and Harold share in common. So obviously, it has to be the sword."

BA stared intently into Tom's face. "That's actually true. But are you just saying that because you don't want to perform the exorcism and because he's your friend, or because it's the truth?"

"This is the unfortunate fate that all of us *humans* are susceptible to." Tom turned his back on BA. "It's not as simple as a normal exorcism."

BA put his hands on his hips. "Well, I can tell you're getting a little snippy, Thomas. Let's just at least *try* the exorcism. What could it hurt?"

"Jericho," Tom replied.

Susie stood. "Tom, I hate to say it but BA's right. What could it hurt? Besides, Caine is one of the toughest bastards I've ever known. He'll pull through."

Tom glanced at Susie and then at BA. He then walked to his office and slammed the door behind him.

"Thanks, Ms. Taki." BA looked at Susan. "At least I'm not the only one who has taken my emotions out of this."

Susie shot out a frustrated breath from her nostrils. "Cut the crap, angel. Don't think for one second that I'm on your side in this. But what you said made sense. And I'd hate to see Tom not even try just because of his relationship with Jericho."

"Fair enough," BA said. "Let's go find Caine."

BA, Susie, and Tom walked a few blocks away from the church to an abandoned coffee shop. BA looked around and waited until he didn't see anyone walking or a car driving down the street. He then kicked open the door. They walked in and fanned away the dust that had accumulated in the place.

"Are you sure we're in the right place?" Tom asked. "Doesn't look like a place an angel hangs out."

"You'd be surprised, Thomas," BA replied. "We've claimed tons of these abandoned buildings around the world to think, pray, and plot our next moves."

"Really?" Susie coughed from the dust. "I would never have thought that."

"Yes, angels are filthy creatures." The Hangman walked in from the back. "I can attest to that. Just look at what they've done with Purgatory."

"Just like a sinner," BA said. "Always blaming others for their misfortunes."

The Hangman smiled. "I'm not blaming anyone, just you."

"Ok. Ok, guys." Tom put up his hands in between the

Hangman and BA. "We're not here for that. We're here to help Jericho."

"For once, priest," the Hangman nodded at Tom, "you and I agree on something."

"Well, isn't that cute," BA cut in. "You two agree on something. Call the wedding planner already."

Susie laughed. "You guys are funny. But isn't Jericho, or Harold I should say, supposed to be here too?"

The fluttering of wings brought forth Arellos. He was tall, as most angels are, with long blond hair. He wore a white trench coat with brown pants and black combat boots. He had on his dark sunglasses just like BA.

"You're right, Ms. Taki," Arellos said. "We have to find Harold and subdue him. I'm glad you came, Susie. We'll need someone to stand guard while the others try to free Jericho. I know where Harold is. Join hands, and I will take you to him."

"No freaking way!" The Hangman walked away from the group. "I'm not joining hands with either of you. You all make me sick."

"Are you kidding me right now, Cromwell?" BA asked.

The Hangman shook his head. "Nope. Just tell me where he is, and I'll join you."

"We don't have time for this," Arellos said. "You others join hands. I will bring the *half-demon* after."

Selby, Maine

Arellos, BA, Tom, and Susie appeared at the edge of the wooded area outside of a small brown cabin. Susie bent over and grabbed her stomach.

"So that's what it's like to teleport somewhere?" Susie breathed heavily. "I don't think I'll get used to that."

Smoke flowed from the chimney stack, so they knew someone was inside. Then they confirmed Harold's presence when he walked past the front window and looked out.

"Let's go," BA said. "It's now or never."

"Ok. But remember," Tom held up his hand, "that body belongs to my best friend. We're here to subdue him, not kill him. Agreed?"

They all nodded in agreement and headed for the front door.

"We'll take the front door," BA said. "Tom and Susie, you guys go around back to make sure he doesn't retreat that way."

BA held out his hand. His battle-ax appeared. Arellos wasn't a soldier angel, but he still summoned his sword to his hand. They walked up to the front door, and BA kicked it in. Harold was surprised, but he was still able to roll across the floor and grab the Sword of Caine from the corner.

"I've been waiting a long time for this, angels." Harold got in his fight stance. "Now we shall see who is right and who has been wrong all this time."

Arellos made his sword disappear. "That tells me how much you have gone astray, Harold. You must go back and give Jericho his body back. It's his time, not yours."

"Save it, Arellos," Harold said. "I had your nonsense in my head for decades. It's time you felt the full force of the slayer."

BA stood in front of Arellos. "Enough of this. Let's just get it on, slayer."

BA attacked with his ax. Harold blocked the initial burst but couldn't block BA's spinning punch. It knocked Harold backward against the wall. Harold's eyes glowed, and his sword floated up out of his hand and shot toward BA. It was too fast to block as BA tried, but the sword struck him in the shoulder. BA fell to one knee as the sword made it back to Harold's hand. Harold then turned his attention to Arellos, who backed up against the front door.

"Your turn, Arellos." Harold raised his sword and approached the angel. "Time to defend yourself."

"Not so fast." Tom climbed through the back window as there was no door. "I can't let you do that, Harold."

"Well, well, well." Harold lowered his sword. "If it isn't Tom Padilla. You like my new body, *old pal*. Does it remind you of someone?"

"I will not let you condemn my friend's soul." Tom put on his brass knuckles. "You will not leave this cabin in Jericho's body."

"Your friend?" Harold glanced over and gestured at Susie, who was attempting to climb into the same back window. "You replaced me as soon as she flashed a little bit of ass in your face."

Susan grunted as she touched down on the floor from the window. "I see that you're not only a body thief, Harold, but you're also a pig."

Harold laughed. "Spoken like a true harlot and homewrecker."

"That's not true," Tom said as he too glanced over at Susie. "And I understand that you're angry, Harold, but I still can't allow you to do what you're doing."

Harold laughed again. "Oh yeah? And who's gonna stop me?"

"You idiot." BA stood. "We're not through yet."

BA's battle armor appeared on his body. He swung his battle-ax at Harold's head. Harold ducked and struck BA's arm with the Sword of Caine. The impact created a spark as the sword whipped across BA's armor but didn't penetrate the metal.

"What's wrong, angel?" Harold backed away after seeing his sword didn't harm BA. "You need your little armor to take me on?"

"No," BA replied. "All I need is this."

BA pointed the Peace Ring at Harold and fired. A white beam of light struck Harold in the chest. Harold fell to his knees. Harold clutched his chest, staggered to his feet, and then began to swing wildly at BA. But BA stepped back and fired another beam. But it wasn't just any beam. A white forcefield appeared around Harold's body. BA balled his fist tighter and applied pressure, causing Harold to drop the Sword of Caine. BA opened and closed his hand again as the oxygen began to drain from the force field.

"Stop it." Tom held up his hand. "You're killing him."

"No, I'm not," BA said. "It'll just knock him out like we need to happen."

Harold finally fell unconscious to the floor. BA released the grip on the force field, and it disappeared. Arellos walked over and picked up the Sword of Caine. He placed it on the table and looked down at Harold.

"Now, we need to strap him to a chair," Arellos said. "He can't be allowed to escape while you're in the sword."

Susie and Tom grabbed one of Harold's arms and dragged him to a four-legged wooden chair. Tom, knowing what was in Jericho's duffle bag, pulled out rope and they tied the huge vampire slayer's arms and legs.

"This should hold him," Tom said. "But I don't know for how long. Jericho's a big guy."

"We'll just need to be quick about it." BA's armor disappeared along with his battle-ax. "Can you handle things out here, Susie?"

"I think I can." Susie glanced over at Harold. "But just in case, you guys need to hurry."

"We will." Arellos motioned for Tom and BA to come closer. "Be very careful in there. Harold controls the sword for now. You must convince Jericho that he's in control. But Harold is like a god inside the sword. He controls everything. It's why, once you're inside, I will return and retrieve Cromwell. You're going to need all the help you can get. There should be a tunnel or portal that leads outside the sword. Once you have Jericho and he passes through it, he and Harold will swap places again. And trust me, Harold will be guarding that portal with his life."

"Is it really that bad?" BA asked.

"Harold believes he died too soon." Arellos reached down and grabbed Tom's and BA's hands. "He will do everything in his power to stay in control of Jericho's body. Are you ready?"

Tom sighed. "As ready as we're gonna be."

BA simply nodded and closed his eyes. He saw a bright light and tunnel pulling him and Tom into the sword. When BA and Tom arrived, it was just like the scene they'd just left. They were standing outside of a log cabin, surrounded by a forest.

"Well, at least we know where Harold got the idea to hold up where he's at right now," BA said as he scanned the area. "The guy's got a thing for wooded areas."

"That's for sure." Tom began walking toward the cabin. "Let's just find Jericho and get outta here."

Tom walked toward the cabin and he bounced off an invisible field. He stepped back and shook his head to shake off the electric shock. BA approached the field and punched it. An electric shock blasted him as well and revealed itself to surround the entire cabin.

"This isn't good," Tom said.

"No, it's not." BA looked down at the Peace Ring, which was fading in and out. "Harold must still be unconscious. His power over the sword is weak. I'd better use the ring while I still can."

BA pointed the ring at the field and fired several shots. The white beams of light from his ring faded in and out as well. However, when the beams struck the field, it pulsated electricity, and the barrier disappeared from around the cabin.

They walked up the cabin steps, and the door swung open. Jericho stood at the entrance wearing only cut-off shorts and his combat boots.

"Are you guys real?" Jericho asked.

"Um, yeah, big guy," Tom replied. "As real as it gets."

"I'm serious," Jericho said. "Are you guys real?"

Tom walked up and hugged the reluctant slayer. "How's that for real?"

Jericho almost collapsed into Tom's arms. "Oh my God, priest. I'm so glad to see you. I thought I'd never see another human being ever again. But how are you here?"

BA walked up and extended his hand to Jericho. "The angel Arellos sent us here to free you and put Harold back where he belongs."

"Arellos?" Jericho shook BA's hand. "He's the only person I've spoken to in what seems like years. How much time has passed?"

"Not long, big guy," Tom responded. "Probably only a few days."

"So, how do we get out of here?" Jericho asked.

BA turned to look back at the forest. "Well, according to Arellos, we have to look for a portal. You haven't seen one while you've been here, have you?"

"No, I haven't," Jericho said. "But in my earlier travels –"

"Earlier travels." Tom cut off Jericho. "How did you get past the barrier?"

"What barrier?" Jericho asked.

BA turned and pointed out to the empty space. "The one we just had to get through to reach the cabin."

"That's strange." Jericho rubbed his bare chest. "I've never encountered a field."

"Um, I hate to bring this up now." Tom closed his eyes. "But can you go put a shirt on?"

Jericho laughed. "Oops. My bad." Jericho rushed inside the cabin and came back with a brown t-shirt and put it on. "Happy now, priest?"

"Can you just continue the story now?" Tom said.

"Well, like I was saying." Jericho placed his hands on his hips as he stared out into the wilderness. "There was *one* place that I couldn't gain access to."

"That's gotta be it," Tom cut in. "Why else would that be the only place you haven't been able to enter?"

"Where is it, Caine?" BA asked.

Jericho pointed. "The other side of the forest. Near the waterfall."

"Let's go then," BA said.

Harold shook his head rapidly as he regained consciousness. His eyesight was blurred as he looked down at the ropes confining him to the chair. He wiggled around to get free but couldn't. He then looked around as he heard someone breathing from behind him.

"Save your strength, Mr. Caine." Susie stood from a chair behind Harold. She walked around in front of him. "You're not going anywhere."

"Ms. Taki," Harold began. "I've watched you with a little admiration. You've successfully ruined the relationship between the so-called Death Brothers. My compliments."

"Only you would think that," she said.

"I'm not the only one. Jericho believes it as well. And though you may all be on the same side against me today, it won't end well for either of you."

"You'd say anything to continue to occupy Jericho's body." Susie grabbed some duct tape from the table. "They left me this in case you woke and did what you're doing."

Susie tore a piece of the tape put across Harold's mouth. She smiled and waved at him as she walked back to sit in her chair behind him. Harold struggled again to get free but then stopped to think. He remembered seeing Arellos with BA and Tom. He looked over at the Sword of Caine sitting in the middle of the table surrounded by candles. *They can only be up to one thing. They're trying to free Jericho.*

Harold tilted his head back, and his eyes rolled back until only the whites of his eyes were visible. He closed his eyes and opened them just as quickly. They glowed white as Harold's essence journeyed into the sword.

Jericho, BA, and Tom trekked through the forest. No one

had a weapon. BA was even missing the Peace Ring. They figured it was the way Harold wanted it.

"Harold must be conscious," BA said. "I can't summon any of my weapons now." As they walked with Jericho up front, he stopped and looked in each direction. He sniffed the air and then raised his fist in the air, indicating for BA and Tom to stop as well.

"What's going on, Caine?" BA asked.

Jericho continued to scan the area. "We're being followed."

Tom turned to the rear. "By who?"

"Not who," Jericho replied. "What."

The sound of broken branches and growling got closer. A full moon appeared out of nowhere even though the daylight still shined above.

"What's that all about?" Tom asked as he looked to the sky. "That moon wasn't there before."

Jericho nodded in agreement. "I think we're about to find out, my friend."

The bushes rattled, and five wolves surrounded them. BA held out his hand to call on his ax again. Again, nothing happened. Tom reached in his inner pocket for his brass knuckles. They weren't there. BA attempted to call on his armor. It didn't appear. They were defenseless except for their bare hands.

A wolf leaped into the air and launched at Jericho. He grabbed the wolf by the throat and squeezed. The wolf exploded into ashes like the many vampires he'd dusted while slaying. Another wolf pounced on Tom, causing the demon hunter to fall backward with the wolf landing on top of him. Tom grabbed the wolf's mouth with both hands to keep it closed as he knew that the wolf's weapon was its teeth.

Two wolves attacked BA, the bigger and stronger of the men. He grabbed one wolf by the tail and the other by the front leg. He spun around in a circle and swung the wolves with him. They burst in ashes in BA's hands. Jericho ran over to Tom and kicked the wolf on top of him in the side. The wolf howled as it was hurled a few feet away and exploded into ashes before it hit the ground.

There was only one wolf left, and it was assumed that he was the leader. He growled, and saliva dripped from his mouth. His chest stuck out and he was slightly larger than the other wolves. His eyes glowed red as he exposed his huge teeth.

Then suddenly, the wolf lurched forward and coughed several times. He fell forward and began to roll around the ground on its back. He got back on all four of its legs and howled at the moon. The wolf then stood on its hind legs and grew. He formed the shape of a man. He became a werewolf. He glared at Jericho, BA, and Tom, moving his eyes from side to side. From behind the creature, Harold walked up and put his hand on the werewolf's back.

"Just when you thought this was gonna be easy." Harold smiled. "I fooled you again."

"Please stop this, Harold," Jericho pleaded. "I'm sure we can figure out something."

Harold raked his fingers through his beard. "Save it, Jericho. And to think, you are probably going to be remembered as the greatest slayer ever. What a shame."

BA stepped in front of Jericho. "Don't waste your breath on this guy, Jericho. He's obviously a madman."

"Yeah, big guy." Tom leaned in closer to Jericho's ear. "Let's just do what we've come here for. There's no reasoning with him."

"I'm glad we're all in agreement," Harold said. "I hope you guys have fun with my friend here."

Harold patted the werewolf on the back and disappeared. The werewolf was the same height and weight as BA. He had long claws and massive sharpened teeth. He leaped into the air and dropkicked Jericho, sending the slayer crashing to the ground. The werewolf got up quickly and backhanded BA, sending the angel sailing across the area to the ground. Tom turned to run, but the werewolf leapt over Tom's head and landed in front of him.

"We're the Death Brothers, Tom!" Jericho yelled from his knees. "We can handle this."

Tom turned and nodded at Jericho. Tom looked down and grabbed his crucifix. Harold had made a mistake when he disarmed them. Tom's crucifix was also a weapon. His eyes squinted first, and then a smile appeared on his face. Tom took off the oversized crucifix hanging from beads. He pulled the bottom of the crucifix off and revealed it to be a knife, and the beads expanded to a wired whip. He let the whip hang and waited for the werewolf to attack. Tom swung the whip and slashed the werewolf's face with the knife. The werewolf staggered to the side, growled, and glared at Tom from head to toe. He especially stared at the crucifix dangling from Tom's hand. The werewolf then turned his attention back to Jericho and BA and decided to attack them instead.

Susie stood in front of Harold and slapped him. She ripped the tape off his mouth. "What are you up to? Why are your eyes glowing?"

Harold stuck his tongue out and licked the saliva that crept out. "You dumb tramp. Do you really think you can come between Jericho and Tom? You're nothing but a sex toy for the priest. He's hard up, and you're the only woman around."

"You can't get into my head, sucka." Susie put her hands on her hips. "I'm not trying to come between them. They're brothers."

"I'm glad you feel that way." Harold smiled. "At least you won't feel like a piece of trash when he discards you like yesterday's garbage."

"You're reaching, Caine. You must really be nervous knowing you're about to lose your grip on Jericho."

"And you must be nervous knowing you're about to lose your grip on the priest.

Susie slapped Harold again. "Shut up!"

"Don't shoot the messenger. It's over, homewrecker. Ha. Ha. Ha."

Part 12

INTO THE SWORD OF CAINE: PART 2

The werewolf grabbed Jericho by his shirt and tossed him across the wooded area. He crashed into and tree and slumped down to the ground. The werewolf ducked a punch from BA and raked his claws across BA's face. BA turned his head to the side and grabbed his cheek. The werewolf then kneed BA in the stomach. BA doubled over, and the werewolf brought his knee up and caught BA in the forehead. BA flew backward and landed on his back. He lay motionless on the ground.

Only Tom stood in his way, but it was obvious that the werewolf's main target was Jericho. The werewolf hesitated as he glanced back and forth at Tom and the fallen slayer.

Tom peered down at Jericho, who had blood coming out of his mouth and then back to the werewolf. "You'll have to kill me to get to him, werewolf."

The werewolf sprang into flight. He tried to land on Tom's head, but Tom stepped to the side. Tom flung his crucifix whip, and it wrapped around the werewolf's neck. The pointed end of the crucifix lodged into the werewolf's throat. The steel from the cross caused the werewolf's neck to smoke as blood dripped to the ground. The werewolf fell to his knees, and Tom pulled harder.

Jericho got back to his feet and teetered over to Tom. BA rushed over to the werewolf and placed his hands in the werewolf's open mouth. BA's hands were on the top and bottom of the werewolf's jaw. The angel ripped the werewolf's jaw apart and let the animal fall lifeless to the ground.

"Jesus, angel," Jericho said. "Had a little bit of extra energy to burn off or what? I know you angels can't have sex, but I didn't know you get frustrated by it."

BA shook his head and laughed. "And there is the obnoxious slayer I remember. Hey, everybody just can't go around sleeping with hookers, Caine. Some of us want love."

"Oh." Jericho's eyebrows raised. "That would explain a certain sorcerer who's palling around with a demon."

BA wiped his hands on his trench coat to get the blood off. "Do you have something you want to say to me, slayer?"

"Yes, I'd—"

"Come on, guys," Tom interrupted. "We've still got work to do here. And, Jericho, don't forget, we're here to help your ungrateful butt."

"Yeah. Yeah. Yeah." Jericho waved his hand at Tom. "I know. My bad, angel."

BA nodded. "Let's just keep going."

They arrived at the edge of the forest. It was just as Jericho had said. A huge waterfall stood before them, which poured down into a lake. The surrounding area resembled a beach as sand and seaweed littered the shore. There was nothing suspicious about the scene, and Jericho wondered where the portal could be. They walked down to the lake and began to walk around it. Suddenly, the water began to stir, and a circle formed in the middle of the lake. Harold emerged out of the circle with his hands on his hips and a smile on his face. He floated on top of the water.

"Remind you of anything, Angel?" Harold's voice boomed and echoed off the mountainous area. "Never mind. But one thing is sure. You all will die or be trapped in here forever."

"You're getting ahead of yourself, Harold," Jericho said. "I'm assuming that you've shown up here because we're close to the portal."

"You can't escape." Harold wagged his finger. "But at least you'll have company. And as soon as I free myself on the other side, I might just find a way to send Ms. Taki here as well."

"If you lay one finger on her," Tom stepped forward, "I'll rip you to shreds."

"Well, let's stop talking and you'll have your chance." Harold floated toward land. "You idiots are in my world now."

BA took off running toward Harold. Harold put out his hand and flicked his wrist. A powerful invisible force blew BA back into the forest. Harold stepped onto the shore. He grabbed Tom by his shirt collars and tossed the demon hunter into the lake. Jericho sprinted and put Harold into a chokehold from behind. Harold grabbed Jericho's arms and whipped the slayer to the ground. Harold then put his boot on Jericho's head and applied pressure. Jericho was lucky it was sand beneath him or his head would have crushed.

Harold raised his foot and prepared to stomp on Jericho's head. "You didn't really think the three of you could beat me in here, did you? This domain is mine's and mine's alone. I knew what your plan was as soon as Arellos helped you break into my cabin. Goodbye, Jericho."

As Harold was bringing down his foot to stomp Jericho in

the head, a red beam of light struck Harold in the back of his shoulder. He fell forward and turned in the direction the beam came from. It was from the Hangman and the Hellfire Ring.

As the Hangman prepared to fire again, Harold held up his hand and transformed the Hellfire Ring into red dust. The dust fell to the ground from around the Hangman's finger. But the damage was done. Harold was weak from the shot. Jericho bounced back to his feet and punched Harold in the jaw. Harold fell flat with his back on the sand. He held out his hand as Jericho walked toward him. Harold strained as an invisible force froze Jericho. But BA had recovered and leaped out from a tree toward Harold. Harold held out his other hand, and the same invisible force stopped BA in midair.

Harold's eyes bulged and the red veins in his eyes grew thicker. He was barely keeping Jericho and BA at bay. Tom made it back to shore and joined the Hangman as they rushed over and kicked Harold in the ribs. Harold was forced to release Jericho and BA. But he waved his hands, and the wing blew all four men to the ground. Harold got up and ran. He used his remaining powers to teleport every few feet to get away from his adversaries.

The Cabin

Susie exited the bathroom. She saw Harold shaking his head as if he'd been punched. She walked over and stood in front of Harold. His mouth and nose were bloody. Sweat streamed down his face as well.

"I know you're going to hate this, Susie." Arellos appeared from behind her. "But you need to help those guys."

"What do I need to do?"

Arellos nodded toward Harold. "Unleash hell."

Susie had a confused expression on her face. However, she slowly reached behind her back and eased out her nunchucks. The confusion was replaced by a smile as the chained weapon dangled from her hand. She whipped around the nunchucks and popped Harold in the forehead, causing a welt to form. She held the nunchucks together and rammed them into Harold's gut. He slumped in his seat and coughed up blood.

The Sword

Harold appeared in front of the waterfall and held up his hand. The water stopped flowing and exposed a hidden cave in the hill behind the fall.

"Do you guys see that?" Tom pointed at the cave. "There's a light coming from there too. It's gotta be the portal."

"I agree," BA said. "Let's go."

Jericho took a step and then turned to the Hangman. "Hold on, Hangy. Thanks for coming and saving me."

"I'm sorry I was late," the Hangman replied and stuck out his hand.

Jericho knocked the Hangman's hand away and hugged him. "Better late than never."

The Hangman gently pushed Jericho away. "Ok, slayer. Don't get in the habit of doing that."

"Jesus, Caine." BA frowned and held out his hands. "Either go get a room, or let's go put an end to this."

They ran up the path they saw Harold take to get to the cave. They couldn't stop the water, so they decided to jump through it. Once they were through, they saw the portal on the far end, and Harold stood in front of it.

"It's over, Harold." Jericho prepared for another fight. "It's time to give it up."

"Never!" Harold said as he unsheathed the Sword of Caine from his back. "You will pay for this."

Harold attacked. The only thing they could do was duck as Harold swung wildly in all directions. Then all of a sudden, Harold fell to his knees and dropped the sword.

Harold coughed up blood and grabbed his stomach. "That damn girl is ruining everything."

Jericho looked in everyone's confused faces. "Damn. Susie must be kicking ass on the other side."

Jericho ran over to take the final shot. He punched Harold in the face, and Harold fell to the ground.

"Go ahead, guys," Jericho said, pointing to the portal. "Go back home. We're done here."

BA, Tom, and the Hangman walked through the portal. Jericho waited until they were through and then stood in front of Harold again. Harold tried to stand, but Jericho pushed Harold back to the ground.

Jericho turned to walk away. "You're done."

Harold reached out his hand with his fading strength. "Don't do this, Jericho. I can be of service to you."

"Yeah, just like you stole my body and left me to be an observer in this sword?"

"You ever realized why you're all alone? That's by design. Slayers are meant to walk alone."

"That's odd." Jericho smiled. "Because you are lying there and about to lose this fight...alone. And I've just had three friends risk their lives to come here and save me."

Harold sighed and held his stomach. "But it still doesn't change my point."

"Goodbye, Harold." Jericho saluted. "You've done something that I didn't think was possible. I've learned to like the angel—a little."

"Don't walk through that portal, Jericho. I can teach you so much more about your powers."

Jericho rubbed his chin. "Hmm. I'll pass, old man. Besides, slowly finding out about my powers over all these years has been fun. I'm in no rush."

Jericho frowned one last time at Harold and then turned to walk away.

"Jericho!" Harold pleaded. "Please don't."

"We're done."

Jericho walked through the portal.

A bright white light descended above Harold. He knew what it was but was too weak to stand and barely talk.

"Harold Caine." Arellos' voice boomed throughout the space. "As much good as you've done in your life, you're still not worthy to enter paradise."

"G-Go to h-hell," Harold said.

"Stand up when I speak to you."

Harold coughed and laughed. "You have no authority h-here, angel."

"And neither do you, Harold. Not anymore."

Harold began to float. He attempted to keep his feet on

the ground but couldn't. Jericho controlled the sword, leaving Harold's essence defenseless. He growled and tried to use his remaining strength to resist Arellos' power.

"Don't fight it, Harold," Arellos said. "We are fair beings. Sending you to the underworld would surely lead to an eternity of suffering because of who you were. So, the decision has been made."

"W-What decision?"

"Harold Caine. You are hereby relegated to Purgatory, where it is hoped that you will earn repentance, find peace, and earn your way into paradise."

"No." Harold flailed about as he continued to float. "Not there."

"Yes, Harold. I was always fond of you and the slayers. I hope that gives you comfort while you're in Purgatory."

The light disappeared. Harold continued to float in darkness. Finally, another light appeared, and the wind picked up. A suction began pulling Harold toward the light. He tried to turn away but couldn't.

"Nooooo!" Harold yelled as he swung his arms as if he were swimming. "Not that place. I don't deserve this."

Harold's powers were gone. He'd lost, and he was sucked into the light.

As everyone made it out of the portal, their weapons appeared again. The Hangman's and BA's rings appeared on their fingers, and Tom checked his pockets to find that his brass knuckles were there.

"Who would have ever thought that a slayer could possess that much power?" BA pondered aloud. "I'm actually amazed we got out of there unscathed."

"Speak for yourself," the Hangman chimed in. "If it wasn't for me, you'd all be dead right now."

"Ahem," Susie cut in as she looked down at Jericho's lifeless body in the wooden chair. "I guess you suckas didn't recognize the blood on the floor around the chair. We all had a hand in this."

"Don't turn on each other now," Tom said. "And where's Jericho? Is he in there now?"

Tom stood in front of Jericho and bent over to look into Jericho's face. Tom gently slapped Jericho in the face a few times. The slayer didn't budge.

"Come on, buddy," Tom said. "Wake up and come back to us."

A white light flashed in the center of the room and over Jericho's body. Everyone covered their eyes as Tom stepped away. When the light diminished, Jericho's body came to life.

"I'm right here, priest," Jericho said as he blinked rapidly. "I had to give a proper goodbye to Harold."

Tom put out his hands. "And?"

"He's not happy." Jericho squirmed to free himself. "But who would be after decades of planning goes up in smoke. Now, can somebody release me, please?"

Susie pulled out a knife and began to cut the ropes. "Oh. Sorry about that. And sorry about your face."

Jericho stood and ran his hand across the welts on his forehead. "It's ok. It had to be done."

BA snapped his fingers. "Now we've gotta regroup for the fight that's yet to come. That demon won't care that we had to go inside a mystical sword and rescue Caine."

"I agree." Tom walked over and poured a glass of water. "We need to go get the wizard and come up with a plan of attack."

"I don't have time for this." The Hangman walked toward the door. "Wait. I have my powers back. Screw this."

The Hangman raised his fist in the air and the Hellfire ring glowed. Red electricity covered his body, and he vanished.

Jericho put his hand up. "Hangy, wait!"

It was too late. The Hangman had vanished. Jericho pounded his fist into his hand.

"Well, I'd like to say, thank you all for coming to rescue me," Jericho said as he stared into Tom's eyes. "I was beginning to question my place on this team, and now I know. And I'm sorry I ever doubted your love me, Tom. You deserve to be happy."

"It's ok, big guy." Tom patted Jericho on the shoulder. "This life wouldn't be the same without you, bud."

BA sighed. "And here we go again. Can you guys knock it off? We have to get ready to fight a war."

Susie smiled with and teared up, but then peered at BA. "Jesus, you angels are unfeeling brutes. Can't we just have a moment to enjoy the small victories?"

"No." Tom nodded at BA. "The angel is right. But along those lines, maybe we need to shed some light on the Damian Red situation that Jericho alluded to inside the sword."

BA put his hands on his hips and turned his back on everyone. He walked out the cabin's front door and stood on the porch. Jericho followed as he knew it was time for BA to reveal the truth. *It's time for that winged bastard to put all his cards on the table. We've given him long enough to come clean.*

Jericho walked out to the porch, followed by Tom and Susie. At first, Jericho stood behind BA. Jericho didn't know what to expect. But then he walked up and stood side by side with the angel.

"It's time, BA," Jericho said.

BA turned his head to the side to glance at Jericho. He then turned to the other side to look at Tom and Susie. They were all waiting for the angel to say—anything.

"Alright," BA began. "As I'm sure you already know, Damian is my son. He doesn't know it, nor does he know he's a half-angel. The demon has been lying to him for years. And I just barely found out when we had to deal with the archangel Michael."

"So, do you plan on just keeping this pretty important information from him?" Tom asked. "He deserves to know. And we deserve to know what you're going to do about him if we should meet on the field of battle."

"Not to mention, the wizard," Jericho finally spoke. "He was included in this because he thought we were dealing with a sorcerer. I'm quite sure his opinion will change if he knows he's facing off against a-a Nephi-whatever."

BA let a small smile escape. "It's a Nephilim, Caine. And I'm sure he'll still want to help. This war affects all who know about it and can help."

Susie folded her arms. "All except angels, right?"

"That's not fair, Ms. Taki." BA glared at Susan. "I'm here, and Arellos risked a lot by getting involved to help Caine. But these are still human matters."

Jericho pointed to his head. "Well, angel, here's something that your bird brain hasn't even thought about either. What 's gonna happen when the Hangman finds out *your son* murdered his wife and possibly his only son?"

"And that's why I was trying to keep this a secret." BA spread out his hands. "I was hoping you guys would do the same."

"I'm not going to lie to him if he asks," Tom said. "He has the right to know."

"Even if it means he won't help us, Thomas?" BA asked. "After all, it was you and Caine's idea to free him from Purgatory. And where is he now? Oh, that's right, he just took off like he doesn't owe us anything."

Jericho walked off the stoop and turned back toward the cabin. "This is getting us nowhere. We'll deal with it when we must. But for right now, we need to go get the wizard and figure out a way to convince Hangy to join us."

"I agree, big guy," Tom said. "Angel, since you're the fastest of us all, you can go talk to Merryweather. Besides, he seems to like you."

"And Cromwell?" BA asked.

Tom smiled. "We'll dispatch Jericho to fetch him. They *did* share a tender moment back there in the sword."

Tom and BA erupted in laughter. Jericho didn't find their humor funny, but then again, he'd said much worse to both at one time or another. He looked at Susie, who had a half-smile on her face. Of course, she had no idea what they were talking about. Jericho just glared at BA and Tom with his eyes tightened and turned to stare off into the distance.

Jericho stepped aside and let BA walk past him. The angel sprouted his wings and took off. They watched him until he was out of their sight. Jericho, Susie, and Tom then walked back into the cabin. They had an important mission. They had to find the Hangman again. It was probably a task for BA as well, but they knew they couldn't bombard the angel with everything. So, Jericho grabbed his duffle bag and wrangled through it. Everything seemed to be in order.

"I'm glad Harold didn't touch my crap," Jericho said as he zipped up the bag. "Still can't believe he pulled off the little feat even if he eventually failed."

Tom walked up and massaged Jericho's massive shoulder. "Yeah, but not to worry, big guy. We'll always have your back."

"I appreciate that, priest," Jericho said. "But now I have an even bigger personal task."

"What's that?" Susie asked.

"The sword and I still have trust issues." Jericho stared at the sword, which still lay on the far table. "We have to find a way to regain that trust and become one again."

"I'm sure you will." Tom prepared to walk out of the cabin. "You two have been together for many years."

"I wish it were that simple." Jericho strapped the sheath to his back and shoved the sword inside it. "I get my power from it, and it gets its power from me being the one true slayer. We feed off each other."

"You could always learn to use nun-chucks," Susan cut in.

Jericho laughed. "Thanks for that."

"Yeah, I thought that would get a chuckle out of you," she said.

Part 13

IN OR OUT?

Harvey, Illinois

The Hangman sat perched on top of his old house on Delaware street and overlooked the block. Every house on the street was empty. Yellow police tape still sealed off some of the homes. And faded white chalk outlines where dead bodies once lay were scattered through the block. No one dared move back into the houses after what the Hangman had done before.

It was about two in the morning. The Hangman stared at most of the houses and remembered his vengeance from before. He'd killed a lot of people during that time, including children, and sent their souls to the underworld as an offering for his second life. As he sat there thinking, he wondered was it all worth it. He'd been killed and came back as a half-demon. He'd taken many lives, and now, his son and wife were dead as well. He hadn't found out who killed Kente Jr, but he assumed it was Hangoctuforre.

As rain drizzled, the Hangman didn't budge. He allowed his robe to get soaked. He took off his hood and let the rain roll down his face. The water soothed his burned flesh. He stuck out his tongue and watched the smoke coming from his mouth as the rain interacted with his acidic saliva.

The flapping of angel wings brought forth BA. "Can I join you?"

"It's a free country," the Hangman replied.

"Since when did you abide by the human's laws?" BA smiled as he sat. "Seems like we've been at this for far too long, my friend."

The Hangman frowned and turned to face BA. "Friend? Since when?"

"Come on, Cromwell." BA slapped the Hangman on the back. "You know you've enjoyed our little cat and mouse game."

The Hangman stared at BA's hand as he withdrew it from the slap. "I haven't. And why are you touching me?"

"Are we gonna be immortal enemies till the end of time?"

"No. I figured one of us would kill the other."

"Fine." BA stood and almost hit his head on a tree branch. "We still need to know your answer. I'll even swallow my pride first, Cromwell. We need you."

The Hangman stared up into BA's face. He knew the angel was being honest, he just still didn't want to let his guard down. After all, the angel had tracked him back to Earth before and eventually killed him. BA took the Hangman back to Purgatory, a place he didn't want to go, which is why he sold his soul to get back to Earth.

The Hangman stood as well. "I'll tell you what. Find out who or what killed Kente Jr, and I give you my word, I'll join your team again."

"But you owe your freedom to me, Cromwell."

"I owe you nothing, *Artherial*. And yes, I called you by your given name as you have called me by mine since day one."

"Ok, Hangman." BA's wings appeared. "I will get you your information in a day or so, and you'd better keep your world."

"I always do."

The Hangman watched as BA took off into the night sky. The Hangman sat down again on the edge of the roof. He wasn't done reminiscing. He remembered the day he met Marla Bingham, which eventually lead to his demise.

The First Day 1985

It was about noon when Kente Cromwell Sr. and his wife Dorothy pulled up in the U-Haul truck. They stared at each other and gave each other a kiss. Kente got out of the truck and went to his wife's side and opened the door for her.

"Your palace awaits, my love." Cromwell spread out his hand and gestured toward the house. "You are now the queen of Delaware Street."

"Now see." She smiled. "Now you're going too far. We don't know anyone around here. We may not even like this neighborhood."

"Pish." Cromwell waved his finger. "We're lovable. It won't take long for people to figure that out."

Cromwell held out his hand for Dorothy. He'd always promised that she'd never have to open another car door when they were together. He helped her down out of the truck. They kissed again, held hands, and stared at their new house. It was all brown with a porch and two windows on the top floor. There were two windows on the bottom floor.

"We did it, honey." Kente squeezed Dorothy's hand tighter. "We did it."

"Let's not celebrate yet, Kente. We've still gotta unpack all this stuff."

"But look at this place." Kent twirled around in a circle. "The street is clean. The houses are nice, and everyone's grass is neatly maintained."

"What's the big deal?"

"I'm just saying; we've come a long way from Hawthorne, Indiana. And I have no doubt that we're the only black family living around here."

"And that's a good thing?"

"How could it not be?"

Kente and Dorothy walked up the steps and onto the porch. Kente pulled out the keys from his pocket and unlocked the door. He scooped up Dorothy in his arms and carried her across the threshold. It was Kente's dream house, and he was surprised that Dorothy wasn't as excited as he was. But then again, Dorothy liked her family and her life in Hawthorne. Her father had passed away, but her mother, brother, and a few cousins still lived in the small town. She didn't even want to change her last name from Tisdale to Cromwell. She offered to hyphenate the names, but Kente wouldn't have it.

She punched Kent in the arm. "Put me down, you big kid. We have work to do."

"Ok. Ok. But I can see you're not enjoying this as much as I am. How's about I send for your brother, Robert, and give him a job at Cromwell Construction. It'll give you a family member to be around and, hopefully, help you relax."

"Oh, Kente." She hugged him. "Really? That would be great. Plus, Robert really needs the work."

"Ok, it's settled then." Kente turned back toward the front door. "I'll call Robert later on, and we'll set things in motion."

Dorothy's uneasiness seemed to disappear and the smile on her face hung around a little longer. They walked back out onto the porch when the neighborhood women came into the yard. They were Marla Bingham, Darla Whitmore, and Janice Wilson. All were homemakers and their husbands weren't around during the day.

Marla, a tall blonde with brown eyes and bright red lipstick, held out a casserole. "Hi. We're the welcoming committee, and we'd like to welcome you to the block. You will like it here."

"Awe, thank you." Dorothy reached out and took the casserole. "You all are so nice. We are Dorothy and Kente Cromwell."

"Yes, we have nothing better to do than to sit around and cook," Darla said. "In case you haven't noticed, Marla and I are twins. We grew up here in Harvey our whole lives."

"I was gonna ask about that," Kente said. "But let me take that casserole off your hands."

Kent reached out and grabbed the glass pan with one hand. He began to walk away.

"Ooh." Marla giggled. "He's a strong one. What do you do for work, Mr. Cromwell?"

"I own a construction business on the other side of town." Kente turned back to the women. "I get my exercise in when I can."

"That's great," Marla said. "I'll have to have you over some time to fix my French imported wooden gazebo in my back yard."

Dorothy's eyes tightened, a look that didn't go unnoticed by Kente.

"Well," Kente turned back toward the house. "I'll take this inside and let you girls get acquainted a little more."

"You do that," Dorothy said. "You strong man, you. I'll be in later to feed you some casserole."

Kente swallowed hard and hurried into the house. There was something about Marla. He couldn't' deny there was a chemistry between them. *Dorothy is going to kill me. I'd better steer clear of the neighbors for a while. At least until whatever that was out there passes.*

Kente Jr. arrived home from school. It was only his second visit to the house since his parents first showed it to him when they were thinking of buying it. Kente Jr. opened the door and entered. Cromwell had on a Reggie Miller Indiana Pacers jersey and pounded his fist on the recliner arms.

"Play some defense!" Cromwell yelled out. "Jesus."

The recliner was the only furniture that had been unpacked

because Cromwell had to watch his basketball game. He was a Chicago Bulls fan, but an even bigger Indiana Pacers fan and they were playing each other that day.

"Early game, Pop?" Kente Jr. asked.

"Yeah. How was the first day of school?"

"It was great. I love this place."

"That's good, son." Kente Sr. clasped his hand together. "I had to cut a deal with your mom and bring out your Uncle Robert for her to get in a good mood."

"I like Uncle Robert. He makes me laugh."

"Yeah.Yeah.Yeah. I guess he's ok.We met the neighbors too. They're ok."

"Nice," Kente Jr. said. "I met one too. She——"

"She?" Kente Sr. interrupted. "This conversation just got a-whole-lot interesting."

"It's not like that, Pops…at least not yet."

"Well get on it, son." Kente Sr. smiled. "I think we're really gonna like it here."

"Me too."

The Hangman snapped out of his daydream. A huge man wearing black camouflage clothing and black combat boots walked down the street. The Hangman held out his hand. His hooked staffed appeared in it. He jumped into the nearby tree and prepared to pounce. *There are not too many humans that are that size and dressed like that. Gotta be a demon.* As the man got beneath a streetlight, his face became recognizable.

"Dammit, Caine." The Hangman jumped down to the street and landed in front of Jericho. "What are you doing in Harvey?"

"Isn't it obvious?" Jericho asked. "I'm looking for your fried-crispy ass."

The Hangman chuckled and then got serious again. "Who sent you, the angel?"

"Yeah, he dropped me off a few blocks from here."

"What?" The Hangman looked over Jericho's shoulders. "He couldn't just give me the information I asked for?"

"And what info is that?" Jericho asked.

"Doesn't matter." The Hangman leaned on an abandoned car. "I'm tired, Caine. I was just thinking about how all this started. I did this to be reunited with my wife and son. Now, they're both gone. What's left for me here?"

Jericho leaned up against the car as well, and they dented the hood. "I don't know if you know this, Hangy, but we really need you."

"And so, I keep hearing, Caine. But no one has told me what's in it for me? Not one person."

Jericho breathed out heavily. "Would it make a difference if I asked you for help?"

"I've already helped save you once. Isn't that enough?"

"I know." Jericho stood in front of the Hangman. "But this isn't just about me. This concerns the whole world now."

"And I don't care about the whole world. It means nothing without my Dorothy and Kente."

"You're immortal, Hangy." Jericho folded his arms. "Who do you think they're gonna come after next once they have taken over the earth?"

"So, let them come." The Hangman dropped his head. "They may be doing me a favor."

"Wow." Jericho shook his head. "I never thought I'd see

the day when you gave up. What if I told you who killed your wife?"

The Hangman straightened up. "I already know. It was a sorcerer named Damian Red. He was looking for the Ring of Light for his master."

"So, you know...*everything*?"

"What else is there to know?"

Jericho reached inside his pants pocket and pulled out a flask. "Hold on."

What aren't these guys telling me? First, BA and now Caine. Something's up. Why does the slayer have to take a drink to get up the nerve to tell me what he knows?

"Are you drinking that for the taste?" the Hangman asked. "Because I thought you couldn't get drunk."

"It's mostly to calm my nerves."

"Is it helping? This info must be damn good."

"It's an interesting little story." Jericho coughed and took another swig from the flask. "I'm sure you would have figured it out sooner or later."

"Spill." The Hangman put his hands on his hips. "This is getting old."

Jericho held up his finger. He coughed again and again. Finally, the coughing became violent, and Jericho dropped to one knee.

"Caine?" The Hangman bent over and slapped Jericho on the back. "Come on, man. What's wrong?"

Suddenly a flash of light appeared a few feet away, and Alexander stepped out of a portal. The Hangman straightened up quickly, only to be shot in the chest by a pulse of invisible energy. He flew backwards about five feet and landed on his former lawn. He got up and called his hooked staff to his hand. He walked back out to the street, stood next to Jericho, and stared at Alexander.

"Step away from him, demon." Alexander pointed. "Or suffer the consequences."

"You must have a death wish, human," the Hangman said. "I'll assume you're a wizard since you're holding a little pick-stick."

Jericho coughed and held up his hand. "N-No."

It was too late as the Hangman charged Alexander.

Alexander held out his hand. "Gladio (sword)."

Alexander now had his staff in one hand a silver sword in the other. He blocked the Hangman's attempted beheading with the sword. The Hangman twirled his staff and launched at Alexander, first with the hook, and then the sword extension on the staff. Alexander blocked both.

The Hangman chuckled. "You're kind of a wimp, aren't you wizard? I've just been toying with you so far, and you're sweating already."

Alexander's eyes widened, and he grunted as he tried to defend himself. But with a few more forceful swings, the Hangman knocked the sword out of Alexander's hand. The sword disappeared once it hit the ground.

"Cicer (pulse)," Alexander said as he pointed the staff the Hangman.

The invisible forced knocked the Hangman backward again. This time he crashed into a tree and banged the back of his head. He got back to his feet and rubbed his hand across the back of his head to check for blood. There wasn't any. He looked back at Alexander and frowned. His eyes lit up and glowed red, as did the Hellfire Ring.

"Enough of this crap." The Hangman walked back out to the street. "Now, I'm pissed."

The Hangman raised his fist and prepared to fire a beam of light from his ring. Jericho jumped to his feet and stood in front of the Hangman.

"Caine?" The Hangman lowered his fist. "What in the hell are you doing?"

Alexander slowly approached with his staff pointed at the Hangman. "Jericho? Do you know this creature?"

Jericho bent over and put his hands on his thighs. "That's what I've been trying to tell you idiots. We're all on the same side. Alexander, this is the Hangman. Hangman, this is Alexander, the wizard."

"My word." Alexander's staff disappeared as he walked toward the Hangman with his hand extended. "I'm so sorry, Mr. Hangman."

The Hangman reluctantly shook Alexander's hand. "Is this what you do, wizard, jump out of portals and just start pulsing people to death?"

"Again, I'm sorry," Alexander said. "I thought Jericho was in trouble."

"I'm ok, Alexander." Jericho straightened up. "But what are you doing here?"

"BA sent me," Alexander replied. "He said you might need some assistance with your mission."

"Yeah." Jericho pointed at the Hangman. "My mission to convince this crispy guy to help us."

The Hangman turned to walk away. "Good day, gentlemen. I wish I could say it's been fun, but it hasn't."

"So, you're gonna just walk away?" Jericho asked.

"Watch me," the Hangman said.

Jericho and Alexander watched as the Hangman disappeared into the night. Jericho knew he was the best chance to get the Hangman to help them. But he also knew, telling the Hangman the truth about Damian and BA would send the Hangman away for good.

Alexander reached out his hand and his Chicago Cubs baseball hat appeared. He put on the hat the snapped it in the back.

"So, how did you guys become so close?" Alexander asked. "Or as close as someone can be with that guy."

Jericho sat on the curb. "I first ran into each other years ago. Both of our situations ran into each other and he decided to trust me. Of course, there was the BA thing, but we were able to put it behind us back then."

"And now?"

"Things are different this time. His wife and son are dead. Back then, he was trying to get back to them. Now he wants to find out who killed them. If he finds out the truth about Damian Red, I'm afraid we may have a bigger threat on our hands than just the underworld."

"The truth?"

Jericho sat and stretched out on the grass with his feet crossed. "It was Damian who killed his wife. And I'm sure you've guessed by now that Damian is BA's son. We still don't know what has happened to Kent Jr, but according to BA, the demon has the Ring of Light that was once in Kente's possession."

"Holy crap." Alexander sat next to Jericho. "I've missed a lot."

"Well, I'm glad you're here, wizard." Jericho stood and dusted off the back of his pants. "I don't think Hangy's coming back."

A few feet away, a red circular glow opened in the center of the street. Five men seemingly floated up out of it. It was about three in the morning, and the sun was still two hours from rising. As the men stepped in full view of the streetlight, Jericho recognized them as vampires. He knew any altercation would have to last long enough to use the sun as a weapon if he needed it.

Alfred Thompson, leader of the New York Thomson Clan, was in sight first. He was followed by his chief enforcer, Michael, who was known as one of the most ruthless vampires in history. Kofee, leader of the Dekayers Clan, was next. He was accompanied by Soji, a vampire who prided himself on being fit. He rivaled Jericho in size. Then there was Boyd Kelley who'd inherited the powerful Ireland Murphy Clan after Jericho killed their former leader Caden Murphy. He was joined by his cousin Liam Kelley, who was average-sized but known to be deadly with a sword. All the vampires carried swords except for Michael, who had an ancient Indian tomahawk.

Jericho pulled out the Sword of Caine and walked into the middle of the street a few feet in front of the vampires. "Well, well, well. And here I thought I was just gonna go home and get some sleep."

"Save the jokes, Caine," Boyd said with his Irish accent. "It's finally time to answer for Caden Murphy."

"Oh, you mean that Irish piece of crap that was dusted not too long ago." Jericho smiled. "I didn't know you suck-heads plotted revenge for dead vamps."

"Yeah keep being a wise-ass, slayer." Kofee stepped out in front. "It's just gonna make killing you even sweeter."

"I see you've been playing well with others, Caine." Alexander raised his staff. "I was told to expect this whenever I was around you."

Jericho smiled, turned to Alexander but talked loud enough for the vampires to hear. "Oh, these little girls. Don't worry about them, wizard. Although, I must say, I'm feeling kind of special that the leaders of the three most powerful vampire clans in the world have come here to be dusted today."

Michael began running towards Jericho. "Enough of this."

Jericho blocked one of Michael's attacks, but Jericho had never battled anyone who wielded a tomahawk. Michael was skilled with the tomahawk and faster than Jericho. He swung the tomahawk, and Jericho blocked it again, but Michael used his free hand to punch Jericho in the jaw. Jericho staggered backward, and that's when Kofee and Soji joined the action. Kofee forced Jericho to focus on him as Soji kicked Jericho in the back of the head. Jericho fell forward to the ground but quickly got back to his feet.

"That leaves you all alone, wizard," Alfred said as he carried his black cane and an older Civil War sword. "We'll allow you to leave. But if you stay, you'll surely die with the slayer."

"Are you insane?" Alexander swung his staff like a baseball bat at Alfred. "Cicer (pulse)."

The invisible pulse struck Alfred in the stomach, and the vampire dropped to his knees. Alexander then turned to Boyd and Liam. Liam charged Alexander with his sword.

Alexander waved his hand. "Supernatet (float)."

Liam stopped and jammed his sword into the concrete. His feet lifted off the ground as he held on to his sword. He struggled and tried to fight the spell. But he didn't' have to as Boyd punched Alexander in the nose, sending the wizard sprawling to the ground. Alexander got back to his feet, but Boyd grabbed Alexander's staff, and they tussled over the wizard's weapon.

"We gave you a chance, wizard," Boyd said. "Now, prepare to die."

Boyd's vampire face appeared as he bared his fangs. He launched at Alexander with his mouth, but Alexander moved his head from side to side to avoid being bitten. Alexander's hold over Liam was released and the vampire fell to the ground. Alexander also felt his grip loosening on his staff. Boyd proved to be stronger than the wizard.

Alexander looked to the sky. "Fulgur (lighting)."

Boyd looked to the sky as well and dived out of the way just as a lightning bolt crashed down in the spot he was standing. Alexander had to cover his eyes as the lighting crashed down right in front of him. It gave Liam time to recover and slashed Alexander's arm with his sword. Alexander dropped his staff and grabbed his wounded arm. He turned around, ran, and jumped behind an abandoned car. He ripped the bottom strip of his t-shirt off and tied it around the wound. He breathed heavily as he knew he had little time to think, but he had to come up with a plan.

Alexander leaned his head back against the car and tried to remember Merlin's spell.

He waved his hand across his wound. "Desierunt (subside)."

He could feel the energy passing through his arm and saw the wound closing. He needed more time and hoped the vampires would give it to him.

Down the street, the vampires took turns attacking and punching or kicking Jericho. He knew he had to neutralize Soji as the huge vampire's punches were the only ones that affected the slayer. But Jericho also knew he had to still maneuver around to avoid being struck by Michael's tomahawk or Kofee and Soji's swords. Soji struck Jericho again, and the slayer fell to the ground. His sword fell out of his hand. The vampires slowly closed in, impressed by what they considered as getting the better of the slayer.

Jericho looked over his shoulder and located his sword on the ground. "Uh oh, you guys shouldn't have done that."

"Done what?" Kofee raised his sword to strike. "Because just in case you hadn't noticed, slayer, we're winning."

Jericho laughed. "You've given me a chance to catch my breath."

Jericho got back to one knee as is eyes started to glow. The Sword of Caine floated in the air and launched itself into Michael's chest. The vampire looked down, dropped his tomahawk, and turned to around to face Alfred.

"Father!" Michael screamed out. Hel—"

Michael turned into ashes. Jericho got back to his feet and grabbed his sword. As he turned back around, he was stabbed in the shoulder. Kofee pulled his sword out of Jericho's shoulder and prepared to stab the slayer in the face.

"Iaculare (hurl)!" Alexander yelled out.

Alexander's staff made a swoosh sound as it sailed down

the street and slammed into the back of Kofee's head. The vampire fell forward, and Jericho grabbed Kofee by his neck with one hand. Jericho twisted his wrist and snapped Kofee's neck. Jericho knew it wouldn't kill the vampire, but Jericho needed a moment to regroup. But Soji wasn't going to allow him that moment. Soji picked up Alexander's staff and tossed to the side. Holding his sword in front of him, Soji eased toward Jericho.

Boyd jumped on top of the car, knocked Alexander's hat off, and used his vampire strength to pull up the wizard by his hair. Boyd pulled Alexander up to the roof of the car and punched him in the stomach. Alexander coughed up blood. Boyd then grabbed Alexander by his shirt and tossed him face-first to the concrete. Alexander was down on all fours and struggled to get back to his feet, but Liam and Alfred began to kick the wizard in the ribs.

"Pick him up," Boyd said as he jumped down from the car. "It's time to end this."

Alfred and Liam held Alexander up by his arms. Boyd put his sword to Alexander's throat.

"We tried to warn you." Boyd slapped Alexander across the face. "Now it's time to learn the lesson that every fool learns who accompanies the slayer."

Suddenly, a red beam of light struck Boyd in the side of the head. He turned, but before he could see where the beam came from, he turned to ashes. Liam decided to act fast. He opened his mouth, fangs protruding and attempted to bite Alexander. However, a read beam of light struck him in his chest. He dropped Alexander's arm and stepped backward.

He rubbed his hands across his chest where the beam struck him. Liam then exploded into ashes.

"I think that even things up a little." The Hangman jumped down from the roof of a house and tossed Alexander his staff. "Time to go to work, wizard."

Alexander glared at Alfred. "I wish I was as merciful as you guys and gave you the same chance you gave me. But I'm not."

Alfred attacked, but Alexander twirled his staff and popped Alfred in the face. Alfred was knocked to his backside and cracked his head on the concrete. Alexander looked over at the Hangman, who merely nodded. Alexander walked over and stood over Alfred. Alfred dropped his weapons and closed his eyes. His body began to shrink, and he transformed into a coyote. Alexander took a step back at first, but then stepped forward and put his foot on the animal's neck.

Alexander raised his staff and looked and toward the sky. "Fulgur (lightning)."

Alexander quickly moved his foot as lightning crashed down into Alfred's coyote body. Smoke rose from the animal as he transformed back into Alfred. Alfred tried to sit up but then burst into fiery ashes.

"I've been waiting my entire vampire life for this," Soji said as he dropped his sword. "I'm going to kill you with my bare hands, slayer."

Jericho stumbled to his feet. "Ah. I get it. You're off your leash with your master blowing in the wind, so now you want to test your boxing skills."

"No. I just want to kill you."

"Fair enough."

Jericho held up his fist of his non-injured arm in a boxing stance and began to bounce back and forth. His legs were wobbly, though. He was tired. Blood dripped from his nose and mouth. He'd lost a lot of blood from the wound in his shoulder.

Jericho's eyes glowed. "Aw, screw this."

The Sword of Caine shot across the street and chopped off Soji's head. The huge vampire's head rolled across the ground. His headless body swung wild punches at Jericho, who easily avoided being hit. The body and head finally turned to ashes. Jericho teetered backward and fell back to the ground on his butt.

Jericho sighed as he looked up, and the Hangman and Alexander walked in his direction. "Took you long enough."

"I had to see if you still had it in you," the Hangman said. "And lucky for you, my curiosity got the better of me."

Jericho reached out his hand for someone to pull him up. "Well, I'm glad we were able to pass your little test."

"Indeed." Alexander reached down to pull up Jericho. "It was more of a challenge than I expected."

The Hangman laughed. "And you both passed with flying colors."

"Well, thanks for the exercise," Alexander said. "But I really must be getting back to the wife and kids."

"Kids?" Jericho asked.

"Yes." Alexander stretched out his staff and created a portal. "You really should give it a try, Jericho."

"Oh jeez." Jericho waved as Alexander entered the portal. "He's a strange one."

The Hangman smiled. "Yes, he is. No wonder he's on you guy's team."

"So now comes the real question, Hangy." Jericho sheathed his sword. "Are you in or out?

The Hangman's eyes glowed red. "I'm in."

Part 14

ORIGINS 4: LEECHADON, THE SOUL EATER

Cairo, Egypt

Econdro, the Demon Genius, rode on a camel fifteen miles away from the huge city. He stared into the hot sun and regretted he decided not to possess a human. He was in his corporeal form. His skin was red with a small horn sticking out of his forehead. His eyes were yellow, and his long dark hair was in a ponytail. He had oversized hands and long sharpened fingernails.

Econdro always knew that he and the other two powerful demon lords would never have enough strength to overthrow Hangoctuforre, so they devised another plan. And although it took more convincing than he wanted, Econdro convinced Zade and Blaelock to agree to create an alternative to Hangoctuforre.

The Conjuring

The year was 1519, and Hangoctuforre had just been defeated again after attempting to overthrow the earth. The demon lords Econdro, Zade, and Blaelock suffered massive losses to their respective clans. Zade almost was destroyed by Michael's fiery blade but was pulled away just in time by his brother Blaelock.

They began possessing human bodies to find the strongest one. Zade had it. He possessed a six-foot-eight bald black man. The man was muscular from head to toe. They took turns possessing the man to make sure he fit into their plans. Econdro had to make sure the man's brain was on par with his own, so he entered a chess competition. He finished second and then decided to kill everyone in attendance.

Blaelock, having lived longer than any other demon, put the possessed man through strenuous physical tasks. He entered a marathon and won. Then there was Zade, the Mad Demon. He wouldn't sign off on the possessed man until he saw a ruthless aggression in the man that rivaled his own. So, one night after a local soccer game was finished, Zade possessed the man, sat on another man's horse, and started humming. He waited till the man came along with his young son who'd just finished playing in the soccer game.

"Excuse me, sir," the dad said. "But, please get off of my horse."

Zade jumped off the horse. "It's a fine animal. I just wanted to make sure it could hold my weight."

"Why?" the dad asked.

"Because after I kill you, I'm taking it," Zade responded.

The son, about twelve years old, grabbed his father by the waist and stood behind him. "Father, I'm scared."

The dad swallowed hard. "Look, sir, I don't want any trouble."

Zade laughed. "Me either. Well, just a little."

Zade lifted his hand, and an invisible force picked up the father. Zade flicked his wrist and flung the father across the lot. The little boy, seeing what happened to his father, was seemingly endowed with courage. He ran up to Zade and began punching him in the stomach. Zade threw his head back and laughed as the punches had no effect. He looked up to the sky and bared his teeth, which suddenly, became sharp like a row of icepicks. His mouth stretched wide like an anaconda snake. Zade then thrust his head forward and bit the little boy's head off. The body twitched as it fell headless to the ground. The father came back and saw the remains of his son on the ground. He ran over, dropped to his knees in front of the body, and yelled out.

"Oh my God, no" The dad put both of his hands to his head. "Not my little boy."

The dad pounded the ground and glared up at Zade. He got up and charged Zade, who stretched out his hand, and an invisible force began to choke the father. Zade then turned his wrist and snapped the man's neck.

"This body will do," Zade said as he watched the passerby's scream and run in fear. "Yes, run, humans. You haven't seen anything yet."

Zade turned around, got on the man's horse, smacked the horse on the hind side, and sped off.

The Underworld

"Aren't you worried those other two demons will revolt when they find out about Zade?" Comet crossed his legs as he sat in Hangoctuforre private chamber. "They've already tried overthrow you once before."

"I could have chosen either of them," Hangoctuforre said. "None of them are loyal. They are all looking for the moment when they can take me down."

"So why kill either then?"

"As an example." Hangoctuforre stood and walked around. "They know they are not powerful enough to overthrow me. Some of their own followers are loyal to me. Besides, I need to know what they're planning. I'm sure it will happen after the war."

Comet shook his head. "That's a grim way of looking at your allies."

"That goes for anyone." Hangoctuforre's red eyes squinted. "*Anyone* who tries to cross me will suffer the consequences."

"Are you referring to me?" Comet asked.

"I said, *anybody*."

Hangoctuforre walked over to his fireplace and waved his hand over it. A fire lit up, and a blurred picture came into focus through the flames. It was Argos in the section of the underworld allotted to Econdro from Hangoctuforre. Argos and Econdro's voices were muted, but the scene was odd, considering everyone knew Argos was in direct daily contact with Hangoctuforre.

Comet pointed at the flames. "It that what you speak of?"

"Yes." Hangoctuforre folded his arms. "Outside of the do-gooders of Earth, Econdro and Blaelock remain my second biggest concern. Argos is a surprise."

"So why not dispose of them now?"

"I need them and their followers." Hangoctuforre's eyes glowed. "But once this war is over, everyone will pay for their treachery."

The Conjuring

As Zade made it back to the middle of the desert, his eyes rolled back, and his corporeal form emerged from the possessed man. He picked up the body and laid it on a stone slab. Econdro and Blaelock had erected a small hut made of rope and straw. Zade entered the small hut and sat at a round wooden table in the center of the hut. Bales of hay were set up as chairs, and one candle sat in a candle holder in the center of the table.

"I'm in," Zade said as he crossed his legs. "This body works perfectly."

"I'm glad you agree." Econdro clasped his hands together. "Now all we need is the book."

"The Book of the Dead?" Blaelock dropped his head. "I hate that book. It brings nothing but trouble. And you know who has it, right?"

"Yes," Econdro said. "Him."

"That son of a whore?" Blaelock stood and paced. "If we ask or take it, he'll know we're up to something. We've got to be careful."

Econdro smiled. "I've already got that covered."

Econdro's eyes rolled back as he spread out his arms. A small portal opened in front of the demons. The candles flickered, and a slight breezed blew in from the small opening. The demons covered their faces as the sand blew around the hut.

"Come forward, my friend." Econdro waved his hands toward himself. "I summon you to this land of sand."

Argos, Hangoctuforre's aide, stepped out of the portal. He wore a thick brown robe. He was in his corporeal form as well. He had the head of a pig and body of a gorilla. He opened his robe and revealed the Book of the Dead.

He snorted. "Be quick about this. He will miss it before long as he plots his next invasion of the earth."

"He won't miss it." Econdro grabbed the huge black leather book with both hands and placed it on the table. "We will be quick. My clan and I cannot suffer another defeat following him."

"And we shall not, brother," Zade said. "What we do here today, not only will we dethrone him, but have a true leader we've created with our three greatest aspects: intelligence, ruthlessness, and immortality."

"So, what are we waiting for?" Blaelock stood. "Let's get on with it."

Argos snorted. "Wait a minute before you begin. I'll go back to the underworld and make sure we're not discovered."

Argos stepped back through the portal. Econdro opened the book to the page they needed. It was a spell to create demons, a similar spell used for when they were created in the underworld. This spell was different in that it required three demon lords, a host body, and one of the five medallions of existence. They had three. They possessed the underworld's medallion, Earth's medallion, and Purgatory's medallion. The last two medallions were Heaven's and the Nether Region's. Because those two were controlled by angels and no demon could enter, they could never possess them.

They stood around the table and joined hands. They'd dragged the huge body inside the hut and placed it on the nearby table made of straw. They placed the medallions in a triangle on the body's shirtless chest. At first, the writing on the page was in Latin.

Econdro tilted his head back, and his eyes rolled back. "Transferendum (translate)."

Suddenly, the writing on the page appeared to move like insects, and the writing was no longer in Latin. It was in English. The demons spoke a different language in demon-speak, so they used English when they were in each other's presence.

Econdro smiled as he peered down at the page, and the others closed their eyes as he read. "Spirits of the underworld bring forth a demonic life into this chosen host. Bring forth a warrior demon that has our strengths and none of our weaknesses. Do this, and we shall pledge our eternal essences to it."

The wind picked up outside and almost blew over the hut. The sky darkened, and rain poured down. Thunder and lightning pounded the surrounding area. The hut collapsed and blew away in the wind, which left their operation exposed. Then finally, a bolt of lightning crashed down and struck the three medallions. The energy pulsated through the host body, and one of the medallions began to glow. Another bolt of lightning crashed down onto the body, and a second medallion glowed. Then the final bolt of lightning hit the body, causing all three medallions to glow.

The host body had taken on enough energy, and it fell to the floor. The demons released each other's hands and attempted to pick up the body. However, when they all touched it, a pulse exploded and sent the three demons flying across the sand.

Econdro got to his feet and walked back toward the hut's remains. "I'll retrieve the book and you two check on the body."

As they got closer, the ground began to shake, and a mound of sand exploded. The huge host body had come to life. Its eyes glowed red, the medallions glowed yellow and were embedded in the body's skin.

Blaelock bowed his head and eased his way over to the demon. The demon reached down, lifted Blaelock's by his neck, and snatched off his head.

"Ahh, you must be Blaelock," the demon said as he looked into the eyes of the detached head that was still conscious. "The Immortal Destructor. That would make you Zade, the Mad Demon, and you are Econdro the Demon Genius. I am Leechadon, the Soul Eater."

Leechadon placed Blaelock's head into its body's hands. Econdro and Zade dropped to their knees and crawled over to their new master.

"Arise, my creators," Leechadon said. "We have work to do."

Econdro stood. "Thank you, my lord Leechadon."

The medallions on Leechadon's chest began to blink. He held his stomach and dropped to his knees.

Leechadon glared up at Econdro. "Sadly, you will now know what my weakness is. My power and comes from what I feed off—souls. Anything with a soul."

"B-But you're not supposed to have any weaknesses," Econdro said. "I made sure to put it in the spell."

"Come on, Demon Genius." Leechadon fell forward to his hands. "You're smarter than this. All demons must have a weakness. It's what gives the angels and humans a chance against our kind, even if it's

only a small chance. No demon created is supposed to be more power-ful than an archangel. That rule was created so that no demon could ever rule in heaven."

"I'm sorry, my lord," Econdro pleaded. "Give me a chance to correct this."

"No!" Leechadon held up his finger as two of his medallions stopped glowing. "But there's no soul within miles of here, and I'm about to fade away. When you need me again, c-call o-on m-me."

Leechadon's last medallion stopped glowing, and his huge frame fell to its side in the sand. Blaelock attached his head back to its body, and the other two demons rushed over to Leechadon's body.

Zade dusted sand from his robe. "This is not good, brothers."

"This is perfect," Econdro said. "We will bury him underneath a pyramid until we call upon him again. But the next time, we shall have enough souls for him to feed and stay with us."

"Brilliant, Lord Econdro." Blaelock massaged his neck. "And when the time comes, that other demon won't know what hit him."

Part 15

A FAMILY AFFAIR

The Underworld

Damian entered the chamber, followed by Ahmya, and looked around. Hangoctuforre wasn't present, so Damian walked over to the fireplace. He looked around for something to light it. There was nothing.

"Now, how in the hell does he do this?" Damian continued looking around the floor for a lighting mechanism. "Kinda rude not to be here when he summons me."

"I have no comment," Ahmya said. "I'm just here to serve."

Damian stepped backward a few feet and stretched out his arms. "Screw it. Ignis (fire)."

The fireplace came to life with flames. Damian looked around again. Again, Hangoctuforre wasn't present. He sighed and placed his hands on his hips. He turned towards the door and prepared to walk away. He glanced at Ahmya as he walked past her. She didn't appear as if she was going to follow.

Damian shrugged. "Suit yourself, but I'm out of here."

Then all of a sudden, a red dot popped out of the fireplace and landed on the floor. The dot grew into the seven-foot frame of the demon lord.

Hangoctuforre laughed. "Hold on, Damian. I've been here all along. I was just waiting to see what you would do."

"Not funny, my master."

"We have to have some fun." Hangoctuforre continued to smile. "Or we won't enjoy what comes next."

"And what does come next?" Damian asked. "Seems like she and I have been on the sidelines ever since I got you the ring."

"You both get to do what you do best, my friend." Hangoctuforre walked over and patted Damian on the back. "Destroy."

"Destroy what?" Damian asked

Hangoctuforre put his arm around Damian and Ahmya and walked toward the door. "In my meditation, I was apprised of a new threat. I wanted to leave the wizard alone, but his off-spring will pose a problem for us in the future."

"And what of me, my lord?" Ahmya asked.

"Your niece," Hangoctuforre stroked the back of Ahmya's hair. "She's all yours. And with any luck, you might even get your revenge on the demon hunter."

Ahmya turned to face her master. "Thanks, my lord. I won't let you down."

Ahmya left the chamber with a smile on her face, leaving Damian and Hangoctuforre alone.

Damian stared into the dark hood covering Hangoctuforre's head and saw his red eyes glowing. "And so, what do you want me to do?"

"Go to the hospital...and kill them all."

A slight smile crept onto Damian's face. "Yes, my master. I will go at once."

Damian walked toward the door and stopped. He had the ability to enter and leave the underworld at will. He pulled out his snake staff. The eyes on the staff glowed red.

Damian waved the staff across his body. "Evanescet (disappear)."

Damian disappeared, and Hangoctuforre sat on his chair in front of the fireplace. His eyes were as red as the flames. *Damian will take care of wizard. Ahmya will dispatch the girl and hopefully Padilla too. And I shall have three fewer enemies. Nothing can stop me now.*

Chicago, Illinois

Alexander sat in the hospital chair next to Emma's bed. He held the female baby, Octavia, and Emma held the boy, Octus. They watched a game show on a TV that was mounted to the wall. Every so often, Alexander would look down at Octavia and then at Emma and Octus. *I'm the luckiest man on the planet.* He wondered what would happen if he went back on his word and decided not to join in on the war. He was at peace with his new family, and he didn't want anything to interfere with it.

Alexander grabbed the remote, pushed the mute button and put his finger over his lip. "Shh."

"What's wrong, honey?" Emma asked. "I don't' hear anything."

"That's the point," Alexander said. "This is a hospital. We should be hearing *something*."

Alexander got up and put Octavia back in the glass crib at the foot of the bed. He took Octus from Emma and placed the boy in the crib next to Octavia's. Alexander rolled the cribs into the bathroom. He looked over at Emma who had a worried expression on her face.

"You're scaring me, honey," she said. "I don't like this. This type of stuff doesn't happen in the hood."

Alexander tipped toward the door and turned back to Emma. "Hopefully, it's just my paranoia. But one can never be too safe."

Alexander grabbed the door handle and prepared to slowly open the door. But then it was blown open by a powerful gust of wind. Alexander flew across the room and crashed into the huge window. He was surprised that the window didn't break; it was just cracked from where he impacted it. He got back to his feet and realized that the door was blown open from a spell and not from an explosion. His fears were correct as Damian Red walked through the open door.

"Damian Red," Alexander breathed heavily. "What in the hell are you doing here?"

Damian pointed his staff at Alexander. "It's time to take you and your family off of the chessboard, wizard."

Alexander instinctively looked at the restroom. "Please, not now."

Damian nodded toward the restroom. "Ahh. Is that where the children are? Your screw up is now complete."

Alexander held out his hand. But just as his staff appeared in it, Damian shot a red beam of light toward the wizard and knocked him into the window again. Alexander dropped his staff, and blood trickled down from his nose. He struggled to his feet once more and prepared to be struck by another beam of light.

Damian walked past Emma and winked. "I'll get to you in a minute."

A bedpan bounced off of Damian's head. It didn't hurt him, but it gave Alexander enough time to call his staff back to his hand.

Alexander pointed his staff at Damian. "Impetu (force)!"

An invisible forced knocked Damian back out of the door and into the hallway. Alexander rushed over to the bed and helped Emma take out her IV. Blood spewed down her arm as the IV was forcefully pulled out. Suddenly, Alexander stopped. It was as if he was frozen.

"Why are you stopping, Alex?" Emma stared into his stone face. "We need to get moving."

"Honey." Alexander barely moved his mouth to speak. "I think we're in trouble."

Damian walked back into the room with his eyes and the snake eyes on his staff glowing red. "More than you know, wizard." Damian flicked his wrist. "Supernatet and Lignum anum (float and stick)."

Alexander was lifted off his feet and floated to the wall behind Emma's bed. He was stuck to the wall and couldn't move. Emma jumped to her feet and picked up the IV stand. She drew back to strike Damian.

He held up his hand toward Emma. "Arcum (bow)."

Emma dropped to her knees. She couldn't move just like Alexander, who fought and squirmed to free himself from the spell.

"Please, Mr. Red," Emma begged. "Please don't hurt my babies."

Damian smiled. "You silly woman. They are the reason I'm here.'

Alexander began to move his fingers. Damian's two spells weakened his hold over Alexander, who used all his strength to turn his head to his staff on the floor.

"Revertetur ad me (return to me)," Alexander painfully spoke.

Alexander's staff vibrated on the floor and then began to float toward him. Damian quickly shot a red beam of light toward the window, and it finally shattered. He then shot another beam of light, and it struck Alexander's staff, causing it to fly out of the window.

"Now, where were we?" Damian said as he walked toward the restroom. "Don't worry. This will be quick. Then I'll return to finish off mommy and daddy."

Alexander had a clear view into the restroom. The breaking of the glass and subsequent wind made the babies cry. Alexander struggled to free himself again. He was a Suma wizard. He didn't need his staff to create magic, but right then, the only thing he could think about was Damian hurting his babies. He was confused and couldn't think of a spell to free himself.

"Please. No!" Alexander pleaded.

Damian put his finger to his lips. "Quiet now."

Damian walked into the restroom and gripped his staff. He prepared to stab Octus in the chest. But then suddenly, as Damian plunged his staff down toward Octus, a blue force field covered the crib. Damian's staff bounced off it. He tried again and again. But nothing happened as he couldn't break through the forcefield. He looked out at Alexander, who was still stuck to the wall.

"You're more powerful than I thought, wizard," Damian said.

"That wasn't me," Alexander replied. "But this is. "Desciscendum (detach)."

Alexander nodded at the TV and then at Damian. The TV snatched away from the wall and cracked Damian in the head.

Damian fell to his knees, and Alexander fell to the floor. Emma stood as well. Alexander held out his hand called back his staff. Once in hand, he turned his attention back to Damian, who had rushed over to Alexander and prepared to stab him with the snake staff. Alexander blocked it and kneed Damian in the groin. Damian doubled over and dropped to his knees again.

As Alexander was about to strike Damian with his staff, Emma hurried over, held up her hand, and stopped the wizard. "No. Let me."

Emma slapped Damian in the face and then kneed him in the nose. Damian fell backward and scooted along the floor on his butt. He got back to his feet and wiped the snot from his nose.

Alexander pointed his staff at Damian. "Cicer (pulse)!"

The invisible force knocked Damian out the window of the third-floor room. Alexander rushed over with his staff pointing down to direct another pulse at the sorcerer, but Damian was gone.

Emma rushed over and stood next to Alexander, who was still staring out of the window. He didn't know if Damian was gone or merely regrouping.

Emma punched Alexander in the arm. "You promised this stuff wouldn't follow you back to our family."

Alexander sighed. "I didn't think it would. I didn't even know they knew you were pregnant."

Emma buried her face in Alexander's chest. "Well, we survived this time. That'll teach his ass to mess with the Merryweather's. Right, baby?"

"That's right, honey." Alexander finally let out a sigh. "But we've got to talk about what happened here today."

"What do you mean, Alex?"

Alexander stared into the restroom at the babies, who lay quiet in the cribs. "It wasn't me who stopped him from hurting the kids. One or both created that forcefield that stopped Damian."

"What?"

"I know it seems impossible because wizard powers don't manifest until the early teen years. But I know what I saw."

"Oh my God, Alex." Emma turned toward the restroom. "What do we do now?"

"We've got to get out of here," Alexander said as he started gathering their things. "If Damian was right, this isn't the last time we'll hear from those guys."

"Dammit!" Emma kicked the bedpan on the floor across the room. "Dammit. Dammit. Dammit."

"Don't worry, honey." Alexander rolled the crib out of the restroom. "It's time I go and do what I was meant to do and help put an end to this. It's the only way we'll be safe."

New York

Tom and Susie entered a department store that was going out of business. The store was rarely open. The windows allowed for some light but not enough to highlight the entire store. Tom was following up on a lead he'd gotten from one of his informants, a demon that didn't want to be involved in the war.

"Are you sure about this, Tom?" Susie asked as he pulled out her nunchucks from the small of her back. "This seems like a sketchy place for demon activity."

"Trust me," Tom said. "My informant has never given me false information."

Susie groaned. "Well, there's a first time for everything."

They walked through the women's area of the store and pressed their way through the nightgowns. Tom picked up one and turned to Susie.

Tom wagged his eyebrows. "Can you ever see yourself wearing something like this?"

"Hell, no." Susie laughed. "But maybe just for you."

Tom turned back around to put the gown back and was punched in the face by a man wearing all black, including a black ski mask. Tom staggered backward but Susie braced him until he regained his balance. Tom looked around and saw they were surrounded by five men, who were all dressed the same.

Tom rubbed his jaw. "Ok. Who's in charge of you clowns? There's always someone in charge."

"That would be me." Ahmya stepped out from behind a mannequin. "You might not know me, Mr. Padilla, but Susie does, and you will too before this is over."

Tom turned to Susie. "Susie? Do you know this woman?"

"It's my aunt that I told you about." Susie spoke to Tom but didn't take her eyes off Ahmya. "But don't be fooled. She's trickier than she looks."

"It's funny." Ahmya walked toward them. "I would swear I sent you to kill this man, Susie, not sleep with him."

"Well, I guess we're both disappointed in each other," Susie shot back. "The only difference is my disappointment is justified."

Another masked man attempted to attack. Tom had slipped on his brass knuckles and cracked the man in the forehead. The man fell backward to the floor on his back. The man began slowly to get back up. *That's not a regular human because a regular guy would be out cold from that punch.*

Tom raked his hand through his slick black hair and turned to Ahmya. "So, when did demons start doing a human's bidding?"

"Since their master told them to," Ahmya said. "And what business is it of yours? You steal my niece, and you dare to ask me questions?"

"He didn't steal anything," Susie said. "The only thing that was stolen here is my trust, and by you. You lied to me."

"Don't be naïve, Susie." Ahmya pointed at Tom. "Look at him. His kind only knows one way of handling our kind."

"Your kind?" Tom twisted his lips. "You're human and you're helping demons."

Susie patted Tom on the shoulder. "No, Tom, she's a witch... and a dangerous one. Damn, I was so blind. You stopped being a human decades ago."

"Enough of this." Ahmya waved her hand. "Kill them both."

The demon-possessed men pounced. Three of them tried to separate Tom and Susie by jumping in between them both. But Tom knew what they were trying to do, so he made sure he didn't stray too far from Susie.

Tom pulled off his crucifix beaded necklace and let it dangle from his hand. It was now a short whip. From what he could see through his own fight, Susie was popping every demon-possessed man with her nun-chucks that came her way. The whipping motion sound against the air made Tom blush. *She's kicking their asses.*

But Tom found himself in a bear hug from behind by one of the bigger men. He could feel the flood rushing to his head as if his head were about to explode. Tom pounded his head backward, and it smashed into the demon's head. He kept doing it until he felt the demon's grip loosening. But another demon punched Tom in the stomach while he was still in the bear-hug. Tom felt the air leave his body from the punch.

Tom kept trying to free himself as the demon continued to punch. Finally, Tom's abilities surfaced. He gained the strength of the demons he was fighting. He broke free from the bear-hug turned and kneed the demon in the gut. He then backhanded the demon that was punching him in the stomach.

"You ok over there, priest?" Susie asked as she kept whipping around her nunchucks. "I thought I was gonna have to come over to help you out."

"I'm ok," Tom replied.

Tom cracked the bigger demon in the jaw with a left and right hook. He then hit him in the stomach. When the demon doubled over, Tom shot an uppercut to the demon's nose. The demon fell backward over a clothing rack and onto the floor. The other demon tried to put Tom in a headlock, but Tom slipped it before the demon could clasp his hands together. Tom dropped to a knee and uppercut the demon sending him backward and crashing into one of the demons that was engaged with Susie.

"You're welcome!" Tom yelled out. "You can thank me later."

"Show off," Susie replied.

Tom reached into his inner jacket pocket and pulled out a small glass vial of yellow liquid—Detox.

He kneeled and grabbed the large demon on the floor by the shirt collars. Tom pulled off the ski-masked and exposed a black man's rotting faced. Tom elbowed the demon in the gut and forced the demon to open its mouth. Tom then and poured some of the Detox down its throat. The demon-possessed man started to hemorrhage. Finally, the yellow demon essence flowed out from his nose. Tom dropped the body. The human had obviously been dead for a while after being possessed.

Tom turned his attention to Susan, who was fighting off the four other demons. Tom glanced around and couldn't locate Ahmya, though, so he went over to join Susie. Tom punched one the demon's in the back of the head. The demon fell forward and right into a nun-chuck strike from Susie. The demon fell to the floor, and Tom pounced on his chest. Tom then took off the demon's mask and poured Detox into its eyes. It took longer, but the demon's yellow essence seeped out through its ears and evaporated. *Two down, three to go.*

Another smaller demon grabbed Tom from behind. Tom reached back, grabbed the demon by the neck and twisted. The demon's neck snapped, but he was still alive. Tom pulled off the demon's mask, grabbed the back of its head, and forced it to ingest the Detox. Tom dropped the demon to the floor. But before he could admire his work, he was punched in the mouth by another demon. Tom staggered backward and almost fell. But he regained his balance and prepared for the next attack.

Tom looked over at Susie, who'd grabbed a demon-possessed man by the back of his head and then cuffed her hand around his forehead. The electricity she emitted while she drained his demon essence, lit up the department store. Tom and the remaining demon had to cover their eyes with their hands. After Susie was done, Tom didn't hesitate as he karate chopped the other demon in the throat. Tom was prepared to use his last bit of Detox on the coughing demon, but Tom hesitated.

"You need some more juice, babe." Tom held the demon by the back of the neck. "If so, I've got a present for you."

"Ah, Tom." Susie clapped. "You shouldn't have."

Tom pushed the demon over to Susie, who immediately grabbed the demon's forehead and prepared to use her ability to drain his essence. As Tom stood back and watched the light show, a hand grabbed him by the back of his shoulder and tossed him across the room. He crashed into the wall and fell, breaking loose the water fountain beneath him. Water spouted all over, but it also kept Tom from passing out as he rested on the floor.

However, Ahmya wasn't done. She crept over and kicked Tom in the face, sending him crashing into the wall again. Tom tried to stand. The little old lady packed a wallop, and the force of the kick loosened one of Tom's teeth.

Ahmya approached slowly and pounded her hands against the air. "Cicer (pulse)."

The invisible force continuously pounded Tom in the chest. He couldn't move as he was trapped between Ahmya and the wall.

"I'm here, babe." Susie ran up behind Ahmya. "Don—"

Without looking, Ahmya backhanded Susie and sent her flying across the room and crashing into a glass jewelry counter. "I'll deal with you in due time, my niece. But first, I'll deal with this wretch of a human."

Part 16

EXIT SUSIE TAKI

The Underworld

Damian returned to the underworld. He walked down a long passageway with torches lit on each side. He'd gotten used to the rotten eggs smell and the cries of tortured souls as he neared his destination. He walked into Hangoctuforre's private chamber, where the demon lord was waiting.

"Is it done?" Hangoctuforre asked.

Damian dropped his head. "No. The wizard and his children are quite formidable already."

"And you dare show back up to me like this?" Hangoctuforre pointed at Damian. "A beaten sorcerer?"

"I will get the job done, my master. It'll just require another plan."

Hangoctuforre dropped his hand, and a fiery whip appeared in it. He'd only used it in battles that he'd lost, so he rarely used it at all anymore. He swung whip and struck Damian in the face. Damian's head was jarred to the side, and a welt appeared on his jaw. His eyes began to glow, and his staff appeared in his hand.

"You dare muster your powers against me...*here?*"

Damian breathed heavily. "That was uncalled for, my master."

The glow in Damian's eyes subsided. He turned toward the door to walk away. Hangoctuforre smiled.

"Remember, Damian," Hangoctuforre began as Damian

stopped walking toward the door. "I made you. You belong to me. And there is nothing or no one who can change that. Now, go back to Earth and await my word."

"Yes, my master."

Damian walked out of the chamber, and Hangoctuforre's whip disappeared. *The humanity in him will likely be his undoing one day, but its a chance I'll have to take until this war is over.*

New York

Ahmya continued to beat up Tom with the invisible pulse. "I will make you suffer, priest, for taking my Susie from me and destroying my mentor Natasha."

Tom back-peddled while sitting on his back. He put up his hands to defend himself. Ahmya crept toward him with her hands in front of her. Her eyes didn't glow, but they were bloodshot with rage.

"You killed my queen, Natasha of Normandy." She continued walking toward Tom. "And now, you will feel the full power of her coven." Ahmya jerked her hands forward. "Electricae (electricity)."

A stream of electricity flowed from Ahmya's hands and struck Tom as he lay on the floor. He yelled out in pain as he was still wet from the water. His powers came from rivaling a demon's or other supernatural creature's abilities. But Ahmya was a witch, and he couldn't muster his powers. He didn't think he could combat her skills. As Tom lay on the floor and continued being electrocuted, he reached out with his hand and tried to reason with Ahmya.

"I-I c-c-cared for Natasha," he said. "I still would h-have if she didn't t-try to k-kill—"

"You dare speak her name, priest?" Ahmya cut in. "Now, you will surely die."

Ahmya strained as she increased the power of the electricity. Tom flopped around on the floor in pain. His heart raced faster, and he felt as if it were about to explode.

Susie rammed into Ahmya's back, jarring the witch forward and causing her to stop the stream of electricity. She put her hands on Ahmya's forehead from behind like she'd done with so many demons.

Tom crawled backward to the wall and tried to get up, but he fell back to the floor. His body smoked. He could smell his skin frying. He wanted to help Susie as she battled her Aunt.

Ahmya tried flipping Susie off her back. "Are you stupid, child? That doesn't work on me. I'm not a demon."

"You've become my own personal demon, Auntie," Susie said. "Your lies had almost turned me to the wrong side. And now, I will not let you destroy the man I love."

Susie's weight forced Ahmya to her knees. Susie pressed her hands harder and concentrated more. Ahmya rocked back and forth, trying to toss Susie off her back.

"If you don't let me go." Ahmya began to sweat. "We will both perish."

"Then we will both perish."

Blue electricity began to flow from Susie's hands. The electricity spread over both Susie's and Ahmya's body. They fell on their side to the floor with Susie desperately still holding on to her aunt's head.

"No, Susie." Ahmya's eyes began to glow blue. "Please. You must stop. I was doing what I had to do for our coven...and our queen."

"But for the demon?" Susie's forehead tightened. "And for that reason alone, you must now be destroyed," Susie said.

Tom looked out the window. Dark clouds had formed over the building and filled with lightning. He finally sat up against the wall and looked back and forth outside, then at Susie and Ahmya. He knew there was a correlation between what was happening outside and with his girlfriend.

"Um, Susie." Tom grabbed his chest and coughed. "I think she's right. I think you should let her go."

"No, Tom." Susie began choking her aunt with one arm while still pressing her hand on Ahmya's forehead. "This coven crap ends today."

Tom slowly crawled over to Susie and Ahmya. "We'll find another way, baby. Please stop."

"No!" Susie said.

"P-Please Susie," Ahmya pleaded. "Listen t-to him."

Finally, an explosion catapulted Susie across the room, and she crashed into the far wall. Ahmya didn't move and lay on the ground. A gust of wind blew Tom back against the wall he'd crawled from. Tom rapidly slapped his head. He used his remaining strength to get back to his feet. He took a step and fell to one knee. He got back up and staggered forward. He stopped and stared at Ahmya as her body began to smoke. The body then began to dissolve into a white milky substance. Tom looked across the room and saw Susie's motionless body face-down on the floor. He couldn't move fast but plodded his way across the room.

Tom fell to his knee as he reached Susie. "Please, baby. Please be okay."

Tom rolled Susie's body over. Blood trickled down from

her nose. Smoke emanated from her body, which was still hot. Tom didn't care. He sat on the floor and draped Susie's steaming body across his lap. He propped up her head in his arm. She was breathing, but that was it. He rubbed her face and wept.

"Susie," he said. "Susie. The fight is over. You can come back to me now."

She didn't move. He hugged her and cried some more. He had an idea of what had just happened, but that thought quickly faded.

No one from his team knew they were there, and he knew he couldn't carry Susie out of the building in his condition. He needed to regain his strength. So, as he held Susie's unconscious body, his body collapsed against the wall, and he passed out.

Golden, Colorado

Damian kicked in the boarded-up door. Surprisingly, no dust flowed out, as if someone had recently occupied the abandoned church. He walked down the center aisle and sat in the front pew. He studied the pew and saw that it was clean, unlike the rest. He looked up and saw a hole in the ceiling. He then stood and with his nose in the air and sniffed. It was the first time he'd done that. He stretched out his hand, and his staff appeared in it.

"Ok," Damian said as he looked around the church. "I know you here. Now, show yourself."

There was no movement and no answer. Damian's eyes lit up, as well as the snake's eyes on his staff. He backed up, so his back was against the podium in the pulpit.

"I'm serious," he said. "I'm a powerful sorcerer, and I don't play around."

Laughter echoed off the old church walls.

"Enough of this crap." Damian held out his staff. "Turbinis vasti (tornado)."

The wind picked up and a small funnel cloud appeared at the top of the church, which turned into a tornado. The wind was strong. Even Damian, who created it, had to jump behind the pulpit and grab on to the railing. Then, a few seconds later, a strong gust of wind blew the tornado out of the front door and it subsided in the outside air.

"Nice trick," BA said as he lowered down from the top of the church with his angel wings exposed. "It's a shame you've learned all this magic and for no reason."

"What do you want, angel?" Damian stood and pointed his staff at the angel. "How'd you find me? Is this about the wizard?"

"What about the wizard?" BA landed and held out his hand to summon his battle-ax. "Never mind that for now. You've invaded my sanctuary, Damian. This is where I come to think."

"I didn't know that." Damian jumped over the railing and back to the main floor. "How's about I just walk out of here without incident?"

"I could let that happen. But this is the perfect time to have a little chat. What happened to your face?" BA pointed to the welt on Damian's face, which stretched from just below his eye and reached his mouth. "Did you run into Cromwell?"

"That's none of your business, angel. And what do you think we could possibly have to talk about?"

"Fine. I'll just get to it. You, Damian." BA sighed, and his ax disappeared. "We need to talk about you and who you really are."

Damian stared intently at BA and erupted in laughter. "This is a trick, right? What do you think you know about me?"

"You are a Nephilim, Damian." BA spread his wings. "And you are my son."

Damian paced, but wouldn't relinquish his gaze at BA. "That's impossible."

"Is it?" BA asked. "You don't know who your real parents are. You're freakishly tall, and you have more power than any wizard or sorcerer."

"And why are you telling me this now, angel? Is it because me and my master are about to hand you guys your asses?"

"Pish!" BA shook his head. "Your master. He is the one who has been lying to you for centuries. He has been using you for your power and attempting to keep me out of this by using you as a shield."

Damian laughed. "You'd say and do anything to win this war. I'm not buying it."

BA put his hands on his hips and dropped his head. "Your mother, Teresa, would be so disappointed in the both of us right now."

"Teresa?" Damian's eyes opened wider. "Is that her name?"

"Yes. And she was the sweetest thing I've ever laid my eyes upon."

Damian stopped pacing and pointed his staff at BA. "Well, why in the hell did you two abandon me? Why?"

Damian's eyes glowed red and shot two red beams of light from the snake eyes on his staff. BA, feeling guilty, could have blocked the beams, but instead, allowed them to hit him in the chest. He fell to one knee. His eyes glowed white for a brief second, but he then calmed himself again.

BA stood. "I didn't know about you, Damian. But maybe you can ask your mother to explain."

"W-What?" Damian's eyes tightened. "What are you talking about?"

BA held up his fist. A white glow emanated from The Peace Ring. "Come forth."

A small bright white dot appeared in between BA and Damian. Damian stepped back a few more steps as the dot grew. The dot floated down to the floor until it transformed into a glowing female. It was Teresa. Her brunette hair was long and curly just as BA remembered. Her skin was mocha brown, and she wore a white gown with sandals.

"Do not be afraid, my son." She reached out with both hands. "I am here to protect you and give you guidance."

"Why didn't you do it back then?" Damian asked. "I could have been more than I am now. I could have been better. I could have been good."

"That was not your destiny, my son." Teresa walked toward Damian. "Your father didn't know about you and had to keep you hidden from the angels. It had just been decreed that angels and humans could no longer have a romantic relationship. But your father, Artherial, and I were in love. So, before you were born, I sent Artherial away and confided in the Archangel Gabriel. I pleaded with him to take you away and hide you of which he did, for your sake and Artherial's. Your lives would have been forfeit."

"Why didn't you come back years later when nothing happened?" Damian asked.

"I, unfortunately, suffer from what all humans suffer from, Damian." She walked over and placed her hand on his shoulder.

"Mortality. I died soon after from complications from child-birth. But I'm here now to set things right between you and your father."

Damian stared at BA from head to toe. "So, this crooked and immoral angel *really is* my father?"

"Ha," BA said. "Look who's talking."

Teresa smiled. "Where do you think you get your temper and aggression from, my son?"

Teresa put her arms around Damian. He didn't relinquish his gaze of BA, who smiled, and his pale skin turned red. It was what he wanted all those years ago when he first broke the rule and fell in love with Teresa. She pulled away from Damian but grabbed his hand. She reached out for BA's hand as well. BA gladly placed his hand in Teresa's. She brought all their hands together as she stared into BA's eyes. Damian sighed finally, and let out a smile. BA could sense the hard-hearted Nephilim's defenses start to melt away.

"No!" Damian snatched his hand away. "This isn't right."

"Yes, it is, my son." Teresa stroked her hand across Damian's cheek. "Don't ruin what we've accomplished here today. It's all up to you."

Teresa stepped back and glared at her son and BA. She smiled and nodded at BA. She'd done what she was there to do, and that was to put her family back together.

BA held out his hand toward Teresa. "Must you go already?"

"I'm sorry, Artherial," she said. "I must be getting back. But I truly enjoyed seeing you both."

Teresa slowly started to fade away. BA placed his hand over his heart. Teresa was the only person he'd ever loved. He'd broken the rules for her. Now he was faced with protecting

Damian from his own team. BA knew they wanted to kill Damian, especially the Hangman. It was now time to devise a plan to keep his son safe.

"Well, what do we do from here on out?" Damian asked.

"First things first, my son." BA stood in front of Damian. "You've got to commit to not hurting anyone else. That's the only way I can prevent others from trying to hurt you. Secondly, you've got to separate yourself from the demon. And lastly, you need to tell me everything about what he's planning."

"I can do all those things." Damian nodded. "But I'll need some more time to accomplish them."

"Take what time you need." BA stepped back and sprouted his wings. "But you must not waste any. The pieces on the board are moving toward the climax. And we could use another hand."

"Do I have wings? And if so, will you show me how to do that?" Damian asked with a smile on his face. "I've always thought that flying stuff was amazing."

"In due time, my boy." BA flapped his wings and flew up, heading for the hole in the roof. "In due time."

New York Hospital

Tom rushed through the double sliding door of the Emergency Room, carrying Susan in his arms. "Someone please help me. Please!"

Two nurses hurried with a gurney, and Tom placed Susan gently down. She'd risked her life and destroyed her aunt to save him. It was the least he could do. He held her hand until the doctor showed up and asked him to leave the room while they worked on Susie. She hadn't been in his life for long, but

Tom didn't want to live in a world where Susie wasn't in it. He sat just outside the small room, and a single tear rolled down his face. Tom thought back to the witch Natasha and how she was masquerading as a nun, whom he'd fell for. When she revealed herself to him, he killed her. He thought about how he would have never met Susie if it weren't for the witch's coven.

Tom put his elbows on his knees and buried his face in the palms of his hands. *But this is the life we've chosen. Is there no hope for the truly good people? I keep sacrificing my life for this job, and I hoped this was my reward…finally. But Susie's strong. Hopefully, she'll pull through.*

Tom jumped to his feet as the doctor came out to greet him. It was a younger doctor. He was twenty-eight. He had brunette hair and a mole on his cheek. He wore a white smock with blue hospital garbs. He walked up to Tom with his clipboard.

"How is she, Doc?" Tom asked. "Is she ok?"

"Hi." The doctor put out his hand to shake Tom's. "My name is Dr. Arnold. Who are you in relation to the patient?"

"I'm—I'm her boyfriend," Tom replied as the shook Dr. Arnold's hand. "She doesn't have any other family."

"Well, boyfriends are family too where I come from, sir. There's no explanation for how, but Susie is in a coma. I can't gauge for how long because all vital signs and bloodwork have come back as normal. What happened to her?"

"We were out, and she just passed out." Tom dropped his head because of the obvious lie. "That was all."

"Hmm." Dr. Arnold scratched his head. "It doesn't make sense. But we'll keep looking for an answer. Are you ok, Father? You look like you've been through something as well."

"I'm fine," Tom said. "I'm, sadly, always the one that's fine. Can I see her now?"

"Of course."

Dr. Arnold walked off. Just as Tom was about to go into Susie's room, a huge man walked through the sliding doors. It was Jericho. All eyes were on the huge hulking man in green army fatigues as he made his way over to Tom.

"What's going on, Tom?" Jericho asked. "Are you ok? I got your message, but it didn't say much."

"It's Susie." Tom glanced over his shoulder at Susie's room. "She's in a coma. She saved my life though."

"Guess you guys are even then." Jericho folded his arms. "Guess she had worse luck than you did from when you saved her."

"Dammit, Jericho!" Tom pointed in Jericho's face. "Sometimes, I don't think you know how insensitive you can be."

Jericho's lips twisted. "What? What did I say?"

"Never mind."

Jericho looked in all directions and lowered his voice. "Well, what happened?"

"She thought she could drain the essence of her aunt like she does with demons and vampires." Tom sat back in the chair. "Her aunt is gone, but Susie's powers were never meant to do that to a human."

"Jeez, man." Jericho dropped to one knee in front of Tom. "What do you want to do now?"

"We're gonna go take the fight to the demon and all of his followers. Starting with the demon who led us into the trap,"

Tom said. "They're trying to take us out one by one. But I've got news for them."

Jericho leaned forward and rested his forearm on his knee. "Oh yeah. And what's that?"

"I'm gonna kill every last one of them."

Part 17

DIVIDE AND CONQUER

The Underworld

Hangoctuforre sat at the head of the table. He glanced around at the empty seats. All of the head vampires were gone. Ahmya was gone. Hangoctuforre had destroyed Zade himself, and suddenly, his army appeared weaker than before. He exhaled and nodded as he glanced at Damian and Comet. Hangoctuforre next nodded at Econdro and Blaelock because he knew they didn't want to follow him, but they'd stuck around to finish the fight.

"The Hangman has once again proven he doesn't deserve my power by joining the do-gooders," Hangoctuforre said. "But it doesn't matter. It's time we launched our assault on the earth."

Econdro sighed. "Please tell me that it won't be exactly like the last time."

"No, it won't be," Hangoctuforre responded. "This time, I have a plan. We won't attack them head-on and all at once. We'll separate them and meet back here. They are stronger together, especially Caine and Padilla."

"But, they're just human." Comet shrugged. "How can they be a threat to us?"

"Have you not been paying attention, angel?" Damian asked as he squirmed in his chair. "They are the Death Brothers. Their abilities feed off each other's. We have to keep them separated."

Hangoctuforre leaned in closer to Comet. "Your hatred for

humans is clouding your judgment, my friend. Those two are dangerous alone. Together, they are extremely formidable."

"Whatever." Comet waved his hand at Hangoctuforre. "What's your plan?"

Hangoctuforre smiled at the disrespect from Comet. "Simple. Since you want revenge on BA, Comet, he's all yours. Damian, you will take the wizard. Padilla belongs to you, Econdro. He's smart, but I think you can match him. Blaelock, you don't die. That's enough to drive any slayer crazy. So, I'll leave him for you. And Cromwell is mine."

"And how do we separate them?" Blaelock asked. "They, no doubt, will try to confront us together."

Hangoctuforre clasped his burned hands together. "That's where my sorcerer comes into play. He will take care of that. Agreed."

Everyone nodded in agreement. Hangoctuforre glared at Comet. The angel had disrespected him in front of his followers. Hangoctuforre knew then that Comet couldn't survive the upcoming battle. *And even if he does, I'll kill him myself. Earth can't have two rulers. I will wait until he destroys BA first. And then he will perish as well.*

New York Coffee House

BA ordered another cup of coffee, and Jericho finished his third slice of apple pie. Tom just stared in amazement at Jericho's dessert exploits. The Hangman sat with his head lowered and his hood covering his face as not to scare the patrons. Alexander filed his staff with a butter knife. They sat in a round table. There were about six people that were also in the diner. The man sitting the counter slid a few more seats away.

"Ok, sorry, Tom," Alexander began. "But we don't have Susie anymore, which means we're short one person."

"You can look at it like that." Tom held up a finger. "I've decided that I'm gonna get some pay-back from those guys. And the way I see it is, as they're down a person too, a powerful witch."

"Not a good way of looking at things, Thomas." BA sipped from his coffee. "Don't let that distract you from the ultimate goal."

"What? The war?" Tom asked. "My Susie is laying in a hospital bed because she killed that w—"

"Yeah. Yeah. Yeah," Jericho interrupted. "Ding, dong, the witch is dead. Let's get this meeting on the road. We have eyes all over us just because the angel is addicted to coffee. Jesus!"

The Hangman raised his hand. "I'm with Caine."

"Oh, there's a surprise," Tom cut in. "Seems like you guys never get off the same page."

"And just what in the hell is wrong with you, priest?" Jericho held his finger up to order another piece of pie. "I'm the one suffering with this crappy pie."

Tom picked up a toothpick from a bowl on the table and threw it at Jericho. "That's right, keep stuffing your face, Jericho. At least we weren't begged to save your ass like your crispy friend here, had to be. Nor Susie, who came along and was barely mixed up in this yet."

"Oh my God." Jericho threw hands up. "What do you want from me?"

"Guys." Alexander pounded his fist on the table, and the other patrons turned to see what was going on. "We're not here for this."

"That's right... *Tom*," Jericho said. We're—"

Poof. Jericho disappeared amid a cloud of smoke. The others jumped to their feet, knocked over the table, and drew their weapons. The sudden action caused the other diner patrons to get up as well.

"Wait!" BA held out his hands. "No one move."

"It's magic!" The Hangman backed up a few feet. "The sorcerer."

Poof. Alexander disappeared as well. The Hangman, BA, and Tom got in their fight stances and tried to stand back-to-back. But, *poof.* Tom disappeared as well, leaving the Hangman and BA staring at each other and wondering if they'd be next.

The Hangman patted down his body and then looked at BA. "You feel anything?"

"Nope," BA said. "Maybe it's because they're human."

They heard a rapping on the window. They looked out. It was Comet. The fallen angel pointed at BA and used the same finger to gesture for BA to come outside. BA took off running and dived through the window. Comet sprouted his wings and flew off. BA did the same and pursued his brother.

Back inside the diner, the patrons had either hid under the tables or ran toward the back. The Hangman looked around at each person. He didn't know if any of them were responsible or was Damian Red in disguise, so he decided to confront them all. He walked through the diner and stared at each human from head to toe. An older gray-haired woman continued to sit in her booth and stared at the half-demon. The Hangman slowly approached and gazed into her eyes. *That's a perfect disguise, grandma. She's probably a witch.*

However, another burst of smoke appeared on the table

behind the Hangman, and a postcard materialized on it. The old woman's hand shook as she pointed to it. The Hangman turned a saw the postcard.

He turned back to the old woman. "This may turn out to be your lucky day."

The Hangman walked back to the table and picked up the postcard. It read "Viva Las Vegas" under a picture of the Las Vegas desert. The Hangman looked around the diner again and raised his fist in the air. The Hellfire Ring glowed, and red electricity covered the Hangman's body. He disappeared.

Wrigley Field, Chicago

Alexander landed on his buttocks on the pitcher's mound. He stood and reached back to massage his butt-cheeks. He was ok. He took one step towards home plate and then stopped as a portal appeared in front of him. Damian Red stepped out wearing his red suit and black top hat. He was ready for battle as he had his snake staff in his hand. Alexander extended his arm, and his staff appeared in it.

"I love the fact that you have Merlin's staff," Damian said. "Defeating you while you have it will make this even better."

Alexander shook his head. "Are you telling me that you still want to fight me knowing the truth? You've got to be kidding me."

Damian pointed his staff at Alexander. "We have unfinished business, you and I, wizard. I couldn't just quit being me, cold turkey. Besides, knowing who the best is will finally settle things in my mind."

"But you're not a wizard or a *sorcerer*. What is there to be gained by us fighting each other?"

Damian shrugged. "Pride."

New York Subway Station

Tom made his way around the platform. People were scattered throughout, so he had to be careful. He didn't know if he was dealing with Damian Red, demons, vampires, or all three, so he backed up against the wall and surveyed anyone who walked by. He stood up straight when he finally saw what he was looking for. Modern demons dressed in suits. Older demons still wore older clothes, almost ratty.

A man pushed his way toward Tom. One hand was behind his back, and he had on an opened brown trench coat with holes in it. He wore a blue tracksuit with white stripes down the side of the pant legs and arms.

"Tom Padilla, I'll presume," the man said. "It's an honor to meet you."

"And who are you?" Tom asked.

"My name is Econdro," he said.

Tom nodded. "I see. You're supposed to be some kind of demon genius, right?"

"Some call me that."

"And you think it was smart coming here to take me on?"

Econdro put his hands behind his back. "You've destroyed or sent many of my brethren back to the underworld, priest. But I can assure you, I am not my brothers."

"Are you gonna talk, or are you gonna fight, demon?" Tom pushed up from against the wall with his foot. "You guys do a ton of talking."

"I would love to fight you, priest," Econdro said. "But I'm going to do you a favor. You can thank me later."

Econdro pulled his hand from behind his back and exposed the Book of the Dead. He held up his finger to Tom. "Give me a second, demon hunter."

"You would dare bring me this?" Tom balled his fists. "You've got some nerve."

"Trust me, priest, I may have the book, but I'm not the one that raided your church and killed your people." Econdro flipped through the pages until he landed on the one he needed. He extended the open book to Tom, who quickly snatched it away.

Tom held the book at his side. "Why are you giving this to me? Isn't your boss gonna be pissed."

"We hate him." Econdro stepped back a few feet. "And I'm giving it to you to go help your friend, the slayer. My plans are already in motion, and I don't need the book anymore."

"So, what am I supposed to do?" Tom asked. "Am I supposed to let you just walk away from here?"

"I'm not your enemy today, priest," Econdro said. "But I'm sure we'll see each other again."

Econdro backed up more until he was behind one of the other demons. He grabbed the demon by the back of the neck and shoved him toward Tom. Econdro and the third demon then turned and ran. Tom punched the demon that was pushed in his direction. The book fell to the floor. Tom then put on his brass knuckles and began to punch the demon in the face. A police officer tried to stop Tom by grabbing his arm. The demon stood, and his eyes turned black.

The officer looked into the demon's eyes. "Oops. This doesn't appear to concern me."

Tom shook his head. "Idiot."

The police officer took off in the opposite direction and talked on his walkie talkie. The demon charged Tom and kneed him in the stomach. Tom bent over, and the demon kneed Tom in the forehead. Tom fell backward against the wall. He wiped his head and braced himself for another assault. However, the demon, seeing his opening, turned and ran.

Tom took a step forward and was about to give chase until he looked down and saw the book on the floor. He picked up the book again and turned to the page that had been marked for him. *Now, let's see what this demon wanted me to see.* It was a teleportation spell. Tom sat on the floor as the onlookers stared at him. Tom smiled because of what he was about to do. He didn't care. *Hell, I've probably just saved them all from a demon attack. If it wasn't for that dumb cop, I would have gotten one of them.*

Tom folded his legs and placed his hand on the pages. "Ut mihi Jericho. (Take me to Jericho). Ut mihi nunc (take me now)."

Suddenly the ground began to shake, and the onlookers reached out to grab ahold of anything that was stable. A portal opened in the floor in front of Tom. Tom glanced around at the passerby's again. Their secret war was now public. He raised eyebrows and shrugged. He closed the book and fell forward into the portal. The portal disappeared behind him.

Big Sky, Montana Foothills

Jericho sat on a huge boulder and waited. He figured he wasn't brought to the destination for nothing. If anything was going to happen, the situation would find him. *This has gotta be the work of that Nephilim, who thinks he's a sorcerer. If I ever get my hands on him, BA and I will have another reason to be at odds, because I'm going to strangle that half-man / half-bird.*

A few feet away, a black portal opened. Blaelock, accompanied by two more demon-possessed men, stepped out. Blaelock had assumed the body of and tall, skinny and balding white man. The other two were black men. One had dreads, and the other was bald.

"Been waiting long, slayer?" Blaelock began. "Don't worry. We'll get to killing you in a moment."

"Big talk coming from a toothpick." Jericho stood. "Apparently, you thought you were coming here to take on the priest."

Blaelock waved his hand. "Silence."

An invisible force knocked Jericho to the ground on his side. He stood back up and unsheathed the Sword of Caine.

"You caught me off guard with that little trick," Jericho said. "It won't happen again."

"Oh yeah?" Blaelock waved his hand again.

Nothing happened. Jericho kept his balance and went on the attack. The demons pulled out swords. Blaelock backed up and allowed the other demons to fight. Jericho swung his sword from front to back and dipped it over his head to block the demon's strike that was behind him. As the demon with the dreads swung in front of him, Jericho ducked, and the demon cut off the other demon's head. Jericho and the dread-headed demon stopped fighting for a brief second as they both looked down at the other demon's decapitated head on the ground.

The decapitated demon's eyes stared at the dread-headed demon. "You stupid bastard. Look what you've done."

The demon's eyes rolled back, and then his yellow essence flowed from its nose. Jericho shrugged his shoulder and focused on the dread-headed demon again.

Jericho nodded at the demon. "Now, it's your turn."

"Never!" the demon replied and drew his sword back to engage Jericho again.

They battled with each advancing and then backing up. Jericho was sure to keep Blaelock in his peripheral vision. He knew the fight would eventually come down to him and the demon lord.

Jericho threw his sword up into the air, and just as he wanted, the demon looked up to see where the sword was. Jericho then reached out, grabbed the dread-headed demon by his dreadlocks, and pulled his head down. The Sword of Caine came down and plunged through the back of the demon's neck. Jericho whipped the sword out of the demon, who fell backward and grabbed his throat. The demon coughed and stared at Jericho. The demon's yellow demon essence then flowed out of his nose and evaporated into the air. *Ha. Ha. Ha. Still a classic.*

Before Jericho could turn around to face Blaelock, the demon stabbed Jericho in the back of the shoulder. Jericho backed up and massaged his shoulder as the blood dripped like a fountain. He ripped open the sleeve of his shirt. The wound closed and slowly began to heal.

"I was aiming for your heart, slayer." Blaelock put up his sword in a defensive position. "Wanted to give you a taste of your own medicine."

"You're about to join the rest of your flunkies, demon," Jericho said.

"I may not be able to move you anymore." Blaelock pointed to the boulder Jericho sat on earlier. "But that doesn't mean I can't move other things."

Blaelock stretched out his hand flat and raised it. The

boulder lifted from the ground. Blaelock gestured his hand toward Jericho, and the boulder zoomed toward the slayer. Jericho sliced the bolder in half with the Sword of Caine and watched the pieces fall around him.

"That little parlor trick is really starting to annoy me," Jericho said.

"Good. Because there's a lot more where that came from," Blaelock replied

Golden, Colorado

BA and Comet crashed through the roof of BA's favorite deserted church. BA was on the bottom as they held each other's shoulders. BA took the brunt of the landing. Comet got up, and BA teetered to his feet. BA looked around to find Comet only to be kicked in the chest by the fallen angel. BA sailed across the church and slammed into a pillar. His head hit first, which caused him to stumble to his feet again. Comet stretched out his arms to the side and called on his armor and his sword.

"Why are you helping the demon, Cometus?" BA managed to say. "I know you're upset that you fell, but this isn't the way to get revenge."

"I'm only helping that filthy demon to dispose of you." Comet raised his sword to strike. "Once I'm finished with you, I'm going to disappear for good."

"So, this is strictly about me?" BA regained his balance. "Because I bested you in the Great War?"

"That's right. You all killed many of our brothers and cast me out. It's time to pay, brother."

"Fine."

BA looked to the ceiling, and his eyes glowed white. Electricity covered his body, and his battle armor appeared. His battle-ax also appeared in his hand.

"Take off the ring, brother," Comet said as he nodded to the Peace Ring on BA's finger. "As the humans say, fight me man to man."

"But we're not men." BA looked down at the ring. "But I'll honor your request, brother. I didn't have or need the ring when we fought before. And I don't need it now."

BA took off the ring, held it in his palm, and it disappeared. He got in a defensive stance with his ax and waited for Comet to make the next move. Comet attacked. The sparks from their weapons lit up the church. It was just as their previous battle unfolded. They took turns striking each other's arms and chest. Their armor was tough, and the glancing blows had no effect.

BA kicked Comet in the chest, causing Comet to fall backward and crash into the pews. The fallen angel then regained his footing and sprouted his wings. He flew out of the hole in the roof. BA sprouted his wings and followed.

Las Vegas, Nevada Desert

The Hangman stood outside with his back to the door of an abandoned shack. Across the field stood Hangoctuforre, Econdro, and five other demon-possessed men with weapons. Hangoctuforre was the only demon in his corporeal form. Gone was his brown robe, replaced by black leather overalls and black boots. The Hangman's attire changed as well. He wore an all-red shirt and pants, with black combat boots.

"So, where's the rest of your flunkies?" the Hangman asked. "Or is it just you seven? That's not nearly enough."

"I like your confidence, Cromwell." Hangoctuforre turned to his side and glanced at his demon contingent. "The others are taking care of your friends as we speak. But I'm sure we'll be enough."

The Hangman's hooked staff appeared in his hand just as Hangoctuforre's sword appeared in his hands. Econdro drew his sword, and the other five demons were ready with their swords. The Hangman's eyes moved quickly around to each demon, staring at them from head to toe. He then focused on Hangoctuforre, who stood out and seemed relaxed as his thumb fiddled with his power ring.

Just as the demons took a step to engage each other, BA and Comet spiraled down and created a huge crater in the ground.

BA jumped out of the crater on the Hangman's side and Comet jumped out on Hangoctuforre's side. Hangoctuforre was visibly upset.

Hangoctuforre leaned closer to Comet. "What are you doing here? This wasn't the plan."

"I know," Comet said. "But plans change. Deal with it."

"Did you miss me, Cromwell?" BA asked. "Just like old times."

"Yeah," the Hangman replied. "Doesn't look as though the demon is as happy about this though."

BA shrugged. "He'll get over it. Cometus was never the type to follow orders."

Hangoctuforre pointed his finger at the Hangman and BA. The demons and Comet attacked. They separated the Hangman and BA almost immediately. Comet and three demons surrounded BA, while Hangoctuforre, Econdro, and two other demons squared off against the Hangman.

The Hangman didn't want to expend a lot of energy on the demons, so he raised his hand that carried the Hellfire Ring and fired. He blasted the two soldier demons first. They fell to their knees, and their demon essence flowed from their bodies.

The Hangman then turned his attention to Econdro and Hangoctuforre. However, Econdro surprised them both by falling to the ground. His yellow demon essence flowed from his mouth and floated into the sky until it was out of sight. He was gone, leaving Hangoctuforre and the Hangman to fight it out.

"It's so hard to find good help these days." The Hangman gestured toward the formerly possessed body that was Econdro. "Now, it's just you and I."

"This is how I've always wanted it," Hangoctuforre said. "I want to prove to everyone that I can kill you, take my powers back, and rule this miserable rock called Earth."

"Let's do it then."

The Hangman and Hangoctuforre clashed. The hooked staff and Hangoctuforre's sword whipped through the air as they tried to decapitate each other. The Hangman's black steel hooked staff was just as dangerous to demons as it was to humans. He slashed Hangoctuforre's leg with the hook and then spun around and kicked Hangoctuforre in the chest. Hangoctuforre fell backward and landed on his back. The Hangman tried to capitalize and plunged the sword end of his staff toward Hangoctuforre's head, but the demon rolled to the side, causing the Hangman's staff to get stuck in the ground. Hangoctuforre, laying on his back, fired a beam of light from the Ring of Light. The blast hit the Hangman in the stomach and catapulted him through the roof of the old shack.

BA, the more skilled of the fighters, decapitated two of the demons upon the initial attack. Their demon essence flowed from their bodies. BA knew he'd have a tougher fight against Comet who attacked BA with a vicious and wild assault. BA did his best to block Comets attack and fend off the other demon-possessed man. Comet was more aggressive than when they faced each other in the Great War in Heaven. As BA blocked Comet's sword, Comet either punched or kicked BA. BA had to act. He was losing. So, as he blocked Comet's sword with his battle-ax, he fired a shot from Peace Ring and blasted the demon-possessed man in the chest. The demon fell backward to the ground and began to hemorrhage. His demon essence left his body through his ears.

"I knew you would use that thing sooner or later, Artherial." Comet raised his sword in an attack mode again. "You're a coward."

"I said I wouldn't use on you, brother," BA replied. "But since I've gotten rid of the flunkies, let's continue."

The Peace Ring disappeared from BA's finger, and he and Comet engaged each other again. Comet was once again the aggressor. However, after he swung wildly with the sword, Comet spun around to back kick BA. BA ducked and chopped off Comet's foot. The foot inside the metal armor fell to the ground. Comet crashed down soon after. He struggled back to his good foot and hopped around until he regained his balance.

"I will give you this one chance to leave with your dignity, brother," BA said. "You can walk away, but never resurface again."

"Don't do me any favors, Artherial," Comet replied. "This is the only way it can end."

Comet sprouted his wings and launched at BA, but BA slid to the side and chopped off one of Comet's wings. The fallen angel crashed to the ground again, but again struggled back up to his good foot. He groaned until he was steady and then hopped toward BA. BA then realized there was only one way to stop Comet. *I'm going to have to put him out of his misery. He's never, and will never, recover from the Great War. Forgive me, brother.*

BA walked over and swung his ax at Comet, but Comet blocked it. Their weapons were locked together, but Comet didn't have the balance to match BA's power. BA shoved Comet to the ground. Comet slid backward on his butt and tried to push himself back up. But BA ran over, jumped in the air, and came down with his knees in Comet's chest. All the air rushed out of Comet's body as black blood spewed from his mouth. BA grabbed his ax with both hands and pressed it down against Comet's throat.

"W-What are y-you waiting for?" Comet managed to say. "D-Do it."

"Damn you, brother."

BA pressed down on his ax and closed his eyes as the ax cut through Comet's neck bone. BA stood over Comet's lifeless body and watched as it started to melt away until only a puddle remained inside of Comet's armor. However, there was no time to celebrate or mourn as three demon-possessed men, all armed with swords, attacked BA.

Part *18*

DIVIDE AND CONQUER: CHAPTER 2

Big Sky, Montana

Jericho dodged a tree trunk, but he couldn't dodge a small boulder that followed. It hit him in the sided of the head, and he fell to the ground and dropped the Sword of Caine. Jericho put his hand up to his head as blood gushed from the wound. He was light-headed and tried to get back to his feet. He looked around for his sword, but his vision was blurred. As Jericho staggered back to his feet, he noticed a blurred dark spot headed his way. He put his fists up to defend himself, but he was hit in the jaw by a skinny fist. Jericho teetered backward and tripped over a branch. He fell to the ground and tried to get up again, but another boulder came crashing down on his back. Jericho again felt around the ground for his sword.

"Looking for this, slayer?" Blaelock held up the sword. "I'm going to kill you with your own sword."

Jericho regained his vision and balance. "You do know that's impossible, right?"

"And why is that?" Blaelock asked.

Jericho's eyes lit up. "Because of this."

The Sword of Caine shot out Blaelock's hand and up into the air. When hit came down, the sword thrust itself into Blaelock's back. He tried to reach back and pull it out but couldn't.

"Let me give you a hand," Jericho said, and he grabbed the sword and ripped it from Blacklock's back. "Whoa! That's looked uncomfortable." Jericho held the sword in front of his face and marveled at it. "Well, I'm glad to see we're back on the same page, my old friend."

Blaelock fell to the ground and then surprised Jericho by laughing. Jericho bent down on one knee and lifted Blaelock's head.

"What's so funny, demon?" Jericho asked. "You're dying."

Blaelock sprang to his feet. "You fool. I am Blaelock, the Immortal Demon. Even your mighty Sword of Caine can't kill me."

"Well," Jericho said as he held out his hand. "Let's try it again for good measure."

Jericho plunged the sword into Blaelock's abdomen. Jericho pulled the sword back out and stood over Blaelock. Blaelock, again rose to his feet.

Just as before, Blaelock stared at Jericho and laughed. "And now, I believe it's my turn."

Blaelock pulled a small knife out of his back pocket. He held the knife out and used his power to launch the knife at Jericho. The knife lodged itself in Jericho's right shoulder. Jericho pulled the knife from his shoulder. He dropped to his knees. He dropped the sword again. He now had a wound in his left and right shoulder. A dizzying effect clouded his mind.

"What did you do?" Jericho asked. "Did you poison me?"

"Of course, I did." Blaelock walked over and confiscated the Sword of Caine again. "It was dipped in a powerful tranquilizer. But because of your healing abilities and the fact that you're a muscle-head, it'll just make you weak for now. But killing you, now, that's my job."

Blaelock reached back with the sword and prepared to chop off Jericho's head. Jericho couldn't move. He fell face-first on the ground. He couldn't even use his slayer abilities to control the sword.

Just as Blaelock was about a strike, a bright portal opened above his head. Tom fell out the portal, still in possession of the Book of the Dead, and landed on Blaelock's head, knocking them to the ground. They got back to their feet, and Tom began punching the demon with his brass knuckles. He cracked Blaelock in the face with the book and staggered the demon. Tom then knocked Blaelock to the ground with a right hook. The demon spat out a few teeth, and his jaw swelled up.

"You have some nerve, priest." Blaelock's mouth sagged open, and he massaged his chin jaw with his hand. "Do you think a mere mortal can destroy me?"

"Maybe not. At least not by myself." Tom walked over and stood next to Jericho, who was still lying on the ground. "But the Death Brothers are more than a match for you."

Jericho strained but was able to look up at Tom and smile. It was the first time Tom had proudly announced they were the famed Death Brothers. *That's my brother right there.*

Tom opened the book, reached down, and grabbed Jericho's hand. "Participes meis (share my power)."

A jolt of energy flowed through Jericho's body. Blaelock's regenerative powers surged through Jericho. The wounds on Jericho's shoulders closed, and the weakness he felt disappeared. He got up and dusted off his camouflaged pants. He held out his hand and tried to call back the Sword of Caine, but

Blaelock had a tight grip on the sword and wouldn't let it go. Jericho began to sweat as he focused harder, and a bolt of electricity burst out the sword. The explosion knocked Blaelock to the ground. The sword floated back to Jericho.

Blood poured from Blaelock's eyes. He turned around and spread out his hands. A black hole opened in front of him.

"Come forth, my friends." Blaelock gestured his hand toward his body. "I need your help."

Ten vampires walked through the portal, and it closed. Blaelock turned back to Jericho and Tom and smiled.

"This is why you good guys will never defeat us," Blaelock said. "We have bodies in reserve."

Jericho and Tom looked at each other. Surprisingly, Tom was smiling as well.

"Ok," Jericho began. "What in the hell is so amusing?"

"I was prepared for this," Tom replied. "It's why I took a little detour before I came."

Tom looked down, flipped pages the Book of the Dead. He found the page he needed.

Tom raised his free hand in the air. "Aperi et venias ad me (open and come to me)."

Tom lowered his hand and a small white light appeared and started to grow. It was another portal. When it reached full size, Captain Sammy Bloom stepped out first, followed by fifteen Dark Hunters. They marched single file until they formed three rows. They all wore black army fatigues with their faces painted black. They all wore gold crucifixes, and miniature crossbows hung from their waists.

Jericho turned to Tom with a surprised expression on his face. "But how did you know?"

"Your friend in DC," Tom said. "He reached out to me while you were trapped in the sword and asked if we needed any assistance. The Dark Hunters don't like fighting demons anymore. But I'll assume they'll be satisfied right now."

Sammy walked up and saluted Jericho. "At your service, sir."

Jericho saluted back and shook Sammy's hand. "Your service is damn sure welcomed, Captain. And as you can see, we have some work to do."

The Dark Hunters stood behind Jericho, Tom, and Sammy. They stared across the field at Blaelock and his vampires. Blaelock turned and walked off. He headed up the mountain. Jericho and Tom decided to follow.

Jericho turned back to Sammy first. "Take care of this, Captain. And I'll be in touch somewhere down the line."

"Yes, sir," Sammy responded.

Wrigley Field

Damian pointed his staff at Alexander. "Augue (fireball)."

A fireball shot out from his snake's eyes and grew as it traveled across the field toward Alexander, who dove to the ground to dodge it. The fireball passed over Alexander's body but did a U-turn and headed for Alexander again. Alexander took off running as the fireball chased him. As the fireball got closer, Alexander turned to face it.

Alexander pounded his staff into the sand. "Fons (Fountain)."

Alexander pulled his staff out the ground, and a gust of water flowed up from the hole and extinguished the fireball. However, Alexander marveled at what he'd done for too long and allowed Damian to strike. Damian swung his staff like a baseball bat the hit Alexander in the jaw. Alexander fell to the ground on his side. He rubbed his hand across his jaw and felt a welt that had been created. Damian ran over and kicked Alexander in the stomach and then in the back. One of Alexander's ribs cracked. He again realized he wasn't dealing with a wizard, but a powerful Nephilim. *I've got to change the scenery. He'll kill me for sure if we stay here. And only BA can stop him now. I've got it.*

Damian attempted to kick Alexander again, but Alexander caught the Nephilim's foot and flung it to the side. Damian was knocked off balance long enough for Alexander to stumble back to his feet. Alexander charged Damian and grabbed in him in a bearhug.

Damian laughed. "Are you kidding me? And what are you going to do now?"

"Take you to the only person who can give you a spanking," Alexander said as he was losing his grip around the bigger half-angel. "This fight has to end now. Invenio BA (find BA)."

A portal appeared right behind Damian. He turned his head slightly, saw it, and began to struggle to break free from Alexander's grip. Alexander knew he couldn't hold the Nephilim much longer, and he brought his knee up and kneed Damian in the groin.

"Oof." Damian's eyes widened. "You dirty bastard."

Damian dropped his staff, and Alexander pushed Damian into the portal. They were surrounded by white light for a few seconds, and when it disappeared, they were about one hundred feet across the sandy battlefield from BA, doing battle with demons.

Damian finally broke free, pressed Alexander over his head, and slammed the wizard to the ground.

"Do really think you've accomplished something by

bringing me here?" Damian said as he called his staff back to hand. "I will still dispose of you and then join my father in defeating the demons."

"We're on the same side, you moron." Alexander scooted backwards on the ground. "Why do we need to keep this up?"

"Call me crazy." Damian smiled. "But I just want to kill you, wizard, for that little stunt you and your family pulled at the hospital."

The mentioning of his family brought back the anger Alexander felt about Damian from that day in the hospital

Alexander called his staff back to his hand while he still sat on the ground. "Cicer e fulgur (pulse and lightning)."

First, a pulse knocked Damian to the ground, and then a lightning bolt fell from the sky and struck Damian, causing him to be set on fire. The ground was scorched around an outline of Damian's body when he stood again.

Damian held out his staff. "Extinctus (extinguish)."

A powerful wind picked up and blew out the flames on Damian's body. His red suit was burned, with holes all over. Some of his skin was even exposed and burned.

"You insolent little fool." Damian breathed heavily. "You'll pay for that."

Hangoctuforre kicked in the door of the old shack. The Hangman lay on his side with his back facing the demon. Hangoctuforre crept over to the Hangman, reached down, and turned the Hangman over on his back. The Hangmen then shot a red beam of light at Hangoctuforre. Hangoctuforre was blasted backward, and he crashed against the far wall.

"One good turn deserves another." The Hangman got

back to his feet. "Now we're both one shot away from assured destruction."

Hangoctuforre managed to get back to his feet. "It's a shame you didn't want to work together. We could have made quite the team. But, oh well."

Hangoctuforre raised his fist to fire another shot from the Ring of Light. But the Hangman tossed his hooked staff and severed Hangoctuforre's hand from his arm. The ring still shot a beam of light, but it exploded out the other side of the room as the hand hit the floor. Hangoctuforre withdrew his arm and clutched his bloody stump with his other hand. His eyes glowed red, and the dripping black blood stopped. His hand regenerated. The Hangman, surprised, stepped back a few feet.

"I can teach you so much, Cromwell." Hangoctuforre waved his new hand at the Hangman. "You just have to swear eternal loyalty to me."

The Hangman smiled. "That's a nice trick. But aren't you forgetting something?"

The Hangman nodded toward the severed hand on the floor, which still had the Ring of Light on it. The Hangman pointed the Hellfire Ring at the hand. Both the Ring of Light and the Hellfire Ring began to glow. The hand lifted into the air and started to float toward the Hangman. Hangoctuforre took off running toward the Hangman and dived toward his hand, but he missed and landed on the floor in front of the Hangman. The Hangman grabbed the hand and took off the ring. He put it on the finger next to the Hellfire Ring. An electric pulse surged through his body from the two rings reconnecting. The Hangman then looked down at Hangoctuforre and kicked the demon in the side. The Hangman reached down, picked up Hangoctuforre, and pressed the demon over his head. He tossed Hangoctuforre across the room, and the demon lord landed face-first on the floor.

Big Sky, Montana

Jericho and Tom pursued Blaelock up the mountain. Blaelock used his ability to launch rocks and trees at them.

"We have to catch up with him, Tom," Jericho said as they ducked another bolder. "Before he takes us out with this crap. You don't have another trick in that book of yours?"

"It's our book, big guy," Tom replied. "And I'm trying to think of something."

"Well, think faster. He's getting awfully close with some of that stuff. Ah, to hell with this." Jericho pulled out the Sword Caine. "We don't have time for you to think anymore, priest."

Jericho tossed the Sword of Caine as far as he could toward Blaelock. The sword landed a few feet in front of the demon.

"Ha. Ha. Ha." Blaelock looked back at Jericho. "You missed, slayer."

Jericho stopped climbing, and his eyes glowed white. "Not quite."

The sword unleashed an electric pulse that was more like an explosion. The impact sent the demon tumbling back down the mountain.

Jericho reached out and grabbed Blaelock by his shirt and looked over to Tom. "Be ready."

Jericho began pounding his fists into Blaelock's face. The demon couldn't defend himself as he was still stunned from the electric pulse. Tom reached into his inner jacket pocket and pulled out the Detox. He crawled over to Jericho, who was still hammering on Blaelock's face. Tom took the top off the glass container and attempted to pour it on Blaelock's black-bloodied face. However, Blaelock's eyes glowed red, and an invisible force froze Tom's arm from lowering the vial.

Tom's strength wasn't enough to break the hold, so he glanced at Jericho. "Big guy, I'm gonna need some help."

"No problem," Jericho responded.

Jericho rolled over, slammed the skinny demon to the ground, and hopped on top of him. He kneed the demon several times in the stomach until the demon's eyes returned to normal. The hold over Tom was released. Tom poured Detox on Blaelock's face. A huge pulse knocked Jericho and Tom backward, and they almost tumbled back down the mountain. But Jericho slammed his fist into the ground and reached out to grab Tom's hand. They regained their balance and crawled back up to Blacklock. The demon grabbed his head with both hands and shook it. The Detox and his immortality battled each other from within.

"Wow!" Tom exclaimed. "This is why they separated us, but then the other demon gave me this book. Detox is the only thing that can kill this guy."

"And where is he now?" Jericho asked.

"I don't know." Tom ran his fingers through his hair. "He gave me the book and ran. This is weird. Something tells me that we need to find the others, especially if we were all separated for this purpose."

"I agree," Jericho said.

They put their hands over their faces as Blaelock's body finally succumbed to the Detox and exploded. Tom recovered the Book of the Dead and searched for the spell he needed to take them to the others.

The Final Chapter

UNHAPPY ENDINGS

The Hangman walked over to Hangoctuforre, who lay on the floor, breathed heavily, and clutched his chest. He kicked Hangoctuforre in the face and watched as acidic saliva dripped from the demon's mouth and burned a hole into the floor.

"Seems like we've been here before." Hangoctuforre wiped his mouth. "Didn't think I'd be on the losing end again."

"It's because you did what you always do, idiot." The Hangman pointed his ring at the demon. "You underestimated those goody-goody bastards…and me."

"That may be true." Hangoctuforre held up his finger. "But did you ever find out who it was that killed your wife and son?"

"Sure. It was your monstrous creation, Damian Red."

Hangoctuforre looked out the window and saw BA still fighting demons. "And why do you think Damian has been allowed to live this long?"

"Duh. He's a sorcerer and has been protected by the lord of the underworld—you."

"No, my friend."

"Don't call me friend."

Hangoctuforre pointed outside to BA. "It's because of *him*."

"What does BA have to do with Damian Red?"

"They didn't tell you?"

The Hangman raised his hooked staff. "Spit it out, or I'm gonna make you suffer before you die."

"He's Damian's father."

The Hangman stepped back against the wall and then dropped the hooked staff. It all made sense. BA had several opportunities to take out Damian since the sorcerer's return, and Damian was still alive. *Did Caine and the demon hunter know about this too? Have I been too friendly with them to see it?*

Once the Hangman snapped out of his trance and looked around again, Hangoctuforre was gone. He turned his attention back to BA. The angel had dispatched the last of the demons he was fighting. The Hangman looked around the area again. He wanted to kill Damian and BA. Damian was on the other side of the field, locked in a magical battle with Alexander. *This may work in my favor. Padilla and Caine are nowhere in sight.*

The Hangman looked down at his hand. He'd taken the Ring of Light from Hangoctuforre and combined it with his Hellfire Ring. He needed BA's Peace Ring to reform the Power Ring and become unstoppable. *All I would have to do is take aim and fire one shot apiece at the angel and his coward son. But then I'd probably have to kill the wizard too. He'd never let me get away with killing BA.*

However, that option was taken away as Hangoctuforre reappeared with Econdro and Papa Rango outside of the shack. Rango had the Amulet of Itsok draped around his neck. When activated, the amulet dampens angels' powers.

The Hangman walked over to the window, stood to the side, and watched. BA was surrounded by Hangoctuforre, Papa Rango, and Econdro.

"Rango," BA began. "You never cease to amaze me. You've aligned yourself with this scum, I see."

"Anything to destroy you, mon,'" Rango said in his Jamaican

accent. "I will finally get to see you die, angel—and hopefully, slowly."

"So, you're selling yourself to the highest bidder then?" BA asked. "The Peddler bought your services before."

"Ending your pitiful existence is my main goal." Papa Rango pointed at BA. "It doesn't matter who I'm working for at the time."

BA pointed the Peace Ring at Hangoctuforre, who was armed with his sword. He pointed his ax at Papa Rango, who had his staff with a skull attached to the top. Econdro pulled out the rare black steel sword. BA looked around at each being. He shot a beam of light from the Peace Ring, but Hangoctuforre blocked it with his sword. The demon was thrown off balance but still stood upright.

"Enough of this." Hangoctuforre looked over at Papa Rango. "Do what I brought you here for."

BA launched at Papa Rango. "Not this time."

It was too late as Papa Rango disappeared and appeared a few feet away. He smiled at BA. Hangoctuforre and Econdro smiled as well.

"Abu Koku." Papa Rango held up his staff and chanted. "Donde Koku Amear."

The necklace around Papa Rango's neck glowed. Just as before, when they faced off, BA doubled over and clutched his stomach. His armor disappeared. BA dropped to both knees and held out his hand toward Papa Rango.

"Your powers are weakened, angel." Hangoctuforre stepped closer. "But I'll make you a deal. Your son of a whore, bastard friend, took my ring. Give me yours, and I'll let you walk away from here."

Papa Rango violently shook his head. "That wasn't our deal dem—"

"Silence, witch doctor!" Hangoctuforre cut him off and turned to wink at Papa Rango. "I'm feeling generous today. Now, give me the ring, BA."

"This?" BA looked down at the ring. "Idiots. The ring's power is not diminished by that amulet. And it doesn't work for demons."

BA jumped back to his feet and shot a beam of light at Econdro. The beam hit the demon in the chest, and he fell to his knees. Hangoctuforre attacked. He swung his sword at BA's head only to have BA block the attempted beheading with his battle-ax. However, because BA was weakened, the force knocked him backward to the ground. Hangoctuforre jumped up the in the air and attempted another strike at BA's head, but BA moved, and Hangoctuforre plunged his sword into the ground. He pulled it out, but not before BA sliced his leg with the battle-ax.

BA was shocked that Econdro recovered. The demon grabbed BA from the back in a bear-hug. Papa Rango then ran up and pounded BA in the face with the skull staff. Econdro let BA fall to the ground.

"Pick him up again." Hangoctuforre reared back with his sword to swing it. "I'm gonna cut off his damn head."

Econdro went to pick up BA again but was met with another white beam of light from the Peace Ring. The blast knocked Econdro off his feet and sent him sailing into the wall of the shack that the Hangman observed from. BA stood with his battle-ax out in front and charged Hangoctuforre. Their weapons clashed, and a spark of lightning from the collision knocked them both backward. Neither fell, and they charged each other again.

Papa Rango pointed his staff at BA. "Scintillae (sparks)."

Red sparks erupted from the eyes of Papa Rango's skull staff and hit BA in the face. BA lost his balance, and he flailed his ax in front of him. Black burn marks appeared around the angel's eyes. Hangoctuforre jumped in the air and kicked BA in the chest, causing the angel to fall backward to the ground. BA couldn't see. He shot random beams of light from the Peace Ring. BA never shot right in front of him, which is where Hangoctuforre approached with a smile on his face. As he got closer, he simply stomped on BA's forehead and almost knocked him unconscious.

BA lay lifeless on the ground. His hands were spread out as if he were lying on a crucifix.

Hangoctuforre erupted in laughter. "Fitting end. You may do the honors, Rango."

Papa Rango pulled out his knife from his inner jacket. He bent down to one knee and kissed BA on the head.

"This is a special blade I had made just to kill you. I made it for me father, angel." Rango then spat in BA's face. "And that was for my Midnight Scavengers that you've killed. And this, well, this is for me."

Rango raised the knife in both hands above his head and prepared to bring it back down into BA's chest. But as he began his downward plunge with the knife, the *swoosh* sound of the Hangman's hooked staffed vibrated off the air. Papa Rango's head hit the ground. His body fell next to his head.

Hangoctuforre jumped backward and got in a defensive stance. "You? What are you doing back here?"

"I never left." The Hangman reached down and pulled the Peace Ring from BA's finger. "And thanks to you, I'm able wield all three rings. Now, I'm about to finish the Cromwell family's business here and now."

"Not this time." Hangoctuforre looked over at Econdro, who had begun to stir. "You can have him instead."

A lightning bolt flashed down from the empty sky and struck Hangoctuforre, who disappeared. The Hangman, already in possession of the Ring of Light and the Hellfire Ring, added the Peace Ring. The rings formed a three-finger ring with the Ring of Light located in the middle. Once combined, the Power Ring's intense energy coursed through the Hangman's body. He clutched his fist to his head until the sensation ran its course. He turned his attention to Econdro, who had recovered from two shots from the Peace Ring, something that wasn't possible even for a supernatural being. But Econdro was The Demon Genius. Before he gave the Book of the Dead to Tom, he'd cast a spell on himself to endure blasts from the rings. But now he faced something different. He faced an angry Hangman, armed with the Power Ring.

"So," the Hangman began as he crept toward Econdro. "They call you the Demon Genis. Well, let's test that theory, shall we?"

"Hold on, Hangman." Econdro dropped to one knee. "I'm not on anyone's side."

"Could have fooled me, demon."

"You've got it all wrong." Econdro clasped his hands together in front of him. "I hate the demon lord. The plan was always to destroy and replace him after we won the war. You could be that replacement."

The Hangman threw his head back and laughed. "No honor amongst thieves, eh?"

Econdro shook his head. "I don't know what you want me to say."

"Nothing actually. I just want you to die."

The Hangman raised his fist and shot a dark pink beam of light at Econdro. As the beam impacted the demon, he looked down and surveyed his body. At first, it glowed dark pink, and then the glow disappeared. The Hangman cocked his head to the side with a confused expression on his face.

Econdro laughed. "See, I told you, I am a gen—"

The demon's entire body exploded into a bloody pile of bones and flesh. There was nothing to identify the demon as Econdro or the human he'd possessed.

The Hangman looked down at the ring in amazement. "Hmm. So much for being a genius."

Alexander put his hands out as if he were holding a ball. "Augue (fireball)."

He threw the fireball at Damian, who caught it. "You're nothing, wizard. Do you know how many wizards I've killed? And yes, some were Suma wizards like yourself."

"Well, you won't kill this wizard," Alexander said. "At least not today."

Damian threw the fireball back at Alexander, who jumped out of the way and allowed it to hit the ground.

Daman twisted his lips. "Who are we kidding? You know, and I know, that you can't beat me. If that fireball was your heaviest gun, then prepare to die."

"That's a good idea." Alexander held out his hands. "Tormentum (cannon)."

Alexander dropped his staff, and a bazooka appeared in his hands. He took aim at the sorcerer and pulled the trigger. The force from the bazooka knocked Alexander backward and off-balance.

"Holy crap," Damian said. "Vis ager (force field)."

Damian created a force field to cover his body in time, but the missile from the cannon still knocked him backward to the ground. He got back to his feet and shook his head.

"You're a pesky wizard." Damian looked to the sky. "Well, let's see if you can handle this."

Damian raised his staff and his other hand to the sky. His eyes glowed red as well as the eyes on his snake staff. The daylight disappeared but just over Damian and Alexander. Lightning clouds moved in, and thunder pounded the air.

"Repeated fulgur (repeated lightning)!" Damian shouted over the thunder.

Suddenly, lightning struck the ground next to Alexander. He moved to the side. It struck again even closer, and then he realized what was going on. Lighting rained down every few seconds. Alexander tried to block a lightning bolt with his staff. However, the electric current was too strong. *Who in the hell am I fooling? I can't defeat a Nephilim. He knows he's one now, which makes him even more dangerous.*

Alexander knew blocking the lightning with his staff wasn't good enough. He needed something more.

He raised his staff. "Vis ager (force field)."

A white glow appeared around Alexander's body just as a lightning bolt struck him. The lightning bolt knocked Alexander to his side on the ground. The force field began to weaken and blinked for a few seconds until it was solid again.

Another lightning bolt crashed down onto Alexander before he could stand. Another bolt of lightning followed. The force field gave way and disappeared. Alexander knew he was done. He couldn't stop the lightning. Thoughts of Emma and the twins flooded his thoughts. *Help me, Merlin.*

Suddenly, Alexander's staff began to glow. A bright blinding light pulsated from it. When Alexander stood and took his hand away from his eyes, the sky was normal again. He looked over to Damian who also was temporally blinded and used his hands to cover his eyes. But the battlefield appeared different. Copper coins were scattered throughout.

Damian staggered backward. He cuffed his head with his hand. He grabbed his stomach. Alexander nodded. *That's right! Copper is the only thing that can kill a Nephilim. I should have remembered that. Thank you, Lord Merlin.*

Alexander looked across the battlefield at BA and the Hangman, who stood over the angel's body. He couldn't hear the conversation. He wasn't concerned with Damian anymore as the Nephilim was temporarily weakened and neutralized.

The Hangman peered down at BA, who was still lying motionless on the ground. He stared at the angel whose eyelids fluttered and opened.

"D-Did w-we get'em?" BA asked.

The Hangman looked around to make sure they were alone. "We did. I couldn't have done it without your ring."

"H-How?"

"How did I use it?" The Hangman smiled. "Well, I now have all three and reformed the Power Ring."

BA's eyes popped open. He tried to sit up, but the Hangman stepped on his chest and forced BA back to the ground.

"W-What are you doing?"

"What you knew I would do if I ever found out the truth."

"W-What t-truth?"

"That tall, big-headed bastard over there is actually your son. And he killed my son...and my wife."

BA coughed up blood. "D-Don't do this C-Cromw-well."

"Do what, this?" The Hangman pointed the ring at BA's head. "I know I'll have hell to pay for killing an angel, but you've had this coming for a long time."

"S-Screw y-you, C-Cromwell."

The Hangman took his foot off BA chest. He fired a beam of light from the Power Ring. The dark pink glow covered the angel's body. "And for the last time. My name is the Hangman. And I'm just happy to know that *you know* who killed you."

The Hangman stepped backward a few feet and stared into BA's eyes. BA also stared at the Hangman. There was no re-spect. Only hate. BA's body started to dissolve into a white milky substance until only his armor remained.

"What?" The Hangman frowned. "No explosion. Damn!"

"Wait a minute," Alexander said as he witnessed BA's death. "What's going on here?"

"Nooooo!" Damian yelled as he looked over at the Hangman still standing over the remains of his father

Damian ran over to the Hangman and engaged him with his sword and staff. The Hangman countered with the hooked staff and a smile on his face.

"Came to join your old man?" The Hangman ducked an attempted beheading. "Don't worry. You will and soon."

The Hangman ducked another wild swing from Damian and slashed one of the sorcerer's legs with the black steel on the hooked staff. Damian dropped to one knee and glanced at his leg.

He waved his staff over his wound. "Sana (heal)."

The wound began to close but not fast enough as the Hangman attacked again. He punched Damian in the face and watched as Damian sailed backward to the ground. Damian didn't move. He wasn't unconscious, but his eyes rolled back. The Hangman looked across the field at Alexander, who was collecting copper coins in his wizard's hat. *Now, what is that guy doing? It's bad enough, I'm having to finish his fight. Oh, I get it now. That's copper.*

Before the Hangman could turn back around, he was hit in the side of the head with Damian's snake staff.

Damian spread out his arms. "Turbinis Vasti (tornado)."

The wind picked up and eventually formed a funnel over the Hangman's head and swooped him up in it. The Hangman couldn't see, and the wind began to crush and suffocate him.

"Supernatet (float)," Damian said as he watched the tornado float into the air and take the Hangman with it. "Continua fulgur (continued lightning)."

Thunder accompanied the dark clouds this time. The tornado was about twenty feet in the air when the first lightning strike hit it. The Hangman yelled out in pain. A few seconds later, another lightning bolt hit the tornado. Again, the Hangman screamed. He then began shooting dark pink beams of light in all directions. He couldn't see Damian, but he hoped he hit him. None did. However, one beam of light landed right next to Damian and forced him to jump to the side and release the spell. The sky cleared. The Hangman began to spiral uncontrollably to the ground. He held out his ring hand and created a dark pink force field around his body just as he hit the ground. He was shaken but not hurt.

The Hangman got to his knees just as Damian attacked again. The Hangman quickly rose and put up his hooked staff to block Damian's snake staff.

"You Nephilims are as dumb as you look," the Hangman said as he strained to repel Damian's attack. "With your big heads and busted teeth, I'm surprised you just can't scare anyone to death."

"Look who's talking?" Damian countered. "With your burnt face, you look as if you were tortured in the underworld already."

"Oh yeah?"

"Yes."

The Hangman turned to Alexander. "Make the damned weapon."

"And why should I?" Alexander approached Damian and the Hangman. "You murdered BA."

"I'll explain that later, wizard," the Hangman said.

Alexander sighed and waved his staff over his hat. "Arma Fabricet (forge weapon)."

Alexander's hat lit up, and the copper melted. The hat blistered and forced Alexander to drop it. When the hat hit the ground, a copper knife fell out of it. It still smoked. The Hangman knew the wizard couldn't pick up the knife, but the Hangman could. He looked up into Damian's face, who was still trying to force the pointed end of his snake staff into the Hangman's chest. The Hangman spat his acidic saliva into Damian's eyes.

Damian stumbled backward and dropped his staff so he could wipe away the saliva. He cleared away most of it, but his eyesight was still blurred. That's when it happened. The Hangman picked up the copper knife and plunged it into Damian's chest. Damian fell to the ground, clutched the knife to pull it out, and couldn't.

"So, this is how it ends, huh?" Damian looked around the field and stared at the white liquid that used to be his father. "I didn't see this coming."

A bright copper light grew out of the wound and covered Damian's body. He turned over on his side and died. The Hangman looked back at BA's remains and then at Damian Red's body. He threw his head back and laughed.

Alexander maneuvered his way in front of the Hangman and pointed his staff at the half-demon. "Now, explain yourself."

The Hangman took a deep breath and put his hands on his hips. "Well, it's like this. He—"

Hangoctuforre appeared out of nowhere from behind the Hangman and stabbed him through the back. The sword exploded a few inches out of his stomach. Alexander tried to react, but Hangoctuforre punched him in the face, knocking Alexander to the ground. Hangoctuforre then picked up Alexander's body and tossed him across the field, knocking him unconscious upon impact.

The Hangman fell to both knees on the ground and tried to pull the sword from his back. He couldn't. It was too deep.

"And who says I needed a ring to defeat you?" Hangoctuforre

walked around to look in the Hangman's face. As soon as you die, I'll just take the ring from your corpse."

"W-Wow!" the Hangman managed to say. "I-I always t-thought it would be BA that got me."

"Oh, yes." Hangoctuforre clapped. "Thanks for dispatching him and taking his ring. You made my job so easy. Your little buddies may have killed all my soldiers, but I'll rebuild and rule the earth."

The Hangman was dying. He tried to lift his hand to fire a shot from the Power Ring at Hangoctuforre. *If I go, I'm taking that bastard with me.* But he couldn't do it. And as he sat and watched black blood soaking through his robe, he knew it wasn't just BA and Damian who were responsible for the death of his family. *Daminan worked for Hangoctuforre. That bastard only told me about the situation so I could turn my anger toward BA.*

"Look at you, *Hangman*." Hangoctuforre laughed. "A cheap knockoff finally getting what you deserve. But don't worry about the rest of your friends. If they're still alive, I'll take care of them too. I just wish it was me that killed your wife and son, you son of a bitch."

The mentioning of his family seemingly gave the Hangman new life. He stopped slouching over on his knees. He put one knee up and pushed himself back to his feet. He staggered forward to gain his balance.

"And what the hell do you think you're trying to do?" Hangoctuforre asked.

The demon ran over and pulled his sword out of the Hangman's back. He punched the Hangman in the back of the head with the sword's handle. The Hangman fell forward. He was too weak to put his hands out to catch himself, and he landed face-first in the sand.

Hangoctuforre walked over to the fallen Hangman. "This is almost too easy. I'm going to enjoying killing you. I can't believe you still think you can win."

Hangoctuforre pulled out a small knife made of the same black steel as the Hangman's hooked staff. He dropped to his knees and turned the Hangman's body over. The Hangman's eyes rolled back.

"I'm gonna cut your throat, Cromwell, stand over you, and watch you bleed out. I'll give you credit though. I didn't expect this. You were more of a challenge than I gave you credit for. Tells me that I chose the right man to use my powers."

The Hangman whispered, but Hangoctuforre didn't hear him. The Hangman whispered again. Again, Hangoctuforre didn't hear him. Hangoctuforre leaned over and put his ear closer to the Hangman's mouth.

"Speak up. I don't have all day."

"I said," the Hangman began, and his voice grew louder with every word. *"Did you expect this?"*

The Hangman grabbed the back of Hangoctuforre's head with one hand, held it down, and jammed the Power Ring into Hangoctuforre's forehead. As Hangoctuforre tried to bring up his knife to stab the Hangman, a dark pink shot of energy burst out of the Power Ring. The energy surged directly into the demon's head, and it exploded in the Hangman's hands. The Hangman held up the ring, and a dark pink field covered his body. It healed his wound almost immediately. He got to his feet and pointed the ring down at Hangoctuforre's decapitated body.

"Just making sure," the Hangman said as he shot another beam of light from the ring.

Upon impact, the beam ripped through Hangoctuforre's body, and it exploded.

"Never mess with a man's family, asshole." The Hangman looked around. "Now, where's the rest of the Scooby gang?"

The Hangman walked toward Alexander's unconscious body. Saliva dripped from his mouth. He didn't want to ask the wizard any questions. Besides, Alexander knowing the truth about Damian Red, the wizard also had seen the Hangman kill BA. *He's got to be disposed of as well.*

As the Hangman stood over Alexander, he reached down and grabbed Alexander by the throat. Alexander remained unconscious. The Hangman merely had to twist his hand in either direction to break Alexander's neck. A bright portal opened above the Hangman's head, and Tom dropped out of it onto the Hangman's back. Tom dropped the Book of the Dead to be able to hold on to the much larger Hangman.

The Hangman dropped Alexander to the ground and fell to one knee. Tom's eyes glowed white as his ability came forth. The Hangman held his fist in the air with the Power Ring. The Ring glowed dark pink and sent an electric shock through Tom's body. He fell to the ground and began to shake.

Jericho then dropped from the portal as well and stood in front of Alexander's body.

"Whoa, Hangy." Jericho held up his hands. "What's going on here?"

"Your *brother* just tried to take me down." The Hangman pointed to Tom. "Surely, you don't think I'd sit still and let him do it, did you?"

Jericho slowly opened the Book of the Dead. "Hold on,

Hangy. Let's just talk about this. Why were you about to kill Alexander? He's on our side."

"The Book of the Dead?" The Hangman's eyebrows raised. "You have no angel. No wizard. The demon hunter is down. Are you casting spells now, slayer?"

"Answer my question first," Jericho said.

The Hangman looked over at the white foamy puddle that used to be BA and then pointed at Alexander. "When he recovers, you ask *him* why. I'll see you all again. And when I do, well, let's see if we all go out for beers."

The Hangman looked to the sky, and his eyes glowed along with a red lighting that surrounded his body. He disappeared.

Alexander coughed as he awakened on the ground next to Tom, who was shaking off the effects of being stunned. Alexander grabbed his throat and rubbed it. The Hangman's handprint was visible. Jericho helped up the wizard, while Tom got to his feet.

"Whoa. Seems like everyone is ok." Tom ran his hand through his hair. "Let's go home."

"Wait," Alexander said.

"What is it, wizard?" Jericho asked. "We need to get off of this battlefield."

Alexander pointed across at the white foamy puddle. "We need to recover BA's remains."

"His remains?" Jericho's eyes tightened. "What do you mean?

Are you saying that, that's BA?"

"Yeah, Alexander." Tom took a step toward Alexander. "That can't be."

"Well, it is. He's gone," Alexander said. "We can't leave him here."

Jericho folded his arms. "Says who? There's nothing to recover."

"Says me," Alexander replied. "We can gather his armor... and whatever that goop is. It would be disrespectful to leave him here. He needs the burial of a soldier."

"You know what?" Tom held up his finger. "Alexander is right. He was a soldier of Heaven and our friend."

Jericho grunted. "Speak for yourselves."

"Not now, Jericho," Tom said. "I'll get the armor. You guys go find something to scoop up the liquid."

Cairo, Egypt

It was about midnight as Argos, Hangoctuforre's assistant, walked across the sandy plain. A museum had grown in the spot he'd last remembered. Three Egyptian people accompanied him: a young woman and two young men. They had shackles around their necks and were chained together, so they walked in a single file. Argos held the chain of the woman in front just in case the volunteers didn't' want to go through with the plan. All three humans carried shovels.

Two security guards patrolled the building, one on the inside and one on the outside. As they approached the guard on the outside, Argos' dagger slid down the arm in his robe and into his hand.

"What the he—"

Argos slashed the guard's throat, and they continued inside the museum. The other guard was patrolling the second floor and didn't have to be disposed of...yet. Argos headed to the basement. Once down in the basement, Argos held out his hand and slowly waved it across the room, which housed crates of antiques. Argos' hand stopped over a spot on the floor. He nodded to the volunteers to start digging in that spot.

An hour passed when the humans' shovels hit something solid—a wooden coffin. Argos grunted and snorted as he was in corporeal form with a pig's head. He stood and ordered the humans to pull the box up to the floor. He ran his hand across the coffin and smiled. Argos used his demon strength to pull the top off. A tall and muscular bald man lay in the coffin. His skin had turned grey with time, but it was still in perfect condition.

Argos' eyes glowed red, and he spread out his arms to the side. "Arise, my lord Leechadon. Arise and feed off the souls I have gifted you."

The humans stared at each other and started to run back toward the basement door. However, an invisible force froze them. Electric currents pulsated through their bodies until three bright light floated from their chests. The electricity stopped as the bodies fell to the floor. Their bodies turned pale and wrinkly. Their souls floated over Leachadon's casket and flowed into his nose. His red glowing eyes opened as he turned his head to the side and located Argos. Leechadon's skin went from grey, back to its normal bronze color.

"What has happened?" Leechadon asked.

"It's time, my lord," Argos said. "The Underground's throne is now empty, courtesy of that vile creature, the Hangman. But it's time to take your rightful place."

Leechadon sat up, his bones crackling from lack of use. He moved his head to each side to crack his neck.

"Let's go to the underworld." Leechadon floated up out of the coffin and gently landed on the floor. "And tell me about *this Hangman*. Although he has done us a great favor, he poses a threat to my reign."

New York

A few days later, the three remaining warriors made it back to Tom's church. They knew if they hadn't killed all the demons and vampires, they'd at least be warned with the supernatural alarm system in the church. Tom pulled out BA's armor from his duffle bag. Even after the angel's death, the honor regenerated from the damage it had sustained. He placed it in a wooden lockbox. Jericho also placed an urn, filled with the white liquid and surrounding sand in the lockbox. The box was closed and sealed inside the wooden pulpit.

They all said a prayer to themselves and breathed heavily as they walked to Tom's office in the back of the church. Tom closed the door behind them as they walked in. After the break-in and fire, Tom didn't want to get the priests and nuns involved again even though they knew what his job was.

"I'm telling you," Alexander began. "I saw it with my own two eyes. He killed the angel in cold blood."

"The Hagman is a lot of things, wizard." Jericho put his hands on his hips. "But killing the angel in cold blood...I'm not buying it."

Tom sighed. "Jericho, you've got to put this bromance aside and realize Alexander is telling the truth."

"What's wrong, Thomas?" Jericho frowned. "Are you jealous?"

Tom burst into fake laughter. "Jealous of a scarred, crispy, half-demon? You've got to be kidding me?"

Alexander stepped in between the two. "Hold on, guys. This is getting us nowhere as usual. Think about it. There's got to be a perfectly logical reason behind it."

"There is," Tom said. "Damian killed his son and wife. He found out Damian was BA's child…the end."

Jericho shook his head. "And while you're wondering about why he killed BA, shouldn't we all be worried about ourselves? I know that guy. I'm sure he's figured out that we've known about it all along as well."

Jericho gave Tom a hard stare one last time and then sat on Tom's cot. Jericho's words sunk in. They were dealing with an angry half-demon in possession of the Power Ring. However, it was the first time since their first encounter with the Hangman that they felt they were his match. But they'd have to get the Power Ring off his fingers first. They knew getting rings was the key, and the most dangerous as well.

Tom straightened up and snapped his fingers. "I have a plan. But it's not going to be easy."

TO BE CONTINUED

Lightning Source UK Ltd.
Milton Keynes UK
UKHW011930070220
358393UK00001B/12